The Grand Summer

Of Spells

&

Other Tales

By, Barbara E. Hill

D1253696

National Library of Canada Cataloguing in Publication Data

Hill, Barbara E. (Barbara Ellen), 1962-
   The grand summer of spells, & other tales
ISBN 1-55369-279-9
   1. Horror tales, American. I. Title.
PZ7.H5378Gr 2002   813'.6   C2002-900812-3

TRAFFORD

This book was published *on-demand* in cooperation with Trafford Publishing.
On-demand publishing is a unique process and service of making a book available for retail sale to the public taking advantage of on-demand manufacturing and Internet marketing. **On-demand publishing** includes promotions, retail sales, manufacturing, order fulfilment, accounting and collecting royalties on behalf of the author.

Suite 6E, 2333 Government St., Victoria, B.C. V8T 4P4, CANADA
Phone   250-383-6864   Toll-free   1-888-232-4444 (Canada & US)
Fax   250-383-6804   E-mail   sales@trafford.com
Web site   www.trafford.com   TRAFFORD PUBLISHING IS A DIVISION OF TRAFFORD HOLDINGS LTD.
Trafford Catalogue #02-0092   www.trafford.com/robots/02-0092.html

10   9   8

ACKNOWLEDGMENTS:

THIS BOOK IS DEDICATED IN MEMORY OF MY FATHER, DOUGLAS E. TIBBITTS, WHO WAS A GREAT ARTIST, AND TO MY MOM, MARION TIBBITTS, WITH LOVE.

"BUT THE MAN WHO COMES BACK THROUGH THE DOOR IN THE WALL WILL NEVER BE QUITE THE SAME AS THE MAN WHO WENT OUT. HE WILL BE WISER BUT LESS COCKSURE, HAPPIER BUT LESS SELF-SATISFIED, HUMBLER IN ACKNOWLEDGING HIS IGNORANCE YET BETTER EQUIPPED TO UNDERSTAND THE RELATIONSHIP OF WORDS TO THINGS, OF SYSTEMATIC REASONING TO THE UNFATHOMABLE MYSTERY WHICH IT TRIES, FOREVER VAINLY, TO COMPREHEND."

ALDOUS HUXLEY: THE DOORS OF PERCEPTION.

"BACK INSIDE THIS CHAMBER OF SO MANY DOORS; I'VE NOWHERE TO HIDE. I'D GIVE YOU ALL OF MY DREAMS, IF YOU'D HELP ME, FIND A DOOR, THAT DOESN'T LEAD ME BACK AGAIN .....TAKE ME AWAY."

PETER GABRIEL: THE CHAMBER OF 32 DOORS
THE LAMB LIES DOWN ON BROADWAY

COVER ILLUSTRATION "MISTICAL FIELDS" CREATED BY SILUS. CONTACT: SILUSATRIUM☐IOL.PT AND WWW.SILUSATRIUM.FR.ST FOR VIEWING THIS TALENTED AND INSPIRED ART GALLERY FROM PORTUGAL; ATTN: MARCO.

Table of Contents:

POEM FOR A GHOST

Last night I said goodbye to my father, who passed away over a year ago.

He was dying and we held each other. We cried in a deep silence. No words.

And then he went. I felt his spirit jump, consumed by a tenuous step across some unknown chasm. I suddenly remembered when I had jumped off a pier for the first time, never having swam before. I held him tight, as he turned into a hundred doves of golden light. Capes of light, turning, rising. Northern lights shooting out from my arms.

I awoke from the dream... Petals dropped quickly from blossoms replete with moonbeams, starfire and rinsing waves. His presence dimmed and flickered from the room, like twilit shadows scrambling for cover. Silence. Still warm from his nearness all around me. I looked out at the dark morning sky. Islands of stars and planets rocked and burned brightly among the sable waves of an endless sea.

Silence hummed inside my room. And I returned, softly swimming out once again, beneath a sharp, sparkling starscape, to a mysterious place, called dreams.

THE GRAND SUMMER OF SPELLS

THE GRAND SUMMER OF SPELLS

A zephyr of mint leaves rode in on a tide of easy summer winds. There was another smell that stole through the wide open window. One of the flowering magnolia or dogwood trees from the graveyard, Ginny thought. She poured the foaming milk over the strong coffee, grating a nutmeg over the top.

Quiet. She loved these moments. She listened to the grandfather clock down the hallway, its deep, slow chimes sounding upon the floors like a heart beating within a deep stillness. The thick rose bushes which flourished around the walls of the entire house felled a steady steam, a pink haze which crept inside in vining, twisting mists, a sweet incense filling the air with its delightful summer magic. Tree frogs, crickets and goldfinches created hauntingly cheerful melodies and sometimes bars and notes would steal into the kitchen and capture her attention.

She heard the front door open carefully and in a moment close.

"Mikey? Is that you?"

No sounds.

"Answer me young man!"

Winged footsteps flew up the stairs disappearing into one of the rooms. She followed him like a police officer trailing a car, ready for arrest. She stopped at the entrance of his bedroom.

Mikey was lowering a large painted turtle into one of his aquariums.

"You better bring that turtle back to where ever you caught it, young man!" She warned.

"Oh mom! It's the only turtle I have that has a shell like this!"

2

And he brought the turtle over to her and held it up-side-down showing her the spectacular red and orange shell. The turtle extended it's neck hissing.

"Take it back buster! You can't keep it!"

"Oh mom, pleeeeeeease! This is the last one. Let me keep him," he pined.

"Mikey, look around this room of yours. You have every shape and size of aquarium in here. You've got salamanders and newts, little snapping turtles, butterflies and grasshoppers together, toads, leopard frogs, frogs so small I can hardly see them yet they fill your room with all this noise.   ...why, there's even a bowl of catfish! And what's that over there?"   She pointed with accusing satisfaction.

"There's a mouse family in there," he noted with regret, looking at the floor for help.

"So that's where all my good cheese disappears to!" She laughed.

"No momma, they eat peanut butter and scraps off my plate."

Her hands braced her hips with eyes narrowing in on him.   "You bring that turtle back to where ever you got it right now and don't drip it all over the house. Put it in a pail and carry it out! How do you ever get to sleep at night with all this noise?"

And Mikey's resilient heart broke one more time and the soul of a little boy had one less dandelion to crown it's bright yellow meadows. A big frown rode his face and he returned the turtle to the lily pond that was just passed the graveyard.

It was a most perfect pond, Mikey thought. Reeds trumpeted the shoreline and bright water lilies rode the caps like flower-rafts that carried the insects and frogs. Dead trees lay with their heads submerged in the pond and their massive trunks elbowed out of the water as wide sun decks for the turtles.

Mikey squatted near the edge of the pond beneath a gigantic sweeping willow tree. Like a giant green octopus the tree threw it's arms and tentacles upon him, riffling his hair as if to say 'hello.' Delighted as willow trees are with children, it quivered and trembled it's soft green fingers and gently cascaded across his face.

A bullfrog croaked and a dragonfly buzzed past dipping and flying two inches above the water.

"Bye, Mr. Turtle," and a fat tear rolled down his cheek and into the pond. The turtle paddled off and in a moment was gone.

Through the heads of the maples Mikey could see an explosion of thunderheads slowly sweeping in. He thought for a moment how each cloud that passed resembled a sea shell. The clouds were the same colors and had the same creamy texture as the inside chambers of sea shells. And sometimes, he thought, when a big tide of wind would blow through the heads of the trees you could hear the sound of the ocean in the same way that you could hear waves crashing by holding a shell to your ear.

The willow smiled upon him, stretching its many arms. For hours, Mikey sat like an Indian in a deep stillness, sensing movements in the weeds and nips at the waterline as little fish traveled. He watched as fine piers of stumps and fallen trees gradually crowded with basking turtles, napping in the bright, warm sunlight, dreaming of juicy minnows and water caves where their hisses echo off the walls and strange glowing bugs snap in the air like fireworks.

At five o'clock the willow tree lashed it's tentacles upon him to warn him of the impending storm. Rivers of wind blew through the heads of the trees. Black shadows flashed across the ground. The thunderheads were shaped like anvils with coal black bottoms. They stretched and spiraled high in magnificent explosions of shell white and coral red. Mikey jumped to his feet with a sudden and thrilling sensation in his stomach and head, and he thought he could smell rain. The tree lashed at him again and he took off running toward home. He was about a mile and a half away. He ran past the apple grove and was out of breath just as he reached the graveyard.

The gates of the graveyard were indeed open and an invitingly sweet air loomed and beckoned for him to come inside and take a look. The dogwood and magnolia trees gleamed in the sunlight, redolent with sweetly flowing curiosity. Mikey entered the graveyard and stood among the ancient headstones. He read the cryptic inscriptions and looked up at the monuments towering above him like gigantic waves which cast him in their foreboding grey shadows. It was only early evening, but the whole sky had darkened with wild winds whorling and whipping all around him. Suddenly, a flood of peach and robin's egg burst from behind the great thunderhead, casting graphite beams across the sky. In the middle of the graveyard there was a dragon water fountain spouting rings of water into a wide pebbled pool, whose tiled floor crept with mosses. One of the talons of the dragon held a lantern and in the other claw, there was a box.

Mikey stood motionless before the creature with his jaw slacked wide. Rolling up his pants, he walked into the pool and touched the swooping wing, frozen in its flight between this world that we see, and some other. He looked closely at the box and gave it a gentle pull. It slid freely into his hands, in want of curiosity, and his eyes widened, with the astonishment of discovery. With no lock to thwart him, he opened its sweet treasures within.

"Wow!" And the flowering trees leaned and creaked from side to side to look within. Indeed, what was inside was a most curious thing! He pulled it out carefully. The trees began to rock slightly, to get a better view. Mikey pulled out a long windchime. It was three feet long and made entirely from triangles of sapphire. He held it in the sunlight and became mesmerized by the deep cobalt colors that now danced in shadows upon his face. The trees withdrew and looked away.

He put the windchimes carefully away into the box, tucked it under his arm and ran home. After dinner with his family he skipped television, even though his favorite shows, <u>Night Gallery</u>, <u>The Outer Limits</u> and <u>Creature Feature</u> were all on tonight, and went straight to bed. Mikey hid the box beneath the bed, fed his pets and went to sleep.

The full moon climbed the sky and shone it's milky path through his window. A massive oak tree shaped like a wishbone stood outside the window and the moonlight bathed it's leaves in an eerie, metallic glow of light. The nightmarish yowling of a cat fight below his window pricked his nerves. He could feel his heart pounding as he lay in the dark, now wide awake.

Blue moonlight poured through the wishbone of the tree. Mikey hopped out of bed and pulled the box out from underneath. He hung the sapphire windchimes in front of the open window and laid back in bed. Mikey watched the shimmering gems as they clinked and tinked in the moon dusted breeze. Indigo prisms rippled along the walls and ceiling, shivering in kaleidoscopes of diamonds.

And as he watched the chimes, something very strange began to happen. A halo of pale blue light, almost like smoke, began to form and then to spin around the sparkling sapphire windchimes. And the halo expanded to a blue mist that filled the room and the air became dense in fragrant clusters of hyacinth.

He got up and walked over to the window, looking out across the dark meadows, filling his lungs with the sweet night air. He looked up at the twinkling starscape with its vivid swirls of galaxies scintillating like billions of crushed diamonds scattered across an infinity of space. And in an instant, as if it were all a dream, a strange thing began to happen. He could now pierce the darkness and see the meadows with its sleeping wildflowers and nodding sedges, and the tombstones of the graveyard became distinct almost to the point where he could read the writing inscribed upon their stone. He turned his head and watched a rabbit nibbling in a knoll of ferns and sweet clovers. He felt so light, weightless as a feather.

And then he bent forward and flew off the ledge.

He swooped like a buoyant torpedo, flapping his huge wings as he traveled over the meadow to the road, and followed the road which led passed the graveyard to his favorite turtle pond deep in the woods. And there he landed upon a generously branching oak, looking out upon his friends. He sat absolutely still, a nuance of shadow. Almost a part of the tree, he stood and listened to the bullfrogs bellow and watched the turtles splashing off their wood tree rafts and sturdy stumps.

"Come over here - come over here," bellowed one frog to another.

Mikey was not surprised that he could now understand their language. In a moment, a huge frog, perhaps two feet long, leaped from the bank and jumped in the water, swimming beneath its warm, comfortable, black surface and popped up near the first frog who had beckoned her company. Her eyes shined at him.

Mikey looked over to the right. A large painted turtle paddled swiftly through the water and bit a minnow hungrily, carrying his dinner while he swam. The turtle emerged with a soft splash climbing up onto a mossy rock and ate. It extended its neck, and for a moment, watched the stars at just the right instant to capture a bright green comet which lit the sky and disappeared, as if it were all a dream. But, as turtles know, life is indeed *very real!*

Mikey meant to exclaim a "wow" at the sight of this comet, but his voice went "Hoooot Hoooooooooooot!" And quickly below a rabbit ran off. The oak tree embraced him, indeed even watched him with its long hollow faces configured by the shadows of the bark. Its thick, beautiful head of leaves shook almost as if from a sudden chill, and then became still.

Mikey watched every movement in grand detail as turtles, frogs, fish and fireflies all sang and feasted among the splendid reeds and water lilies. Fireflies blinked along the bank and a water snake moved its body in a continuous movement of inverted S's across the pond to rest upon a pier of rocks.   Its tongue flickered in quick flames, tasting the mouse which was lying in a bed of violets, watching the moon.

I better get back home, Mikey thought to himself. He was filled with the excitement of the pond's secret language: of the numerous croaks, chirps and buzzing sounds which now became ideas, impressions and songs. I can feel everything, he thought, flying away back home. Flying was like swimming, he thought, except easier. He flew over the road so as not to get lost, and landed back on his window ledge, the windchimes still clinking.

He hopped off the window ledge and back onto his feet, springing up off the floor with wells of excitement which made his eyes sparkle and his skin tickle. He unhooked the windchimes and placed them back into the box, slid the box beneath his bed and went to sleep. He dreamed deeply that he was riding a dragon to a new land, someplace faraway, or was it that he had traveled into the future?   And he awoke the next day with a kind, warm wind blushing the air of his room in tender colors of pink and peach. Outside, crickets and treefrogs hummed and buzzed the air imperceptibly beneath the sharp, high cheerful songs of the whistling birds.

Mikey kneeled before his aquariums. He looked into the glass tanks where his pets now lived and spoke softly to them. "Hello little turtles! You should have seen that comet last night, boy, it filled the whole sky with glowing lights!"   And he animated his memory of the comet by swooping his arm through the air, his fist the thrust of the comet.   But not one of his turtles appeared to be listening to him today. Instead, they sat with their necks retracted in their shells. He looked over at his butterflies, their wings pulsing open and closed in the stale air. The butterflies climbed upside down beneath the screen which held them within. The tender film of skin beneath the chin of the toad clucked in and out quickly, while its beautiful eyes stared at him and then seemed to look beyond, from its mysterious lens, at the room. He reached his arm down into the tank which contained his salamander and pulled the sticky amphibian out. "Don't you like your little tank?" Mikey whispered into his face. What a beautiful salamander, he thought, he'd never seen one with such bright yellow spots before. It began to squirm in his hand and he released it back into its room of bark, leaves, sticks and mud. He grabbed his mist bottle and sprayed the tank, simulating a gentle rain storm.

"Well," Mikey said rubbing his hands together, "I've got to go, I've things to do today!" The animals stared blankly at him as he disappeared down the stairs. Mikey went into the kitchen and sat down at the table. His mom brought out a basket of fresh cinnamon rolls hot from the oven, with warm frosting that melted in his fingers. She set out a platter stacked with sausages and bacon, a bowl of fresh strawberries and raspberries and a big glass of juice. She returned again with a bowl of poached eggs and the thinnest, most tender crepelike pancakes, a bottle of syrup, and then sat down beside him, hands folded beneath her chin, wondering, smiling.

"So how's the zookeeper this morning," she aimed. "Are you going to the pond today?"

"Uh huuuu," he said, stuffing his mouth with a tooth-shaped strawberry as big as a baseball.

She looked at him and smiled to herself. His plump, pink lips, his blushed, tanned cheeks, his animated smiles and sparkling eyes, 'what a fine boy,' she thought. 'What a fine boy indeed.'

"Why don't you let them go?"

"Because they're my pets, mom.   They're my friends."

"Couldn't they just as easily be your friends, if you set them free? You could visit them at the pond, that's where they belong, Michael, you know.   How'd ya sleep last night?"

"*Really* great!"   And he laughed with a tone which betrayed his special secret.

"So what's my boy up to today?   Baseball with Brent and Cody? Fishing? Hide and Go Seek with Nicholas out by the river?"

"I thought I'd bring my net out to the pond today!"

"No sir! No more animals, we talked about this yesterday."

The front door opened and Nicholas came in, just in time to save him from the growing trouble all around him at the breakfast table.

"Hello Mrs. Greenfield - hello, Mikey," he said, sitting down and stuffing a roll in his mouth.   "Let's go out to our treefort today!" He announced.

And the three of them ate breakfast together, laughing and telling stories and jokes, and two hours later, the boys loaded a basket with cookies, jawbreakers, sweet tarts and candy bars and disappeared out the door.

"Bye, mom!"

"Bye Mrs. Greenfield!"   They shouted, running down the road.

They ran off the road into the woods, passed the old house they called "haunted," through Mr. Skullcap's pumpkin field, passed the cornfield and down to the river bank. And standing there before them was their tree. It's strong, ropey green arms quivered to see them in a kind of mysterious wave hello, and swayed in the breeze. They carried the basket into the treefort and set it on the table. The great willow overlooked a slow, rippling river, wide and deep, with mossy boulders and misting waterfalls.   The bank of the river was resplendent with bright orange and silk white clusters of lilies, emerald knolls of ferns, berry bushes, thick hedges of wild mint and soft beds of violets, buttercups and shooting stars.

Nicholas grabbed onto the tire swing hooked up just outside the back door, and shot out, swinging over the warm river, and letting go, jumped into the sparkling watercaps. They slid down mossy boulders into deep pools with arms held high, shouting and laughing. They dried off at a sandy bank, lying in the sun, scaring each other with homemade ghost stories, and later went back to the fort.

Mikey looked out the window below at the bright reflective sunlight which poured down upon the river, making it hard to see. He turned around tearing into the basket and popped a large sweet tart into his mouth, sucking and biting on it with the savoring flair of a connoisseur. A whippoorwill regarded the fort from its lair in the woods, turning its head and listening to the bright laughter which shook the sprouting shags of the tree.

"You know, Nicholas," Mikey pondered, "something strange happened to me last night."

"What?"

"Well, maybe it was all just a dream, you know, but I don't think so. I could see the darkness, I could smell things I've never noticed before. I could hear mice hopping in the meadows, pushing through tall grasses. And it's all because of this windchime I found in the graveyard."

"You stole the box from the dragon?"

"Well, I'm sort of borrowing it, you know."

"Put it back Mikey, it's got a spell on you! That's a magic box guarded by the dead souls of the graveyard. They're gonna come after you Mikey!"

"I flew away last night, off my window ledge, over to Nightshade Pond! You know, our turtle pond!"

"Mikey, you stole something from that graveyard, no one's ever touched that fountain. It's a fountain of secrets. They say it's trouble, Mikey. There's a spell on you! Bring it back! There's spooks watchin' us, Mikey!"

"Oh, I'll bring it back tomorrow, okay!"

"Ya, you look funny today, there's a spell on you Mikey, I can see it!"

"Can *not!*"

"Can too, see it," and Nicholas shuddered, as if he'd just seen a shadow move.

As the sun began to set, the boys ran home, this time running through a part of the cornfield with arms open flicking the tall, hard stalks with their fingers, they leapt over the rows of the pumpkin field and they even stopped to steal a peek into the old haunted house, their small faces peering through a broken window. They ran down the overgrown driveway where a stand of strange gnarled chestnut trees entwined their fingers together at the top creating a sort of gateway which they ran beneath and back out onto the road. At the roadway they parted: "goodnight Mikey," shouted Nicholas, waving while he ran.

"See ya!"

Their timing had been good, as Virginia Greenfield began ringing the cowbell outside to bring him home for dinner. And tonight was spaghetti night, perhaps his favorite night of the week. After dinner Mikey watched The Outer Limits and Night Gallery and went into his bedroom. His pets, it seemed, had not moved a wing nor a tail, why not even a little new clawprint touched the sand. They all sat in the exact same positions from which he had left them. He fed his friends, and went to sleep.

And this night, once again, he was awakened by a shrill, sickening, eerie cry from outside his window. He sat up in bed thinking it must be very late, and he remembered the windchimes. He hung the windchimes in the window, and again the full moon washed the room in mysterious blue lights that began to spin and tremble. The massive arms of the oak tree outside his window waved at him in the moonlight. The windchimes clinked like delicate magic bells, as a blue smoke began to crawl upon the floor, folding in wings and hands, and in a moment the air smelled like flower blossoms.

He walked slowly to the window ledge, wondering if he would be able to see, smell and hear the world outside in that new and clear manner as he could before. And in a moment his senses bounced off places and objects like a sonar system. He could, in fact, now smell the pond from two miles away. He could smell the duckweed and the water lilies, he could feel the presence of the cattails, the thrust of the reeds, and the blowing flower seeds drifting in the air. He looked up, but instead of peering out the window through the big oak, he was now looking up beneath the most beautiful, endless night sky. The sky enfolded its sable, sparkling wings around him, embracing him in its infinite sea.

No longer in his room, he slid off the log whose soft moss gave him an even, level landing into the warm, black water below. And he swam, neck extended above the waterline, and watched shooting stars and the deep, swirling, sparkling dust of the galaxies and the spotlights from the burning planets. Death blew past him toward the town of Woodbine, prompting an owl to speak, "Hooooot Hoooooooooooooooooot!" Is the song the owl sang upon the passing of this messenger ship, but what he really said was: "...be gentle, my good friend..." Death's sudden chill lifted as its wind blew into Woodbine, down Hickory Avenue. A street lamp flickered for a moment, far off, and the animals became quiet.

Mikey swam slowly in a creamy flood of moonlight, other turtles, like himself, dove off stumps and crawled off the shoreline dipping into the water. They popped up around him, bobbing, staring at him, as if to say "where is our mother?" And Mikey, knowing this, felt ashamed, "why she's at my house, safe. I'll return her tomorrow..." And the others swam off. And at this moment, a huge snapping turtle drifted over to him. 'It's so much bigger than myself!' He thought. Mikey back paddled in the water, but it's big mean face broke the water staring at him. "I won't hurt you, you have my little ones, I want them back!" Spoke the snapping turtle, "I am miserable without them. I have so much to show them, soooo many fine mud caves, such juicy fish, they could ride my back in lightning storms," the animal hissed, "bring them back to me, it's soooo lonely for me..." And she disappeared with a splash beneath the surface, her heavy body swimming beneath him and rocking him in a wave.

Mikey swam to shore, dejected and sad, for he had learned that he had trapped the spirits of his pets by keeping them for himself, and that indeed they should now be set free. For no green comet, no swirling galaxies could be seen from inside the aquariums and tanks which held them back. And turtles, with their perfect water bodies and generous claws, loved to swim and hunt, and could no more hunt, than they could watch the stars and the falling rain. No more could they bake their shells in the warm, summer sunlight, telling stories to each other, spellbound with fresh air and good fish to eat. And they could no more listen to the chirping, whistling music of the crickets and treefrogs, whose chorus entertained them on so many fine nights. Gone were the sunsets and the deep water dives, thought Mikey, remembering how he too, loved to move about freely. What if I could never leave my room, he thought to himself sadly. Never again to swing over the river, letting go in mid air, splashing down into the deep, warm summer river whose buoyant arms captured him in its mysterious currents. Floating, nay, flying over the bottom with his eyes open, watching clams and fish below, like an astronaut suspended in space. "What if?" He said outloud.

Mikey remembered his room, he could see the window ledge shadowed by the giant oak. Moonlight shimmered into his room as he slid off the window sill and onto the floor, soaking wet. He dried off and went to sleep, dreaming of the vortex of death which blew over the pond tonight, and of the fat mouse sleeping in a knoll of shooting stars and buttercups, sleeping under the same moonlight that touched his own life, too.

And when he awoke the very next morning, he returned the baby snapping turtles, the large painted turtle and all of the frogs, toads and salamanders back to their home, the pond. The wildflowers trembled, listening to the reunion of families, and indeed it became a day of celebration for the animals of Nightshade Pond, both small and large, as they enjoyed their birthright songs of freedom and their love of simple things, as from these simple things, flowed love.

CHAPTER TWO

Thinking deeply, Mikey had decided this: He liked turning into owls and turtles! With his fist beneath his chin, he pondered the mountains of clouds framed by the sharp turquoise summer sky. 'So still and yet so noisy, was this summer forest,' he thought. He listened to the whippoorwills and morning doves, his hands still folded beneath his chin on the window ledge of the treefort, thinking, looking out upon the world. A bright orange butterfly drifted among the water lilies and landed upon the ledge right next to him, pulsing its wings. The butterfly didn't leave, rather, it continued to investigate this boy who had so many thoughts.

'I'm not going to return those windchimes!' He mused to himself. Why, tonight I shall go out again, go back to the pond. Perhaps more lessons awaited him among the spells of its diamond lights and sweet apple blossom mists. 'Why, I could go even further than the pond, maybe tonight I will fly among the bright stars!' And he whistled to himself, a rather nimble, magical little note, all his own, like an elf in a tree. And the woods answered back, whistling also, as Nicholas, his friend, appeared from the foot trail below.

"Hello!"

"Hey Nicky!"

"Whatcha doin'?" He asked.

"Countin' Clouds! So far I've seen three shells, two mountains, a billowing squall and one lost ship."

"I know Mikey!" Exclaimed Nicholas, as he climbed up the ladder, "let's camp out tonight in our fort!"

"Cool!"

"Yeah, let's do it! I'll go home and get sleeping bags," Nicholas offered, "and my dad's battery lantern.   ...and you go home and have your mom pack us up a supper and a big jug of soda!"

"Rootbeer!"   They beamed nose to nose.

"Poles!"

"Full moon's always a good time for fishin', Mikey!"

"You said it!"

And the boys disappeared like a gust of wind through the woods, by the corn field, leaping across the pumpkin field, passed the haunted house and out to the street, where the regular, common world enfolded them. They turned around and looked back down the tunnel entwined by the fingers of the chestnut trees where yellow and purple shadows danced in the knolls and the moist smell of the sweet earth loomed and beckoned them back inside with wooden fingers waving and long, hollow mouths sighing softly in a shadow play of thought.

"See ya!"

"Meet ya at the fort at six o'clock!"

And the boys returned to their homes with the thrill of some great expedition charging the air around them. Nicholas gathered camping gear, pillows, sleeping bags, his night cap and the lantern. Mikey, on the other hand, began weaving tales of treasures his mom could give them from the lofty shelves of her pantry.

"Well, what do you want honey? I'll make you boys whatever you'd like. I'm so very proud of you for freeing your pets! How about your mother surprising you. I'll fix a basket dinner for you two Huckleberry Fins, with lemonade and soda. You go pack a bag with an extra sweater and socks."

And indeed Mikey did pack his extra warm clothes, and his fishing pole, hooks and rubber bugs. And he even packed something extra. With quiet tinkling sounds the box of windchimes slid into his backpack with the anonymity of a secret made sacred from a patina of having been well kept. And as Mikey had no more pets to feed, he was out of his room in a wave of smiles, skipping down the staircase and tasting the wonderful air of his mother's kitchen. Packages and containers of unknown origin were carefully placed in a large picnic basket, and she fastened the latch of the basket with a smile.

"I want you back early tomorrow morning. And I know I don't need to say this, but I'm gonna say it anyways: No salamanders, no toads in your pockets, no turtles smuggled in by your backpack, nor any fish in the empty food containers. I'm very serious, Mikey! Very serious!" She warned, pointing at him as he ran down the road to the tunnel of trees. "And we're going to have a garage sale and get rid of all those aquariums you don't need anymore, young man!"

But he could not hear her, for the piping treble notes of the reeds chirping, buzzing and echoing with its colonies of newts and frogs, waterbugs and cicadas, and those things that fly and drift, and swim and crawl, all filled his senses with their presence. So his mother's warnings became lost in these tender, beautiful sounds. His heart sang as he flew down a tall row of corn stalks and along the narrow trail of the deep woods.

Mikey pushed the basket across the floor and climbed up into the fort. He slid the pack from his shoulders and dressed into a pair of shorts. Squatting on the window ledge, he unhooked the tire from the wall, with the thick rope of the swing looped around his ankles and a tight grip with his hands, he leaped hard into the air and swung low over the river. The heels of his feet skimmed the surface, the warm water spraying through his toes. Once, twice and he was flying. He let go and was caught by the buoyant deep river with its copper eddies and bobbing water lilies. This was his favorite place to swim, with the rifts of sand to walk on, the clear waters, cool, then warm, and bright lights that were captured upon its reflective lens. Individual lights cascading images of leaves and dragonflies, petals and clouds, all this together, flowing and moving, one bright scintillating surface of stars, capturing for a brief moment, never to be the same again, this special part of the world. He floated on his back, holding on to an arm of a felled tree, its bare skeleton arched above and then buried below the waters. Above on this hilly river, scattered boulders created a small waterfall whose swift current bubbled and rained all around him in a whirlpool of rootbeer foam and lilac mist.

'I could stay here forever,' he thought to himself. Like delicate butterfly wings, his eyes closed. The sun was full and warm, his skin flushed in orange lights. He drifted among that twilight space, not asleep, and truly not awake, but feeling and sensing all around him in a tender abandon. He noted the songbirds, the nearness of dragonflies buzzing and the sounds of the water surrounding him in purling reveries.

Floating on his back, he felt as though he were beginning to dissolve into the world around him. It was as if *he* were the forests, the gentle eddies of warm air and the phantastic cumulus mountains that swept forever upwards in explosions of shell pink and coral red. He had to look at his body to reassure himself that he was still actually in it: that he had not taken flight from some dream...that he was not a cascade of stars glistening fast upon the river; that he had not become a butterfly, opening and closing *his* wings upon a fern, or that he was not the fern itself, or gentle whirlwinds breathing across the sandy riverbanks.

So peaceful... When suddenly, a jar to his senses, *CRASH!* And up splashed Nicholas shaking his head like a dog.

"Hey, thank your mom for me!"

"For what?"

"That awesome dinner she made!" He grinned, laughing.

"You didn't! You monster!" Mikey shouted, releasing the tree and his place of dreams, and he climbed out of the river and up into the fort. He set the basket on the table and peered inside. Perfectly in tact, he fished up a large chocolate chip cookie and bit in, watching as Nicholas climbed inside and grabbed a towel, and sat down beside him.

Nicholas laughed. "See, I didn't do it," he assured him. And they reached in and pulled out paper plates and various containers.

"What's in here?" Asked Nicholas.

"Why, it's fried chicken. .....and here's a cherry pie!"

"Wow wow, Italian beef sandwiches...deviled eggs...wow, wow, wow..." he said, jumping up and down to make his point, "chocolate pudding," Nicholas said, rubbing his hands together. "Gimmie, gimmie," he pleaded, and Mikey passed him the basket.

The boys stacked their plates with a bit of everything, Mikey reached into his duffle bag and pulled out some of his favorite monster magazines.

"Alright!" Connected to each other like brothers, and to the tree fort so embraced and supported by the great willow, they chewed and laughed, flipping pages and exchanging memories of various movies they had seen, both together and alone.

"Look," exclaimed Nicholas, "here's the Creature From the Black Lagoon, you know that movie was filmed on this river!"

"Was not!"

"Was too!" Nicholas said.

"Who told you that?"

"I've seen him," Nicholas declared.

"When?"

"Oh, it was last summer, at night," he boasted.

"Wow!" Exclaimed Mikey. "How'd ya get away?"

"I flashed my lantern on him and he jumped into the water. He swam along the bottom until he was gone. Pass me some more chicken and those creamy eggs, Mikey!"

"Wow, here, take 'em."

"Did ya ever see <u>Attack of the Giant Leeches?</u> I did! Saw it five times now," bragged Nicholas.

"Yeah! That cave under the river was cool, where the leech kept all the bodies it was sucking on. That was a cool sound it made. Somethin' like that could never happen though. A monster leech," Mikey reflected, biting into a piece of big sandwich.

"Sure it could," Nicholas assured him.

"Don't lie, leeches are little. I picked one off the leg of a baby snapping turtle once."

"Yeah, you think so? I was out in my row boat last spring and somethin' was pullin' on the bottom of the boat. I thought maybe I got stuck on a water stump? When I looked down into the water, I saw this giant creature, it was bigger than my boat, like a giant eel, but with a big suction cup lined with millions of razor teeth for a face! It saw me and disappeared right down to the bottom of Hag Lake."

"You mean Hager's Lake?"

"Naw Mikey, I call it Hag Lake cause all the weird things in it. Why, the bottom is a thick mud quicksand that'll pull ya down and kill ya, if ya let it."

21

"Oh, no!" Exclaimed Mikey, completely transfixed.

"Oh yeah, Mikey! I found a human jaw bone and a pair of glasses there once, why, I even saw a human finger tangled up in the seaweed!"

"Well, I never go there anyways," Mikey comforted himself. He looked at a big dill pickle with relief, and, CRUNCH!!!!

"I heard that the monster leech grabs your face with his razor mouth and sucks your brains out, like drinking soda pop with a straw, slowly, and then he sucks out all the inside organs, and your body is left behind like a pile of clothes," Nicholas smiled, knowing he was spookin' Mikey.

Mikey laughed nervously. "Naw Nicky, there ain't no monster leech. That's all Hollywood movie picture stuff made to scare you and me, that's all it is Nicky, really, believe me. There ain't no spooks in the world. No witches, no goblins, why, there ain't even a Sanny Clause! And there's no Easter Bunny either Nicky," Mikey stated with the authority of experience, "and there ain't no Tooth Fairy cause I waited up for him and it was *just my mom!* .....so there can't be no Devil Leech neither!" Mikey concluded his address against the nature of spirits and spooks with a mouthful of cherry pie.

Before them their celebrated mess sat like a trophy. A plate piled high with chicken bones was over there, an empty pudding container was stacked together with a confetti of crumbled napkins, spoons licked clean with cherries on the handles and bits of sandwich all sat before them.

"Here, gimmie that copy of Tales From the Crypt and Famous Monsters, Mikey."

"Okay. I'm gonna roll out the sleeping bags. You gonna swim some more?"

"Naw, do some fishin' later," he said, gazing at each page with utter fascination.

Mikey put his backpack over in the corner, listening with a smile as the chimes delicately clinked together. 'Just wait 'till later,' he thought, petting the bag.

Hours passed like minutes. The boys played Chinese Checkers, and then played a game called the I Ching, pondering over the course of their lives and the things that *could* happen.

At nightfall, the boys stood along the bank of the river casting their fishing poles. The lilac bushes exhaled a dense, sweet perfume, trembling in the stillness. The moon rose up above the canopy of forests, gleaming down upon them in a lurid flood of ivory and bone.

"Sometimes," Mikey reflected, "the moon doesn't look all that big. And then there are other times when it seems so enormous, so gigantic, as if the sky was one big magnifying glass."

"It looks cold and lonely," added Nicholas.

"Yeah, it does. It's got a ring around it tonight."

"It's got the whole world lit up tonight!" Nicholas pondered.

"Oh ya, I can see all the way across the river."

"I got one Mikey!" Nicholas shouted.

"Maybe it's that Devil Leech you're pullin' up!" Laughed Mikey.

"It's a whale, I caught a whale, Mikey!"

"It's that leech and he's gonna jump up on your face and eat your brains!" Mikey giggled.

"Ya want me to throw ya in now Mikey?" And Nicholas pulled up a pretty little sunfish. He slid the hook from its lip and handed the fish to Mikey.

At once, Mikey gently tossed the fish back into the river.

"Should'a kept it, Mikey, could'a put it in your tank!"

"Naw, can't do that anymore. I let all my pets go."

"No ya didn't!"

"Ya, I did."

"Why, what in the world would you do a dumb thing like that for?"

"Well, maybe I can better explain that later."

"Naw Mikey, it just don't make sense. Those tanks were so cool. You had the best collection of animals of anyone I know."

"Yeah, and I let them all go. They're free now, like your little whale-fish is!" And he laughed, watching the watery moonlight.

Nicholas shook his head, "boy, I just don't understand you sometimes."

"You'll see," Mikey explained with a mysterious tone.

In the fort, the boys whispered quietly so as not to wake the trees.

"Sssshhhhhhhhhhhhhhh....." Mikey said with his finger over his lips. He hung the windchimes in the window ledge. The moonlight instantly set the sapphires ablaze in glowing blue lights that sparkled and chimed. Mikey climbed into his sleeping bag as Nicholas quickly sat up in his.

"No way!"

"Just wait...we can't get hurt."

"You were supposed to bring it back to the graveyard. Oh, Mikey, there's gonna be a spell on us both now!"

"Maybe a spell cast by trees."

"Now you sure don't make any sense anymore, Mikey. I'm packin' up and goin' home."

"Yeah, you're gonna walk passed Mr. Skullcap's old spooky house alone in the dark? I don't think so! Get back in your sleeping bag and watch the windchimes! I've done it before, Nicky. I'm still alive and safe, ain't I?"

"Well," and Nicholas leaned over and stared into his face lit by the ample lights cast by the lantern. "Why, I guess you look the same. But you sure act funny sometimes, now. Givin' back all those turtles just don't make much sense to me, Mikey. And....and you've been lookin' kind of pale lately. Worries me about you."

"Now you know I'm perfectly fine. And if the chimes don't hurt me, they ain't gonna hurt you either. So where do you want to go tonight?"

"Well, what kind of a foolish question is that Mikey? I want to lay in our bags and tell stories all night, and then I want to fall asleep and dream about summertime and Halloweens and Christmas Eves to come."

"No, silly, I mean, if you could go anywhere in the world, maybe even in the universe, to any time you wanted, say far into the future or back to the past. Where would you wanna go?"

"Why, Mikey, I don't know yet. Maybe to that *faraway place of secrets,* so that we could find out if there really is magic in the world. If Santa Clause exists. If ghosts are real and if there's life after death. Then we could talk to Uncle Bob again. We could find out if wishes and dreams can really come true, and if all the terrible and wonderful things we always talk about are truly, really, real!   Spacemen and mind travel, all of it Mikey.   I want to know!"

"Well, let's watch the windchimes and think about where we want to go and what we want to be.   Like playing the I Ching, concentrate Nicky, *concentrate.*"

"Just lay here and watch 'em?"

"Oh yes! It's all we gotta do!"

So the boys laid in their sleeping bags, watching the prisms of blue light cast in shivering apparitions upon the walls of their treefort. Watery shadows trembled all around them, circling, wanting, waiting...

"What was that?"   Shouted Nicky.

"That was a tree branch scratching the fort. It's windy Nicky. So tell me, what do you want to do?   Wake up the dead and ask them what it's like?   Ride with a flock of witches through the moonlit sky like black boats in a sea?   Ummmm, we could ride a dragon far into tomorrow and see what the world would be like. Maybe, maybe we could go to another planet way beyond the furthest stars."

"Why, where will we go Mikey?"

"Certainly not the moon. It seems so barren."

"No, not the moon. At least not tonight."

"I've never seen a real castle before,"   wondered Nicholas.

"There's a lot of 'em in my books at home. I wonder if they're all haunted? We could go someplace where there are ghosts, ya know! Why, we could even go to Nightshade Pond, then you would know why I let all my pets go."

"It all sounds so silly," mused Nicholas. "....but, can't we get into trouble?"

"No, I'm sittin' here, aren't I?"

"Why yes, of course, Mikey."

"And I've been to one of these places before."

"No!"

"Oh yes! And I came back home safely again," he confided, pulling the sleeping bag up under his chin, staring off at the chimes. "Where should we go...lot's of places we could go...hummmmmmmmmmm.....I wonder if there's a planet with nothing but piles of candy on it? Rock-candy hills like granite rocks, sweet koolaide waterfalls, chocolate trees with mint leaves..."

And the boys waited, wondering about magical things. With their heart's pounding hard, they waited to be transported to another land or perhaps another time. Someplace, for sure, that would tell them that the world is *truly* full of magic.

"We could pet a dinosaur."

"......And get eaten by one, too! I wanna go far into the future."

"Ah, where to go; where to go..."

"You sure that thing works?" Challenged Nicholas. "Nothin's happened yet. Aren't we still layin' here?"

"Oh yeah, but you'll see...be quiet and watch..."

One, two and then three hours passed.

"Well, I can't keep my eyes open any longer. So much for magic," Nicky sighed, "I'm goin' to sleep..."

But Mikey was already ahead of him, sound asleep.

And that's when it happened.

A fragrant blue mist crawled over the floor covering them. It filled the air like cirrus clouds billowing up above their sleeping bags, but they did not know. The willow tree woke, thrashing its long, whip-like branches against the walls, trying to wake the boys. And the mist crawled, moving around the room, thickening and turning round, opening its shimmering night hands.

"P p p p p p p p p p p s s s s s s s s s s s s s s s t t...
................ppppppppppppppppppppppppsssssssssssssssttt.........."

"What?" Said Mikey.

"You awake?" Nicholas poked him. "That thing didn't work, we're still lyin' here!"

Mikey sat up in his sleeping bag.   He smiled, thinking how Nicholas had an expression of relief on his face.

"I don't know, things seem the same. Though, things aren't always what they seem anyways."

The boys wandered among the pumpkin fields. The warm, melting sunrise with colors of orange and red and purple, stained the world as if they were contained by a colored glass dome.

And immediately they knew the windchimes had worked. For the world seemed new again.

"Ouch!" Complained a vine, as it curled away from Mikey's foot.

"I'm sorry!" Mikey cried.

And the pumpkins of the field stretched and rustled about, and the sky dimmed a rich purple red.

"Strangest sunrise I've ever seen. Who ya talkin' to over there, Mikey?"

"Why, haven't you ever talked to a pumpkin before?" Asked a large pumpkin whose face instantly flickered with carved expression and a glow from within its empty head.

"Wow! Cool! You talkin' to me?"

"Why, yes, son, I'm Jake," and the pumpkin shook its vines. The tall pumpkin leaned back, addressing a row of other pumpkins, and spoke: "Let's do Sixteen Tons for the boys."

And with this, all the pumpkins of the field sang together, their faces flickering hard with many varied Halloween expressions. They sang songs that the boys loved from school music class, that lent a special mood to living. And then, after many songs, the boys sat in the field cross-legged, among their friends, and the pumpkins gathered and dragged themselves in a great circle around Jake, and he began to tell the most deliciously scarey ghost stories that the boys had ever heard. Tales spun with literary narrative, and that masterful art and tone of a pumpkins' enthusiasm filled their imaginations with new worlds of terror and delight.

"Why, Nicky, *if everything is alive*," explored Mikey, "then let's go see the apple orchard! Why, I wonder what the trees could tell us? I wonder what the worst thunder storm was like? And the oaks, Nicky, the oaks live over a hundred years, they could tell us about the Indians."

And with that, the boys bid goodbye to their new friends, the pumpkins, and thanked them for so many a fine story and song.

"Why, you'll always be at my house when the year turns to autumn and big leaf piles are raked and burned at night, with the long, cool smell of the woods, you'll be waiting inside the window for me, until after Halloween night!"   Mikey assured the bright orange faces, as they ran toward Mr. Skullcap's house, coming closer and closer towards the apple grove.

"Hello!"   Addressed the boys to the ripening trees.   "Hello!"

The branches of the apple trees were filled with flocks of crows. Big, black shiny crows. Or were they ravens? They were almost too big to be crows, the boys thought.

To their vast disappointment, not a single tree replied. No leaves shook in murmuring words, nor did the bark configure its crested shapes into slender mouths bearing fruits of history and adventure. Instead, the sable capes of the crows with their squawking words and silhouettes stark against a sharpening sky, sharpening like the presence of an ocean glowing and thundering in the darkness, filled the twilight dusk around them.   The profiles of the crows, vivid and intense, moving and exchanging calls upon the myriad branches of the gnarled apple trees, began to shift.   The boys stood, watching the shadows of the trees melting together with the movements of the birds.

"Wow!"

"It's like the Northern Lights!"

Bending in nebulous forms, winged, tufted and now protruding, what once were beaks were now hats, tall and familiar. What once were sheaved feathers, became long arms.   And what once begot the sky with wings, was now captured by long sticks. Broomsticks.   And cackling laughter, pitched high and shrill, drown out the cawing calls of hopping crows. And upon this tree, danced witches. Treelimbs turned to broomsticks, upon whose flight the sky was filled. The moon's bright orb cast surreal lights upon the flocking witches, who sprung from the trees as branches dissolved to brooms, and trees to mist. And the orchard was no more!

Suddenly, the boys were lifted up like leaves in a fast turn of wind, and thus strode behind a hag! Higher and higher, climbing among the purple clouds they rode. Thrilling sensations of height leapt their bellies in vertigoes of terror like runaway Ferris Wheels spinning off towards the cream lights of the moon. Sensations of flying turning to swimming, immersed in deep waves of sky, warm and light, buoyant and shimmering sweet among the burning stars. Thrilling fear waned to reveries of being taken into deeper waters of higher climes. Exhilarating motions that felt like swimming made them fly.

And fly and fly they did, beyond the limits of a wonderful green ceiling of swimming clouds, like passing through a cool, wet membrane purifying them in strange moving lasers which vibrated deep into the very marrow of their thoughts and bones. They passed through the ceiling membrane of the green clouds, and beyond into golden skies shining brilliantly, piercing them with a brisk clarity like millions of lights reflected off clear watercaps, *making senses once hidden, come alive.*

Magnificently twisting labyrinths of castles climbed up above the cloud ceiling, and seemed almost, as if they too were alive, watching them, waiting. Steep turrets flagged with myriad bartizans, whose cat-like window eyes blinked at them. Grand battlements formed sinister smiles with their giant teeth, like grinning tombstones defending the house with its murder-holes and shielding merlons. The gaps of the embrasures between the merlons were sometimes peopled with marble statues of saints and angels, of prophets and martyrs, some holding lanterns in their eternal frozen sojourn over the castle, some holding harps, swords and giant bands of keys.

Closer and closer they approached the many steepled castles whose great towers were entwined together by eloquent connections of stained glass halls, catwalks and curtain walls. They floated buoyantly just above a courtyard like leaves drifting off branches, branches that had once turned to broomsticks, and broomsticks which now dissolved into nothing, as gentle hands of air lowered them into the courtyard.

Grey and precipitously descending, a stone cliff connected the castles with the world below, a winding cliff whose foot was lost below in boils of clouds, green and cool.

Silence.

"Now how we gonna get back home?" Whined Nicky.

Nicholas and Mikey looked all around. A streak of brilliant light wandered like a fish over the grey stones of the courtyard and beyond. They entered a great hallway of giant stone faces, whose conversations suddenly felled a curdling silence.

"I sure wish you had brought those windchimes back to the graveyard when I told you to, Mikey!" He elbowed.

"Sssssshhhhh."

"And who are you!" Bellowed a stone face.

"Why, why, I'm Michael Greenfield, and this here is my friend Nicholas."

"Nicholas! Michael!" Shrieked a wall. "I don't believe it!"

"Yes, ummm, yes....that's us......, but we'd be happy to go home now," offered Mikey, shuddering before the giant face of an owl.

"If you were happy at home you wouldn't be here now, would you boys? Out looking for a little magic today, boys? *Bored?* Magic doors abound in the common world below, but they shouldn't be opened without first knowing what you truly need and feeling it with all your heart. Now *you* have the windchimes! Those windchimes are a sacred relic. The windchimes conjure reveries of the supermind or ultimate consciousness, which is the key to unlocking the mysteries of the universe. You have leaped across a chasm which separates the three dimensional world from the limitless dimensions of *true reality*, flying beyond the outer limits of the sky which broods over the common world below, into greater regions, a *terra incognita,* where new, unexplored lands await you. You have passed through the mirror. These lands are the physical terrain of your own imagination, your dreams and talents, and the sum of your fears. It is the outer world of the inner subconscious. And you have also unearthed a treasure, a treasure chest of great knowledge and power - where the ultimate secrets of reality are kept. What shall you do with it? What do you want? Maybe you will help someone you know, who is suffering?" Questioned the owl.

"Why, mister, you speak rather well for a rock!"   Nicky said smartly.

"Everything is alive!   Everything is alive!   Everything lives!" Declared the stone face, as if an alarm had been suddenly sounded. *"Hoooot Hooooooooooot!   Life is everywhere!* I suppose you think the trees are dead? They are not!" The owl declared, talking rapidly and flapping its wings, creating a sudden draft. "I'm alive, aren't I? *Hoooot Hooooooooooot!* I want to know what you're going to do with the magic windchimes, it was guarded by the dragon of the graveyard! Trouble follows you now!"

"Mikey and Nicholas! I don't believe it! I don't believe it!" Mocked the weasel comically, as if in a hurry to get a word in edgewise. "Brave little fellows you are!"

A tortoise stretched his head and looked over at the boys, straightening his glasses. "Be warned! There exist certain magical places and objects in the common world. They have the power to awaken our greatest potential which normally lies buried deep within the mind awaiting billions and billions of seasons of evolution. These sacred forces unlock inner realms and dimensions of awareness which are our infinite connection with the universe. These relics bridge the finite to the infinite."

"It is you who sleeps, you who is dead to life!" Interrupted the owl. "It is the rocks and streams which sing, and the trees which whisper words rich in wisdom and history."

The tortoise continued: "There are geometric boxes, windchimes, magic waterfalls, pyramids, haunted trees, mystical caves and crystal pools that if you swam in, you'd be sure to emerge back onto the shores of a new and different world. Let me see," he said, straightening his glasses again, "...there is great power in the desert and canyons, too, I've seen it! But boys, these are sacred objects and sacred places which should not be disturbed. There are enchanted forests so amazing, so beautiful, so you see that many things abound all around us, everywhere, all the time, and that which is commonly known to be true, call it reality, call it life or time, call it anything you like, is only an infinitesimal and minute understanding of a tremendous mystery, like a single grain of sand from a vast and wondrous beach of possibility, without limits, without end, and evermore reaching beyond even the greatest comprehension."

"Why, yes, that's right." Agreed the owl. "Nicely put, I was going to say that!"

"I don't believe it - I don't believe it! - Mikey and Nicholas! I don't believe it!" The weasel announced with comical flare. "Why *I'd* never mess with *that* dragon!"

"Sometimes," the tortoise continued, "the objects are found in certain holy locations, like graveyards, cathedrals, mountain peaks, beneath the ground and at the bottom of oceans."

"Why yes," blinked a rabbit, "even camping tents can have it!"

A deer turned its regal head of antlers, and added: "Tents? Preposterous! Why do you think such nonsense could be true? A tent is a tent! Ha!"

"Much imagination and wonder has been created in tents at night, why," spoke the bunny, "ghost stories have been woven, and thunderstorms witnessed - why, even the animals that like to chase bunnies like me prowl around tents at night trying to listen, that's why!" The bunny spoke, suddenly cleaning his paws in a rapid movement.

"Never mind!" Gestured the owl, "I want to know why you stole the windchimes from the dragon? The dragon guards the dead souls of the graveyard, and you disturbed a protected and sacred object." The owl pointed at them with his wing accusingly.

Nicholas and Mikey looked at each other quizzically. "Why, what do you mean? We only wanted to travel to faraway places, to see *if magic is really real.* If there really are spacemen; and if people don't ever die really ."

"Nothing, dear boys, is more real." Confided the tortoise. "It lies just beneath the surface."

And with that, the great hall of faces began laughing. Kind and beneficent, the faces laughed knowingly. "Is magic real? I don't believe it! I don't believe it!"

The laughter gathered around them in a warm mist of embracing unseen arms, laughter that echoed in a foreboding sense of destiny, for indeed they knew *not* what lay ahead. But for certain - a cauldron of mysteries whorled in the air all around them.

Suddenly, the hall grew icy cold and a shrill wind blew down the strange corridor and all the giant stone faces froze. The hall hushed to a dead silence. An eerie howling and wailing mourned the castle walls.

"Why, what's that?" Nicholas asked the dolphin. But the dolphin did not reply. The animals froze in their immediate expressions, and an eerie soundlessness flooded the great hall as if they were sitting in a boat in the middle of a sea...rocking, waiting, ... *and then!* ...the ground shook, and a great thud of mountainous footsteps felled the corridors beyond. Bulwarks shook and tapestries trembled as each footfall grew nearer and nearer, heavier and heavier. A high pitched shriek, shrill and long, filled the air, and from around the corner a giant snout protruded barring horribly jagged razor teeth and a long, serpentine black tongue which slithered down the hallway towards them, moving rhythmically like a snake, and then retracted suddenly into its cave of fangs. Then came the sound of claws stomping down with terrible scraping, shearing sounds echoing throughout the corridors. The brushing of enormous wings dragged behind, which acted as a sort of cape for the sharp taloned arms of the Dragon.

"It'll be my head, It'll be my head!" Roared the giant. "I must find them!"

Nicky and Mikey looked at each other in a numbing fright. Quickly they climbed and hid in the open mouths of the walls.

"Who stole the magic windchimes?" Long torches flamed wildly from his nostrils scorching the walls in pulsing red flashes.

The Dragon shrieked again and lumbered down the hall, drawing closer and closer. Well hidden in their peculiar alcoves, the boys watched the monster as it passed them. Its face was characterized by a snout which opened into a long cave of teeth, deadly sharp, with a wicked long tongue for grabbing its prey like a rope and dragging it back down into the pit of its throat.   Six bloody eyes raged wildly as it labored passed the boys like the giant head of a fly, clumsily dragging a sort of dinosaur-like tail behind, which scraped the floor in an eerie metallic sheering sound.

"Look Nicky!" Mikey whispered low, it's got a tongue like that Jackson lizard I once had - you know, when he'd nab a fly, his tongue zipped all the way across the tank, and he didn't even move..."

Nicky said nothing.

"Whoooooooossseeeeee there!!!!!!!!!!!!!!!!" Stomped the giant. "Whooooossseee got my windchimes? The dead souls from the graveyard are after me now; they want my head!" He stomped in a thunderous gait, flames flaring from his nostrils. "It'll be my head! It'll be my head!" He roared.

The Dragon stopped at a large circular door in the ground with wrought iron handles, "It's those insipid trolls!" He said, rubbing his claws together. He pulled up the door and climbed down below, all the while bellowing and shrieking with fires blasting from his nostrils. The dragon's roaring passage faded in macabre echoes, a shadow lost among the shadows of a nightmare, as he thundered further down an obscure mazework of tunnels and caves beneath the castle. Suddenly, screaming echoed from below. It was the wild, shrill, high-pitched panicked screaming of being eaten alive. Unfortunate elves, trolls, dwarves and goblins were roped and dragged mercilessly into the Dragon's mouth of unspeakable teeth whose jaws were more formidable than a shark, and as quickly devastating as the savage hunger of a school of piranhas. Many scrambled up from the trap door running down the corridor passed Mikey and Nicky. The long black snake tongue hissed up from the floor like a cobra, roping an elf, dragging him back down into the echoing caverns below. The elf's eyes were wild with delirious fright as he held on to the giant black tongue which constricted him, dragging him down the hallway and towards the fetid jaws of the giant. For an instant the elf saw Nickys' terrified little face watching him, hidden from beneath a giant nose, as he was swiftly dragged below and out of sight.

And oh, that awful screamin' and thrashing! The boys held their little hands over their ears, but the horror of it all stained their minds with sounds of torture, with the unthinkable experience of being eaten alive, one limb, then the next, watching yourself disappear piece after painful piece. It was a hollerin' from something that sounded like it had lost its mind, followed by a long mournful wailing of soul which can never be appeased or saved for the world, as the maddening notes curled the air all around them rising in a morbid, unseen funereal choir. Hell lay just beneath the floor, its infernal chorus straining their nerves. Indeed, even the stone eye of the dolphin moved inconspicuously toward the wrenching-agonizing sounds and immediately froze again.

"Where are the windchimes?" The dragon blasted. "Tell me! Where are they? Where are they?" He bellowed, holding the little elf before his burning eyes, blood and strips of muscle streaming from his jaws, "tell me!"

"I've been stirring potions all day; I've never seen any windchimes!" He cried.

And with that, Mikey and Nicky slid out from their secret hiding places in the wall, and ran down the hallway *never looking back.*

And run and run they did, however, the hallway never ended, but rather continued, narrowing inwards closer and closer the further they ran.

"Oh, Nicky, here he comes!" Cried Mikey.

"He's behind us, I can see him." Nicky shouted, running with terrified leaps. And indeed behind them a shadow as black as night dilated into hundreds of bats growing nearer and nearer, their frenzied flapping and maddening squeaking casting a witchery of horrors within the hallway. And the hallway became narrower and narrower until the boys were almost running shoulder to shoulder.

"It'll be my head! I'll be my head!" Wailed the monster.

"We can't go back!" Screamed Mikey.

"I know! He's gonna get us...he's gonna get us!" Cried Nicky. "Where do we go now?"

Mikey quickly turned around as the black cloud of squeaking bats shape-shifted back into the dragon, whose head thrashed from side to side with scorching flames and scraping talons.

"You've got the windchimes!" The monster roared, laughing maniacally.

Sweat covered both their faces, a new terror they had never before experienced. "I don't want to die," cried Nicky. And before them, the hallway narrowed to a fine point ending nowhere and fortunately for the boys, they did not notice but continued to run hard, looking back at the dragon who changed once again into a cloud of whirling bats, picking up speed behind them as they ran straight through the end of the hallway and disappeared...

Falling like leaves, they could open their arms to slow down and almost float, or fold them and spiral downwards in a thrilling and refreshing wind. Up above, they heard roaring and the shearing sound of the heavy tail scraping back and forth across the floor, but saw nothing for they had escaped the dragon's terrible fate with their newfound magic, running right through the parallel wall of one place, and into that of another. The boys felt like they had just ran through the looking glass of a funhouse. But where were they? Falling and falling, and *splash!* The boys bobbed up from the waters as if they had merely dived off from a small beach cliff.

"Why," said Mikey, "this must surely be the most beautiful place that I have ever seen!"

"We must find the windchimes and return them right away," Nicky implored.

"I know that Nicky, I just about got eaten by a dragon! I know that!" Mikey snarled, panting.

"But where are we?" Asked Nicky feeling utterly lost, the relief of escaping the dragon turning now into a new and stranger fear. "Why, where is this place?"

"Well, I don't think we're any nearer to our treefort yet. Do you?"

"No."

And the boys climbed up onto a giant boulder, misted by the perfumes of vining lilac, rose and hyacinth trees which wound and climbed up and around the walls and ceiling of the glowing cave, surrounding them in dizzying floral arrays of sparkling colored lights. The cups of the blossoms were so gigantic that the boys could easily climb inside and sit among the cool nectar pools. And beneath them in the clear river watercaps, schools of skeleton fish blinked in dense shimmering curtains of yellow, emerald and blue. Suddenly the schools of fish moved together in a graceful and singular turn upwards, dreamlike and surreal, and then in an instant, the sheets of scintillating water stars flashed in traveling columns to the right, scattering quickly outwards and swimming out of sight. Jellyfish pulsed with ribbons of iridescent blue and purple lights, trailing glowing shadows whose fading water dust streaked like comets shooting down and down and down into the vast fathoms of the mysterious river cave. The surface of the river was like a looking glass magnifying the crystal waters. Lights flashed so far down that they had to agree that indeed there seemed to be no bottom at all! Imagine that, a river without a bottom, without end. And the boulders they rested on, why, what were they? The peaks of mountains? And who had ever heard of a never ending mountain? They agreed that they were very lucky, for sure, that they were both good swimmers, for to fall into this river without being able to swim would be to drift downwards forever among the glowing red seaweeds that flowed and swam like mermaid's hair and to meet with creatures strange and new. It was like watching spectacular fireworks exploding underwater, and it was as if the northern lights had been stolen right out of the skies and cast to dwell in this haunting waterscape, with its vivid and thrilling sceneries which they could not describe. The boys watched in utter fascination, begot by the utter abandon of its spell, forgetting for the moment that they were still a long way from home. Such things they had never seen before, and such things they could have never even imagined existed, but for the visions which beheld them now, they did!

"Wow!" Exclaimed Mikey. "What's that?"

"It's a, ...it's a swimming reef!" Said Nicky.

"Can't be. There's no such thing!"

"It's a coral reef as big as a house and it's traveling under us, and it's going that way!" Nicky pointed. "Wow!" The boys watched as the reef slowly passed below like some kind of strange, slowly floating space ship with polyps, gorgonians, coralbells, clams, sea urchins and millions of tiny flowerlike animals pulsing from its bones in a spectrum of phosphorescent colors, with close nipping reef fishes darting here and there.

"Look, Mikey! An eel!" Nicky exclaimed.

"Wow."

And the boys laid on their bellies looking down into the endless clear waters below, watching as the magnificent coral reef drifted passed, and moments later, a group of manta rays swam by, rocking the surface of the water, as one of them swam so close to the surface that Mikey was able to pet it as it traveled passed. Hours passed as the boys watched fishes that have been long extinct over centuries of time, swim below. Gigantic whale sharks cruised passed and eel-like fish as big as trains traveled below, and all of a sudden, the boys found that they were being stared at from below by a school of seahorses which gathered near the surface looking up at the boys, their gossamer wings rapidly fanning.

"What do they want, Nicky?" Said Mikey.

41

"Probably never seen nothin' like you before!" Laughed Nicky.

The cave echoed with the dripping sounds of falling nectar, which rose in a cirrus of fragrant mists, shining in deep prisms and shadows of petals, drifting further down the river like balloons toward the end of the cave.   Deep into the cave at its furthermost end, clusters of lightning storms struck and sparked in brilliant flashing vines. Behind the root systems of rippling lightning, raged torrents of waterfalls that did not crash straight down, but rather surged across like an extension of the cave in a raining lip of cyclones.

"But how do we get home from here?"   Asked Mikey to Nicky. The seahorses turning their heads now to Nicky.

"I don't know," answered a gigantic rose nodding its head downwards, "but if I were you, I'd follow the cave to the end, for if you go through the wall of lightning, you'll cross over into even greater dimensions. It could even take you home, if that's what you really wanted?"

"Nicky, did you say something?"

"No. It was *that rose* over there!"

"I keep forgetting that we're not home."

"You're always at home where ever you go, if you're content with yourself." Spoke the rose, opening wide.

"I don't like riddles!" Complained Nicky.

"Me neither!" Exclaimed Mikey, and the boys jumped over the tops of the boulders and journeyed toward the end of the cave where silver-blue skeletal lights flashed wildly. Beyond the fiery curtains they heard the roaring drop of a waterfall, whose precipitous cliff crashed wildly in thundering torrents like a raging sea. They looked through the veil of lightning, *the door in the wall,* and saw to their amazement that the waterfall did not drop down, but rushed straight across like a river, a river with sheer space underneath and all around it. Almost like a tube - a tornado - a sort of slide...

"Why up seems down and down seems up here!" Said Nicky, shaking his head.

"Yeah, and nothins' gonna seem like anything if that dragon catches up with us!" Warned Mikey, skipping over boulders while staring down at the magnificent lights of the undersea fishes and wandering reefs.

"How can a waterfall fall across, and not down? And lightning strike under the ground in a cave?" Nicky wondered outloud.

"Why, it's easy," whispered vines of lilac. "It's very easy. Come with me to the end of the cave," it beckoned.

"Well, as there's really no other place for us to go, and we're already headed there, we'll probably beat you to it!" Said Nicky. "...common'...."

And the vines trembled across the ceiling of the cave in delicate lanterns of lavender and blue, just keeping pace ahead of the boys as they traveled further down towards the storming lights.
Surreal rings of jellyfish pulsed in vermillion moons, as flying skeleton fish leapt from the waters and propelled steady flights swimming along with the boys, in an eerie escort of glowing bones. And all at once, the rippling lilac vines and jumping fish disappeared beyond the veil of lightning and surging waterfalls and the boys were suddenly alone. They stopped just before the curtains of branching, scoping lightning, reaching an arm through the soundless, flashing wall, touching the waterfall. And as they did so their arm disappeared; for when they pulled their arms back out, there was nothing there, yet, they could still feel them and use them!

"It's an invisible ray machine!" Announced Nicky.

"I want my arm back!" Shouted Mikey. "Where'd all the fishes go?"

"I donn' know."

"I can feel it, but I can't see it! Wow! Mr. Sampson in science class won't believe this!" Said Mikey, bragging.

"Nobodys gonna believe nothin' we've seen, ya hear me Mikey, Nothin', " Nicky assured him.

"Who cares, I just want to go home!" And Mikey's eyes welled with tears: tears that fell in gentle raindrops upon the magic waters, and each teardrop turned into a snow white dove that immediately flew away beyond the door of lightning, and in the sudden wake of their flight, an eerie, haunting, lonely echoing coooooooing sound faded to nothing. The only other time that Mikey could remember feeling this deeply sad, was when he returned home from a vacation with his parents from an ancient country far, far away, and having been picked up at the airport and brought home, he woke up the very next morning with the sad call and song of a distant land just there at the back of his mind, like haunting memories drifting up to the surface of wakefulness from his subconscious mind, so richly alluring and beautiful, filling his heart with wonder and possibility, and this moment indelibly impressed upon his life a yearning to forever seek out such reveries and magic again - *for beware the emptiness...*

"Remember that huge fish I caught in the river?" Nicky asked, jolting Mikey from his thoughts of knowing that some new door was about to open, as the other had just closed forever behind them. "Why, I doubt that anyone's gonna believe *even that!*" Nicky whined, folding his arms in defeat. "And it was a true giant, remember? My whale-fish!"

"No way! It was a minnow. You're dreamin," laughed Mikey.

"I'd have to be, to be in a place like this!" Nicky answered him stubbornly.

"So? Are we gonna do it?" Prodded Nicky.

Instantly the cave began to shake! Rocks and giant blossoms fell from the cavern ceiling, and fishes and waterlife swam down and down and down, far out of sight, as the lights of the undersea worlds disappeared. An eerie soundlessness filled the cavern: there were no echoes of dripping nectar, no sighing flowers nor singing reeds, the lights had simply vanished as if a Christmas tree had suddenly been unplugged!

It was a strange, spooky silence that summoned and invoked a brooding flock of vultures, clutching trees in their dusty, worn vests and lowering red eyes in a sort of superimposed desert landscape that faded to and from the walls of the cave.

Suddenly, and with the terrific force of a giant, the dragon burst from the waters below and stood face to face with the boys. The vultures faded to glowing red eyes which lit the darkened cave as the monster swiped at the boys, and in that instant moment they dove head first beyond the door of lightning and into the wilds of the falling river beyond.

They rode the crashing waves which carried them swiftly passed skies of coral and shell peach. They watched the theatre of the skies as it beheld ancient ferns and dinosaurs. Stars collapsed consuming nearby planets in an infinite wake of darkness. Suns dimmed to cold orbs and comets soared. New worlds struck bright with life burst in solar flares and beacon lights, signaling the vast and endless seas of the universe its simple single message. Barren planets wept with ten thousand years of rain; and things crawled from oceans and lakes, and apes dropped from trees running with food in their arms. Paintings and journals became inscribed and recorded upon the walls of caves - trembling antiquity in torch-lit shadows of tomorrow. Continents split and volcanoes flared. Giant insects and birds eyed eclipsing suns and moons with curiosity - fleeing from lightning and the mysterious booming of thunder. Diamond galaxies scintillated in a spiraling dna of scattered islands among shoreless oceans of space. Grounds split and shattered as mountains broke the sea, and majestic peaks became submerged among the deep of the silent seas.

They soon saw their own town long before their homes were built. The general store and post office was now framed by dirt roads, and not the smooth paved roads they knew so well from so many a bicycle ride. The toy store, too, looked different, and was now a soda fountain! But why would an entire store just sell ice cream and soda pop? They wondered, when now, it could be bought in packages? Life must have been different then, they pondered.

Suddenly, the boys were flying, or were they falling? ...down and down and down through a passage of outer space, pulled within a phantasmagoria of solar spheres and dimensions of light and sound and color flashing passed them with a speed and an immediacy they new not ever before. They were transported beyond sparkling configurations of stars and planets and suns and moons. Comets flashed passed as suns waxed and waned in distant fields of space. The passage of No Time turned, and the boys fell off into bridges of rainbows which gently captured them, slowing their descent, when all of a sudden, and quite by surprise, they hit a solid ground and were sprawled upon the floor of their treefort.

"You okay?" Asked Mikey.

"Yeah. How 'bout you?" Asked Nicky.

"I'm okay, I think. Wow, what a ride!" Said Mikey. "Remember those pterodactyls?"

"Yeah! Sure do. But howd' they turn into the smaller birds I have in my yard at home?"

"I donn' know!"   Said Mikey.

"Wow, what a world!"   Nicky exclaimed, looking around their treefort with relief.

"Let's hurry, gotta get the windchimes back to the graveyard before the dragon finds us again." Said Mikey.

"He's gone now, Mikey." Nicky advised him.   "He couldn't follow us here."

"Yeah, that's what we thought before, 'common!   Let's go!" Mikey implored.

"Yeah Mikey, ya know, you're right! *Anything's possible!*" And with that, the boys carefully placed the magic windchimes back into its box and ran toward the graveyard.

For a spell had woven itself about their lives in an indelible web of enchantment, with lifelong memories to behold and possibilities to imagine and explore.   And therefore, it had indeed been a most grand summer of spells, for they knew now for sure, that no such thing as *boredom* has ever existed and that magic is truly real. They knew not how long they had been gone, for it seemed like many months.

"I wonder what time it is? I hope summer's not over!" Nicky said, running passed the pumpkin field and entering the rows of corn.

"What if we missed Christmas?"   Mikey pined.   "What if my parents are..."

"Dummy, your mom's probably in the kitchen right now makin' a pie. And there's no snow, so it can't be winter yet either! And I don't think it's midnight, 'cause I can see."

"We don't know that for sure!   It's that spell, Nicky, we're not back yet!"

" 'Common, let's hurry."

And the boys ran like the wind passed the spooky house they called haunted, "I ain't goin' in there! That's for sure, Nicky." Mikey said, pointing at the house as glowing eyes blinked back at them from the dark shadows within. The boys ran into the tunnel of trees and out onto the road.

Mikey began crying, holding the box close to his chest.

"What is it?" Nicky said, looking around fearfully.

"My house is gone! I knew somethin' terrible happened. We're being punished."

"Oh, no! It sure is." Said Nicky. "Maybe it's just the spell. Maybe this isn't happening! *Or maybe it's just happening here.*" He told him, quizzically having perplexed himself by what he had just said.

"I want to go over there and see what happened." Said Mikey.

"No!" And Nicky grabbed his arm, pulling him the other way running passed the apple grove. There before them stood the menacing gates of the graveyard. Steel grey clouds turned black with gusting winds, as vortexes of gravel and dust blew at them off the road. The trees were bending in a shrill wind which rose in eerie choruses of wailing voices as the boys walked up the driveway and unlatched the banging gates. The spired, iron gates squeaked like thousands of bats scattering wildly all around them from an unseen cave. They ran into the graveyard among the sombre headstones. A skeletal arm reached up from the earth grabbing Nicky by the ankle, pulling him down.

"Put it back!" Nicky shouted at Mikey.

Mikey reached the dragon water fountain, sliding the box of windchimes back into its empty claw against the cold gusting winds. Immediately the roaring winds and wailing voices stopped, and they knew that the spell was now over, for songbirds sang and whistled, and thickly growing buttercups shined in sunlit knolls and the world was the same again. Nicky pulled a large tree branch off his ankle and looked over at Mikey in desperate relief.

No storm clouds raged the skies and the air was warm and kind, the sun ablaze in brilliant fires of yellow and rose, saturating their skin with the smell of wind and rain and warm earth.

However, although they were back, the world was *not* the same. For they had learned that it is truly filled with a sublime and endearing magic always; with a wizardry of doors where wonderful adventures await us all, just beyond that transparent film of thresholds, permeable by imagination and courage. It is a place where time stops and truly begins, from so simple a place as a frog pond full of dreams and a yearning for truth, *and therewith the sweep of its magic wand, it had been a most grand summer of spells...*

THE LIGHTHOUSE

THE LIGHTHOUSE

CHAPTER I
THE ACCIDENT

All around me lightning branched in electric green and silver flames from the black hulls of the thunderheads and squalls gusting over the wild sea. The wind blew shrill and hard as icy waves slapped against my boat and across the floor boards, sagging and spinning me down inside a quaking maelstrom.

And then it happened. In an instant, all was grey foam and shocking cold. I climbed up onto the overturned bottom of the boat, and through the blowing foam of the surging waves was able to see, if not from the tumult and delirium of my horror, a beacon light from a tower standing lone upon a dark forested island. I let go of my life-raft, the boat, and swam in the direction of the broadening and pulsing light. Whether it be a ghost-vision produced by my hysteria and panic, or a real place of sudden beatific refuge, I had released my only safety, the raft of the boat, and now expended the whole of my energy in swimming towards what could sharpen into focus as being merely a phantom shore.

Icy pipelines of waves crashed against my face, forcing me under. If clever gnomes of luck had been hiding near me anywhere, they should be with me now in this moment of death. The currents dragged and pulled me like a dead fish to the stony thorns of the forest shore. Cragged peninsulas stormed with shooting geysers that blew up from the boulders as waves exploded against the steep, rocky cliffs.

I was exhausted, and crawled out on my hands and knees from the raining surge of the ocean. I don't know how long I laid on the shore, but I knew this: That when I awoke, seagulls swirled above in pacific satin tides of sky, and the echo of their calls became lost among the brightly shining watercaps in a quiet, sullen dream of sight and sound. Gentle winds fanned the surface of the sea, and then lifted again as the surface became a glassy smooth mirror, a gigantic clear eye upon whose watchful brow I had escaped. Against the shore quietly rocking among scraps of timber and pine, was my boat.

I grabbed onto sharp boulders and pulled myself to my feet. Climbing over to a sandy section of beach, I stretched and bent around, sensing and feeling the contours of pain my muscles had absorbed. The morning sun had dried me, and the nightmare of the accident from the night before seemed unreal, as if I were a spectator, as if it had happened to someone else. But I stood, looking over at the broken boards of the boat, gently rocking up onto the shore, it too, trying to elbow itself out from the dangerous rage of the sea not trusting its present mood either for naught too long.

The fine emerald line of the horizon wrapped itself around the world as far as I could see. I had no idea where I was or how far lost I was from the area where I had started my boating journey. A journey I now regretted with bitter remorse, for I had heard over the radio that the storm was coming, but tried to out-race it for the sake of sheer excitement alone. I would remember to find other sources of excitement, should fate remunerate my efforts in having survived.

A narrow, unkempt trail wandered upwards beyond a crowd of boulders. I followed the trail which brought me to the round wooden door of one of the largest and most beautiful ancient cobblestone lighthouses that I had ever seen. The yard was a bramble of neglected gardens and thicket bushes, which bore the ground in a fence of green and red, keeping the old stone graveyard just behind it set apart.

I felt weak to the point of being dizzy, and looked up at the narrow windows above and hoped that the keeper would be in. I banged the door with the iron knocker and waited.

Nothing.

I knocked on the door again, the echo rising up the firmament of the tower.

Being a lady of sound and civil mind, had my circumstances been any different, I would not have entered the lighthouse. However, I needed help and felt that this fact warranted the uninvited interruption of my company.

"Hello," I offered the long echoing chambers. "I need help!"

But my own voice echoed back from the reaches of the great tower. Way up above, the light which saved my life beamed out, swinging round.

The entryway was a boot and coat room with benches, shovels, rakes, gardening tools, fishing gear and rain coats. I ascended the wrought iron spiral staircase to the first plateau. A kitchen area and a pine table with chairs occupied the room. Dried flowers, chili pepper swags and braided heads of garlic hung from the wall near a grated window sill. An old, ornately sculptured double sink of light green marble with generous counter space joined a cast iron wood-burning stove, whose chimney vented directly out the side of the stone wall. A small refrigerator system and a section of pine cabinets curved around. I explored the cabinets immediately.

In my hunt for food I found cans of peaches, sardines, salmon, jars of pickles, eggs and various vegetables and peppers. I sampled different jars until I was absolutely stuffed, sitting by the waning light of a candle.

My fear disappeared to amusement with my predicament, and I decided that since no one was around for now, and it would only be a matter of time before I would be rescued, that I should make myself at home in this most unusual place. I began to explore the lighthouse like a child on an Easter egg hunt, awaiting treasures of blissful delight. I ascended to the next platform and found the entire level devoted completely to refreshments for the body. A stand-up clawfoot bathtub, a toilet, and an ornately carved wooden table with mirror and cushioned chair decorated the room creating an atmosphere reminiscent of long ago, with Victorian rose patterned carpeting flushed in rich, dark shades of ruby. There were ample shelves and racks stacked with towels, blankets, sheets, pillow cases and a collection of dark blue bottles of lavender water. I looked inside the drawers of the table and discovered accessories that would make a princess smile. Bottles of rose and gardenia perfumes were on the table, and facial creams as tender as pudding and fragrant of cucumber and camomile lay within. There was also an ornately carved mahogani couch with generous fabric cushions of cerise and claret roses which were entwined in a florid eloquence with the carpeting. A large pirates' chest contained toilet paper, soaps that smelled of Lily of The Valley, tropical shampoos, band-Aides, razors, and many other fine amenities of esthetic personal care. I have to admit that the notion of never leaving this place absolutely crossed my mind. It was a dream, as if specifically designed with my favorite things to comfort my fall from the terrible storm. My whole life seemed to be a succession of falls and failures from the things that I had pursued with love, destroyed by the hands of enemies or well-meaning friends. To say that I had become a loner in my adult life would be an understatement. I was beginning to loath people. No friend that I had ever kept was ever true to me, making this new adventure so intensely poignant, with all the restful solitude, as if I actually slumbered just beneath the enchantment of a magic spell. It was not really such an unfortunate predicament as it appeared to be. To have been washed ashore all alone on such a beautiful island with a want for nothing and total privacy, I scarcely could ask for more.

I explored the next platform, and found an office library. A generous writing desk with ample drawers was stocked with pens, pencils, a ruler, paper and a dictionary, all thoughtfully organized. The desk was positioned in front of a window looking out to the open sea. There was a table next to it with a typewriter and gigantic telescope. Book cases were filled, and each wooden bookcase had vines of Tiffany lights winding round, illuminating the books in a sort of dappled, silent reverence. Thoughts and ideas settled solemnly like autumn leaves over the room. There was a dark leather couch, a leather side table with Victorian lamp, and a wood stove in the room which afforded an academic air of study and solitude. A large oil painting of a sea captain smoking a pipe hung near the window. The captain was standing near a window that looked out upon the vast ocean. It was a painting of this very room. A rush of chills struck me upon my realization. An icy air wrapped itself around me in a cloak, as if suddenly I stood in the cold of a black night. The painting seemed eerily alive somehow. I stared at it for quite some time, waiting to see if a hand or an eye would move. The chill deepened the longer I stood there. I stepped back, and all became warm again. I stuck my arm out into the space where I had previously been standing, and it was icy cold. It was a precise area that seemed as if a circle of air was refrigerated. I walked around the space reaching my arm in and out again, and it was absolutely unbelievable! My family would never believe me. All of this was sure to disappear like the abruptness of a broken dream once I made contact with someone from the outside world again. The dark blue and grey Victorian carpeting was patterned ornately in palm fronds, and the floor seemed to be moving now in watery shadows. I rubbed my eyes. I could hold my arms around the area of the cold spot, but its circumference was too wide to reach my finger tips together. It was like hugging an invisible cold tree.

Life's pendulum of time had stopped. The lighthouse had its own separate atmosphere apart from the regular world, something I noticed immediately upon entering. It was like walking through a time zone; through a permeable wall, as shadows slipped from parallel spaces, and an enchantment came over me in a sense of rapture. I was sparkling. The lighthouse was indeed steeped in things mysterious. Air still and motionless was now broken like a spell cast long ago, and the house slumbered no more. I walked among gigantic invisible cobwebs whose delicate strings and chords vibrated and resounded upon the ground of another world. I had stepped into a dizzying magic carnival where mirrors could make you look eight feet tall; where strange creatures lurked around corners, half human, half reptile; where pictures of old sea captions moved and dolls rocked in their chairs. It was a place where children play with unseen friends, where music boxes open suddenly and begin to play, and doors close quietly by themselves. It was a place where curtains blow in windows like sheer rippling ghosts. And it was a place where the wind lived, too. Yes, the wind. Tides of air sighed and rose in shrill eerie voices against the screens of the windows, banging doors and pressing faces against the screens, then whipping them back and forth wildly.

I felt as if I had walked through the mirror of my physical self to the other side, the nonphysical, upon entering the lighthouse. And so beneath the things that I discovered - the inviting rooms, the lovely accruements, some uncanny thing began to pierce the air like an evening star, something just around the corner, waiting. It was a ghost, I thought to myself, or some wandering energy field left behind from things that had happened here long ago, a sad music that never stopped playing that I could not hear, but only feel. Some thing that had now been awakened from a deep sleep, conjured up by the stirring of my movements. Whatever it was it listened to my footsteps, waiting patiently for me to blow out the last oil lamp, or for the last red ember to extinguish itself in a soft grey dust upon the hearth. It seemed that every time I looked away from something, it moved. It traveled just at the corner of my sight, and I felt no fear at all.

I climbed up the spiral staircase holding onto the railings, looking straight up and wondering what treasures lay further ahead. I was not frightened by the otherworldly feeling that the lighthouse gave off, a presence of something unknown following me. Rather, I felt enchanted, it delivered me from the ordinary boredom of familiar things which the world had always been. I looked upwards as I ascended the steeply climbing staircase. How wonderful: a place to rest my head! A bed with sidetable and lantern, a chest for clothes, as well as a table occupied this room. A picture of fairies peering through flowers hung over the bed in a kind of strange enchantment. There was another picture near the window of a beautiful spider's web dressed in morning light. Gargoyle wall sconces peopled the parameters of the room. A stand-up table sink with a flowered porcelain water bowl flushed with lilacs with matching water pitcher on the sideboard, and side towel rack stood before the window which overlooked the crumbling graveyard. A bottle of rosewater rest upon wisps of lace over the table near the bed, never having been opened before.

I opened the window and sweet currents of sea air flowed through in an alchemy of salt and flowers, and icy bottom waves hulled from a vast darkness - sea air that washed inside in refreshing winds dappling chimes which hung from some unseen place in delicate little sounds like a sudden burst of songbirds coming from the walls. What a lovely place to rest, why the deepest and most refreshing sleep should be found in such a room, I thought to myself, for I frequently suffered from insomnia. An antique sand-colored quilt lay over the bed, and I wondered why so many priceless antiques would be left behind in such a beautiful lighthouse. Where was the keeper? Who operated the tower light?

Nothing of the lighthouse seemed damp, musty, neglected or of ill-use. In fact, it had a clean, decidedly lived-in feeling with comportments of great care taken to create comfort and pleasure for the solitary caretaker of the lighthouse; certain rewards for the sometimes lonely predicament of the job. And I thought further on this, for there was an area for a garden outside, and fish from the sea, as well as clams and the like, that a person could live quite happily in such an oasis apart from the turmoil of the city and the conflict of people. The person who was obviously here sometime recently had made fine use of the garden which would account for the jars of tomatoes and other canning found. Small onions and garlic had been carefully woven, braided and hung, and jars of herbs rested on the shelf near the wood-burning stove with knowing intent. Wood stacked and stored, and a well-pump outdoors indeed completed what needs a man or woman could have. And the price? To maintain and observe the giant light at the top. To man the brave lighthouse which served so many ships during wild storms. Such a person saved lives.

It was a giant towering lighthouse which stood more like a castle, with thick tapestries of ivy crawling up the cobblestone walls winding 'round windows.   There was plenty of island space to garden, fish, sunbath, and otherwise bemuse and bewitch oneself from the building. I had discovered a kitchen, a bathroom, a library office and a bedroom, and perhaps a ghost or two.   I looked up wondering what waited beyond. I couldn't remember when I had experienced so much excitement in my life.   First the wild storm that had left my boat in pieces, then my luck in being washed ashore by the compass of the tower light which I had followed, and now the adventures inside the lighthouse. The light swung round steady and slow only two more platforms up.

I continued up the spiral staircase wondering if the keeper had the common sense to store a bottle of rum for those cold nights when the wind howled through the windows and flames from the fires danced high.   Long black nights when the aloneness of living in a lighthouse tested a person. I wondered about the rum while slowly walking up the spiral staircase, my heart filled with the beauty and peace of the ancient chambers of the tower house.   Lights from the sea shimmered in through the windows at the next platform flooding the room in a penetrating brilliance. The view from this area was stunning.   The room consisted of an assortment of very comfortable "viewing" chairs near the three long windows, nigh save for a small table with a lantern astride each chair, large ashtrays, and a waste can. On one of the tables was a silver serving tray and accessories for tea.   There was an inlaid china cabinet in this room with small lights within the shelves.   A magnificent collection of silver sugar spoons filled the velvet drawers, and there were also crystal figurines in the cabinet among the splendid tea cups.   One of the dizzying aspects of the lighthouse is that I had expected the walls to all be round inside. Some rooms had round walls, but most were not. This was a perfect entertaining room, I thought - but to entertain whom?

I kept thinking about the rum and began wondering if there might be cigarettes someplace, too.   Then even when I was rescued, it would be doubtful that my departure from this palace would be voluntary, for it seemed that I had found a new home - a place of total contentedness. I would restore the gardens and grow deep red tomatoes juicy with sunshine, and the most fragrant herbs and lettuces. And by God, I just knew there was a bottle somewhere and that, I too, would find.

Up and up I climbed to the apex of the towering lighthouse, unhooking a latch and sliding the overhead trap door open, crawling out. The enormous light rotated slowly round, and a good, solid railing framed safety at the edges of the platform which now brought me entirely outdoors. Hands of wind moved my hair and the ocean swelled forever outwards in sparkling streaks of indigo and jade. Before me the sun set. It was the first moment that I had stopped to think about time, and the fact that I had spent the greater portion of the day exploring the rooms of the lighthouse. I had also forgotten that I was in a boating accident and was now stranded on an island. A perfect orb of vermillion, descending in glowering fires of plum spilt over the horizon and disappeared, as shadows were thrown up to the sky in comets of purple and rose, against the sharpening darkness. It was the perfect last room of the building, like a fine dessert, transporting and blissful. It was sacred like a church, and breathtaking in its magnificent height and vision like an ancient bell tower which signifies its chords to a town in a variety of meaning, yet the light had a singular purpose, and bespoke to the sea, not land. To spirit, not flesh. The sweet mysteries of the sea and sky.

CHAPTER II
THE RESCUE

I spent many days watching the sun rise and set as its colors played upon the changing canvass of the vast sea. I soaked up invigorating winds of juniper and pine from the forests below, and salty moist air thrown wild by the waves, as well as that deep water smell carried by the wind from the great depths of the ocean floor, evoking images of a vast darkness; of shipwrecks; and of seascapes of underwater mountains and ravines, and precipitous cliffs whose vertical drop overlooked deep, bottomless chasms. I imagined that if I drifted from the top of one of these mountain cliffs, I would glide downwards in an endlessly falling space where schools of luminous fish and jellyfish would swim in shimmering constellations all around me, indeed, whole new worlds awaited me beyond the door of the lighthouse. Beneath the cover of the sea was a place where whales resounded solitary songs and tales of their adventures around the world, and their knowledge of things to come.

As I sat back with the pure, fresh wind coming in through the windows, I began to see images of vast undersea deserts, a seemingly endless matrix of frozen rippling sand stretching outwards forevermore, with sculptured barren dunes and hills rolling out and beyond. It was a place where labyrinthine caves blinked with glowing fish and mysterious eyes. Many of the caves would be wide enough to permit the diver a steady swim through, and sometimes those tunnels would suddenly open into vast auditoriums of caverns not to be believed. Hidden worlds were concealed by the narrow black passageways of caves opening into the sides of undersea mountains. All this life lay just beneath the surface of the sea, a surface I pondered each day, as the days pondered me. Perhaps at this very moment a giant octopus had its tentacles wrapped around a whale in a fight to the death so many miles below the surface. I wondered many times what it would be like to explore these unknown regions, as I sat sipping on tea in the golden, glowing lights.

This room, whose only inhabitants were the thick cushioned chairs set easy for viewing outside, and the small cherry wood tables with antique fitted glass tops, and the gigantic, ornately sculptured china cabinet, became my sanctuary. The books I read during the rising and falling lights of the day; the vast perspective for observing dark storms over the sea, as well as cloudless, tender days filled with the haunting echo of seagulls, and bright, reflective sunlight shimmering off the sea, with rich earth spices flowing in through the windows became a daily tonic for me, it grounded me, and yet it also imparted a most ethereal quality to the content of my days.

I kept score of the days I was stranded by noting the weather in a diary, numbering the days from the first of my accident. Twenty score today, I thought to myself, closing the ledger. I looked out across the morning horizon, sipping my orange tea in the quiet of this thoughtful room whose serene presence kept me company, as days washed in and out of sight. I looked back again with quickening pulse. A boat! A boat coming this way and it was as clear as a bell on this beautiful blue day. I began shaking with excitement, and set my cup down almost breaking it. I walked quickly down the spiral staircases to the ground floor, running out of the building and along the forest trail and down to the shore.

I waved my arms up high, back and forth, for surely they must see me. So close. And closer and closer the boat approached. They've heard of my accident and are searching for me, I thought. Or else, they are coming to check on the lighthouse. Perhaps it was the original caretaker coming back to his home out in the sea. It all seemed unreal, like a dream. They must have been able to see me, for they headed directly towards me. I was both excited beyond words, as well as a bit saddened. What a lovely vacation from the mundane and common world I've had. I felt sad, thinking about having to leave the lighthouse. It had become my home. The boat grew into focus larger and larger, nearer and nearer, until it sounded its horn at me, threw anchor, and lowered a smaller boat down which jetted to the shoreline before I could even believe what I was seeing. Faces sharpened into view. I waved, but they did *not* wave back. They looked rather serious, and tired, too.

There were two men who approached the shore, pulling their boat up. How rude, in fact, how strange, for they didn't even greet me! "Hello!" I implored to them. I followed the men and quickly walked in front of one of them to stop him, to demand his attention, and all of a sudden the man walked right through me! A sudden thick warm air that smelled of sweat pressed against my bones for a moment, as if someone had quickly leaned hard on me, as the man walked through me and beyond. "Hello!" "What's happening here!" "Can't you see me?" And then I heard the man say something to the other man.

"Just had a sudden chill, Bobby, really strange it was! Like walking through a block of icy air." He shivered.

"Out on the open sea many strange things can happen. The shore absorbs so much of the cold ya know." Smiled Scott, trying to comfort his friend, understanding the look of worry on his face.

"Yeah, I guess you're right about that. Cold boulders and rocks, it was."

"Oh yeah, that's all it was mate! Naw 'common, we've got to collect the body and bury it. I told me wife I'd be back before dark."

"What body?" I asked the men. They ignored me again. I decided I would follow them. I thought for a moment that maybe *they* were ghosts and that I was reliving a scene from the past. Things like this have happened before, you know. I've read about it. I watched as they winced, lifting up a body that had been wracked against the shoreline and picked over by birds. Oh, what a grisly sight, I had to look away as they enclosed someones body in the bag. They zippered it way up, pinching their noses.

They brought the bag to the old stone graveyard near the entrance of the lighthouse and began digging a hole, using one of the spades from a nearby tool shed. Leaning up against the walls of the shed were apparently a couple of old pine coffins. One of the men dragged one out, and they lifted the body bag down into it. Perhaps they were in too much of a hurry to notice that they had not remembered to nail down the lid? Although it didn't slide around, it still should have been nailed down properly, I thought. Funny, I mused, the things people will do when no one is supposedly looking; the things people think they can get away with.

"I could get you a drink, men. Lemonade, water, tea? I have coffee, too. And I even found a case of rum inside, might make the digging go a bit easier? I know it's taken the chill from my bones on those long cool stormy nights when fires are stoked high and shutters rattle. How 'bout a drink?" I offered them. But no reply came forth. I shouted at them to see if it were their manners which were absent, or *if they* really didn't even exist. Still no response. I watched as they lowered the crude coffin down into the grave. It wasn't even that deep, I thought with a very critical disdain for these men. They really didn't care at all about what they were doing. If this had been a more civilized, populated area of the country, they would have brought the body to a morgue and notified the police. Who knows? Maybe they had. It's true that when a person dies out at sea on a ship, that the body is dropped in the sea. Perhaps a report had been written up on this? There was no way to really know for sure. I sighed, feeling helpless. They began to quickly shovel dirt over the grave, almost covering it enough to come equally level with the ground. The men looked up now and then at the darkening skies. It must have been about four, maybe five o'clock in the afternoon, I would guess, and one of them returned to the shed and replaced the shovels, coming back with a blank stone gravemarker. The gravemarker was not quite important looking, not austere at all, I thought grimly, in fact, it was very small. But it was a marker much the same.

"Who'd we just bury Scottie?"

"Dunno'. Just another routine assignment. Bossman said it was out here, no record of an accident or any missing person. Just a mystery, I guess. All the paperwork's been done. And no one's called in to report a missin' person. Must 'ov been out here a while now. My instructions were to bury the remains right here. If anyone steps forward to claim a missing person, then we know where to go. No one around to step forward and claim the body and pay for a funeral and all the other final expenses. Bossman said he and the chief of police were out here two weeks ago and found it; guess the paperwork got lost on the desk again. All the usual inquires have been made and contact with the newspaper, but there has been no response at all. And this body ain't gettin' any prettier." Bob told him.

"No family?" Asked Scott.

"Not necessarily. We just can't locate any kin. And in this condition, it's impossible to identify the remains. With the jaw cracked off the skull, the finger tips rotten, and with the body havin' been picked over by the birds leaving only a partial face left... well, you saw it, mate."

"What happened, sharks?" Asked Scott.

"No. Boating accident. Some planks were found over there." And he pointed down at the beach.

"Do we say a prayer?" Asked Scott.

"Could." Bob replied.

And the men bowed their heads and began to pray. I, too, bowed my head for the unknown stranger.

"Dear heavenly father, please put to rest this unknown soul and may this person find peace in your majestic arms." And with that, the men put their caps back on their heads and walked up to the lighthouse.

I continued to follow them, even though they had never acknowledged my presence. Maybe *I'm* dead? I thought, and laughed to myself. *No. I can't be. I feel so alive, so real.* The skies are so vividly blue, the air so clear and crisp. The moon burns bright in the evening. I've never felt better. At least, for now, I think I am alive. *What if we are only that which we think we are?...*

The men opened the door slowly as if a ghost were about to jump out at out them from around the corner. I laughed at their trepidation. They entered the ground-level coat room and looked up into the vastness of the tower.

"How long has it been shut down?"

"Dunno. It was too expensive to man, way out here and all. Plus, no caretaker would ever stay here more than a night or two without radioing in for help to get off the island. Some say it's haunted, but I don't believe in them ghosts." Replied Scott. "I think it was just too damn expensive to operate."

"Gezzz, would 'ya look at all these spider webs. Sure looks haunted to me." Said Bob.

I had no idea whatsoever what the men were talking about, for I had kept the lighthouse in spotless condition and the rooms were very comfortable. It was definitely the most comfortable place that I had ever lived. And since I had found seeds to start a garden with, I also ate quite well, too. And I never noticed any dead body before washed up along the shoreline, on those days when I searched for clams and mussels with my basket. Never. No cold spots at the beach, no mangled bodies. Who are these strange people, I wondered. Why can't they see how beautiful my tower castle is? Why, my days had been dedicated to cleaning, gardening, and storing more wood for the fires when not in my 'sanctuary,' my reading room, as I liked to call it, drinking pots of tea and reading the days away. These men were certainly very offensive and getting on my nerves.

"Get out! Get out the both of you right now! I don't like this game you two are playing, get out of my house right now!" I shouted at them.

They looked at each other. Relief. I thought sure, now they'll be polite to me, now they'll talk to me. I have to shout at them right in their faces to get their attention. Jug heads, probably descendants of dirty seaboard pirates from long ago." I cringed with all my English propriety.

"Did you hear that?" One of them said. I became infuriated. Hear that? Of course they heard that, I was screaming in their faces.

"Sounded like a voice in the wall telling us to get out." Said Bob, his eyes watering now.

"Why don't we? I heard it, too! It's a real good idea." Agreed Scott nervously. "It's getting dark out, 'gotta get home anyways, Bobby. Think I'll stop at the pub on my way home tonight, how 'bout you?"

"Oh, yeah." Bob answered, swallowing hard, "throat's dry."

The men pulled thick cobwebs down off a bench and looked around in disbelief.

"It's a bit depressing when a place goes on untended like this. What's that dripping sound? It's coming from under the floor. Must be underground caverns. Hey, maybe it's a wine cellar?" Bob added with hope. "Big ole' barrels of juice just waitin' to come to papa!" He smiled.

"Or a torture chamber or crypt." Sighed Scott.

"Well, whatever it is, I ain't goin' down there. Look, there's a passage over there behind the wall." Bob pointed.

"You mean a catacomb. It must tunnel down and outside to that graveyard." Said Scott. "One thing's for sure: ya couldn't pay me enough to stay here overnight. Not even with you, Bobby, I'd never stay here."

"Yeah, know what 'cha mean. Let's go..." Bob said, trailing out the door, his voice echoing up the firmament of the great tower.

"Hear that Bob!"

"That was just my voice echoing back from the towers." Said Bob. "You're starting to scare yourself." Bob paused for a moment, turning around: "Booooooo!" He shouted, laughing, shaking Scott's arm..

Scottie shrieked and slid on some loose stones. "Ya *dumbhead* Bobby! 'Ya almost stopped me heart cold dead," he screamed at him. "Stone dead, 'ya hear me? 'Ya hear me ya dumbhead!" He retorted back in his face, almost spitting.

Bob held his belly laughing, his wide red cheeks kindling in a glowing cheer, when suddenly they both shook as if an electric current had just gone through them, staring at the castle tower. *"Get Out!"* Bellowed the voice. The voice was not the voice of a mortal man, nor was it the voice of any woman, for it was demoniacal and guttural, blasting out from a great pressure like a valve suddenly opened. The voice erupted into a sudden foul gust of storming winds, surrounding them in darkening veils of impending evil. The hair went up on the back of their necks and along their arms. The castle tower watched them, its shadows lengthening across the yard, reaching for them. Its long macabre arms stretching... almost touching them...

The men ran down the trail that led to the shoreline and exited on the small boat, riding over to the main one. I laughed at their sudden flight from the lighthouse, for I had no idea what could have frightened them so. I did not follow them, but instead walked slowly upstairs with a candle in my hands, to my sanctuary room, my room of comfort no matter what. I sat back in the same chair where I was when I had first spotted their boat out on the open sea. I sipped on my tea, which was now cold, watching them leave. They traveled further out, staring back at the lighthouse as if it were some anomaly, some house of horror. I did not feel lonely, for I found these men to be rather insulting and low-brow. A cellar mouse would have made for more apt company, I laughed to myself. I wonder why they wouldn't talk to me? Maybe they were ghosts, she mused to herself curiously. She stood in the window looking out, her long white dress billowing in the wind.

The men looked back at the lighthouse.

"Gonna look up the history on that place sometime. Bet something horrible happened there. What a spooky place." Bob shivered. "Look Scotty! Look over there!" And he pointed at a window in the tower.

"What! Oh my God, I see it! I see it! Wow!"

"It's a woman in a long white dress, and she's watching us." Said Bob.

"What? She's gone now. I saw it. I sure saw it!" Exclaimed Scotty, rubbing his eyes. "I believe you! She was holding a candle! I hate that place!"

Bob accelerated the boat and the men headed quickly back to the office to check out from what had been a very long day on sea duty, and indeed they did go to the local neighborhood pub telling their story to the barkeeper, like a couple of spooked children after a night of trick or treating, over a stout lager or two.

I watched as their boat disappeared to a fine point along the horizon and disappeared. I lit the lamps on all the tables and decided to bring up a blanket, a bowl of hot soup and a book from the library and retire here until late, to shake off the strange events of the day. Rescued? What was I thinking? Had I seen a ghostly re-enactment from long ago? Who was buried out in the graveyard today? So many questions, no answers. I changed my mind and retired my pot of tea for the brisk bottle of rum I held in the pine cabinet. After long hours of sipping rum, looking out the window, and wondering what was really going on, I decided this: that the only way to find out was to go out to the graveyard myself, even in the rain which had just begun falling in solemn grey showers, and dig up the remains. Whose body was it? Why wouldn't they talk to me? I suddenly remembered the warning of Pandora's Box from traditional literature, and wondered if I should leave all well and alone, for I was very happy in my home, not afraid. And I was at home; finally, I belonged somewhere. I thought again carefully on a phrase that had been important to me all my life: *'what if we are only that which we think we are?'*

I dismissed my reservations, quite fortified by the fine rum the caretaker had left behind and went downstairs. I zipped up my raincoat, grabbed a large flashlight and headed for the shed. I laid the flashlight on the ground and began digging in the misting, fogging rain. I looked up at the windows of the lighthouse, warm yellow flames from my lanterns burned bright. I dug and dug and then rested a bit, leaning against the shovel. I had to admit the novelty of the whole situation to myself: standing in a graveyard in the rain, in the darkness; digging up a dead body; living alone and stranded in a lighthouse. I heard a noise behind me and turned. I saw a gothic-looking mausoleum, brooding and sinister in the darkness, and upon whose funereal walls no vines would climb, hidden by the obscurity of the night. It had tall wrought iron spired gates, and the gates had now blown open, banging back and forth in the wind. The banging of the spired gates brought my attention to the mausoleum, which I had never noticed before, however, it was not my regular habit to hang out in the graveyard anyways. The gates piqued my attention in much the same way a person clears his throat to gain notice. Eerie, how the loud squeaking sounds of a gate in a graveyard can make one feel so alone, and yet so utterly surrounded by things mysterious and unknown, as if not really quite alone anymore. The rain continued to fall in steady showers as darkness deepened in the echoing graveyard, as if I were descending further and further down into some unknown realm with the passing of each moment. 'I shouldn't be here,' I thought to myself for a moment. Yet I couldn't shake the curiosity of knowing who had been buried here today. I had seldom been able to resist the things I thought I wanted in life. And here I was now, surrounded by headstones that felt more as if they had all landed and flocked around me like big grey vultures, watching, waiting, as I became increasingly unnerved by the sounds of the creaking gates, swinging back and forth just behind me.

I climbed down inside the grave next to the coffin, and slowly slid the lid off. I would rebury the body tomorrow, but for tonight, I wanted to know *who* they had buried. I mean, it probably wouldn't have been anyone I knew anyways, but I needed to know, just to make sure. The slant of light from the flashlight on the ground made the rain seem as if it fell in slow motion, as if the entire situation were a dream. Fog whorled over the ground rising in surreal ghosts which stood flowing in the falling rain, almost as if they were gathering around me now, watching me, coming up one after the other from the surrounding graves. The mausoleum in its infinite charm reminded me that it stood waiting just behind me. Was it trying to draw my attention away from what I was doing; was it throwing me a warning; or did it simply need to be oiled? - I laughed to myself in the crowding gloom. What was that depressing looking building trying to tell me? For I had just run over there only a moment ago to secure the gates, and no wind since then had come that could have been strong enough to jar it open again. And yet, the gates still squeaked back and forth now, banging and rattling in the wind. A crawling, glowing grey mist wandered down off the ledge of the ground, settling and wrapping around the bottom of the coffin as if the coffin itself were actually smouldering. I slowly unzipped the bag, wondering if I should have left all that was well enough, alone. ah. I reached for my flashlight, and as I shined it down at the coffin, in that moment just before seeing anything, the lamps in all my windows immediately went out, all at the same time. 'Strange,' I thought, I had just refilled all of the lamps the other day.

I looked down again: I looked down now at a face which stared upwards in a macabre and sightless gaze, and *began screaming!* I dropped the flashlight and scrambled out from the mud of the shallow grave, running back to the lighthouse, screaming as I ran. *"No, No, aaaahhhhhhhhhhhhhh!"* Upon entering the coat room I slammed the door behind me: I was delirious with terror, a maddening, thrilling, sickening horror and realization completely overwhelmed me. I couldn't breath. I was in shock, not believing what I had seen. And I could not believe *what I now saw*, for cobwebs hung in thick grey draperies covered in dust, hanging heavily like despair which wept from the walls and across the staircase. The wet smell of must, stagnant and moldy, rose up the walls of the great tower. A quiet dripping sound echoed from someplace below. I listened as heavy footsteps walked above, and could now smell the smoke of a burning pipe throughout the gloom.

I looked upwards into the vast darkness of the tower, as the lanterns had been extinguished by some unknown hand, and climbed up the spiral staircase knowing every turn so well, even though I couldn't see, and knowing now, for sure, *that indeed, I had been found.*

THE RIVER

THE RIVER

"Political language is designed to make lies sound truthful and murder respectable, and to give an appearance of solidity to pure wind." George Orwell.

"Sick cultures show a complex of symptoms, but a dying culture invariably exhibits rudeness. Bad manners. Lack of consideration for others in minor matters. A loss of politeness, of gentle manners, is more significant than a riot." Robert Heinlein.

"Although a certain amount of hypocrisy exists about it, everyone is fascinated by violence. After all, man is the most remorseless killer who ever stalked the earth. Our interest in violence in part reflects the fact that on the subconscious level we are very little different from our primitive ancestors." Stanley Kubrick.

PART ONE: THE MYSTERIOUS DISAPPEARANCES FROM MANGROVE LANE

It was as if I suddenly stood before a flooding, blinding, white sun, pouring all around me, even through me, as if I were transparent, a mere film or negative of a person. I could see nothing, squinting was useless. I was no longer terrified by what had happened, it was as if I had watched it all on tv, that it had happened to someone else, Jeff thought, as he stepped forward into the blinding light, now unbound, as the snake suddenly dove downwards into deeper waters...

The detective leaned back in his chair, scrutinizing the reports which all had one thing in common, each one of the missing persons' cases was from Mangrove Lane, in Lakeland, Texas.

"Jeff?"

"What," the detective replied, annoyed.

"Coffee, sir?" His assistant offered.

"Yes Linda, that'd be nice. Thank you."

And she walked right in with a mug and thermal carafe, anticipating his needs. "It just doesn't make any sense, Linda. All children. All missing. All from the exact same 5 mile area, off of Mangrove Lane."

"A serial killer."

"It would appear so. It's single handedly this counties' worst crime spree ever. This is a small town, everyone knows everyone else and all of their business as well. Figure news would have come out on suspects from the coffee shop already, or the barber shop, or the town bar. Four missing children, completely gone without a trace, as if they had all stepped into thin air, all within a week. I'm stumped." He said, turning towards his computer and completely shutting her out again.

"Almost like the Bermuda Triangle right here in good ole' Texas," she said, leaving the office. He scowled at her, twisting his moustache with his fingers, but she never saw. Jeff was a very handsome man, but, if life had made him an animal instead of a detective, he would have been born a mule. Stubborn wasn't the word for him, he was much worse than that. But he wasn't stupid. He'd been a detective now for 15 years with a remarkable success rate in resolving local crimes, as well as matters that were beyond county jurisdiction. Linda just wondered why this dedicated bachelor had no girlfriend and never married. Maybe he was one of those men with no sex drive; or a tightwade who wouldn't spend a penny on a rose or a bottle of wine, if it exceeded his own budget interests. She knew for sure he wasn't gay, for in such a small town, everyone would know; then all the women, including the postal carrier, would stop flirting with him. But his refusals only made him more interesting and mysterious to women. He never sat at the local gin mill with the boys, really, he lived and related almost 24 hours a day, to his computer. He loved coffee and cigarettes, and frequently, it was Linda's duty to keep the file cabinet stocked with not only computer disks, notepads, and other miscellaneous office supplies, but with cartons of cigarettes as well. His office newly painted, bore that dim yellow patina of tobacco smoke upon its walls, even with the windows open. Perhaps, she thought, she was too plain for him. Divorced, surviving on his average paying wages, with two children of her own and plenty of expenses, she had too much baggage. Here was a handsome, successful free man. No child support payments, no dirty unscrupulous rages with an ex-wife or ex-girlfriend, no gossip known about him because he kept to himself, and really, nothing bore him down except a simple life primarily consisting of his work. That was it, she figured, he was married to his work. Besides, he was 40, and she was 39. Eligible men didn't seek out women over the age of 29 anymore, or women whose figures were not a petite size 6 or 7. But he seemed like 'real people,' not brainwashed by superficial generalizations. He was a leader, not a follower of masses. As he was stumped on this case sitting at his desk, Linda sat down in the front office quietly pondering this man, her fist beneath her chin, while she was stumped on him. The phone rang, jolting her from her hormonal trance.

"Mr. Thompson's office," she said.

"Yes, this is State Trooper Blair here, and we seem to have another missing person from Mangrove Lane. Is the detective in?"

"Yes, sir, please hold the line," and she buzzed Jeff Thompson's office announcing the call.

"What! Another one? Give me the address and I'll be right down."

"Got any more of those fancy ceegars, 'ya like to smoke there detective Thompson?"

"Well sure I do," Jeff answered, twisting his moustache. "I'll bring some along."

"Pretty boy, don't need to comb your hair first, we've got some hysterical parents on our hands here, hurry up!"

"Fuck you too, Trooper Blair, be right down." And he hung up the phone scowling. Jeff turned one of his fishing portraits around to reveal a mirror on the other side. He combed his hair and his moustache, poured himself a quick shot of bourbon at his desk, relocking the drawer, grabbed his briefcase and was off.

"I'm leaving." He said to Linda.

"I know." She smiled.

"Lock up at 5 if I'm not back by then." And the screen door swung hard behind him.

The drive to Mangrove Lane took about 20 minutes. It was located in the swampy, wooded back country of slow, deep flowing tannic rivers which wound and split like pluvial mazes into the dense green forests. This was the first place where the roads would flood when the weather got bad. You could smell the water in the air, the land was so verdant and green. Moss and airplants hung lazily from the steeps of trees. The drive evolved from the small town and its bustling daily routines, and twisted through straight, sharp, jagged hills and down a straight lane into the waterlands of Mangrove Lane. He didn't need a map in such a small local community. There was a local police officer and the state trooper already parked in the drive of the home, lights flashing.

The trooper greeted him. "Got me my ceegars?"

"Yeah, Don, they're in my briefcase. Shouldn't we look for the dead body first though?" Raising an eyebrow at Trooper Blair. The trooper gave him a quick unfriendly glance as if he had just trespassed the fence of their already precarious relationship once again. For it was always the detective who had solved all of the previous crimes that they were mutually involved in, no matter how much additional search time the trooper had put in to apprehend the criminal. The men walked up to the house, and the parents and the officer came out, standing in the hot July sunshine, meeting them. The woman was crying, and the husband was pale, holding his wife by her side.

"Detective, our only son is missing. He's been gone now for two days. We reported it immediately, and we requested your involvement right away, but the officer insisted upon exhausting the regular routine checks first, even though other children are missing. What can we do? Where is our boy?" He pleaded, as if an absolutely positive answer would come forward now.

"Have the other missing children been found?" He added.

"No, sir, they have not been found. It's been exactly one week since the first child disappeared. We have no clues at this point in time. We are exhausting every single possibility at this time and I assure you, Dr. Young, that your boy will be found, and the other children will be found as well." Jeff informed him.

"Officer Truit," Jeff turned, "do you have search parties out?"

"Yes sir, we do. I have people combing the countryside looking for anything, a piece of clothing, a doll, a shoe, anything at all. We've come up with absolutely nothing in each and every case. It's like these kids just walked off into thin air, it's the most baffling thing I've ever seen, sir."

"Yes, or at least, one of them." Jeff added. The trooper stood silent, observing the matter.

The trooper, who was missing an upper tooth which bore him a distinctly nasty, red-neck unorthodox demeanor, an occultation of pestilence, added: "We've obviously got a serial killer on our hands here."

And the woman cried harder now, as if she instinctively knew that her only son was dead.

"Ah possibly, only a serial kidnapper, I mean, mam'."

"Looks like we just found one of the shoes," winked Jeff, looking at the trooper.

The report was handed to detective Thompson. "I need to see the child's room, and take a look at the house." He said, after quickly reading the report. "Officer Truit, did you walk the yard area?"

"Yes sir, I did."

"And found nothing, I'm presuming."

"That is correct, sir."

At that moment one of the chairs from the swing set along side the house, began to rock in the windless, stifling afternoon air.

"My wife," the husband stated, "she's not well. She hasn't slept in days. Let me take her inside and I can answer your questions for you."

"Fine Dr. Young." And they all went inside. The doctor walked his silent wife into the bedroom, returning a moment later, shutting the door behind himself. "You gentlemen do whatever you have to do. I'll be in my study waiting for you after you look around. I've already shown the officer every square inch of the house. He can show you." The doctor looked weary and defeated, as if he, too, assumed his son to be dead, but reserved emotion upon proof.

"Looks like we've got quite the photographer here," said Jeff. A variety of cameras were on a table in the boys room, with beautiful photographs on the walls of sunsets, rivers and one of a large snake.

"Must'ov got that one from a zoo," pointed the trooper. And the officer, trooper and detective walked the house taking notes, and returned to the doctor in his study in a solemn air of respect. As if approaching a grieving man.

"Dr. Young, we have what we need now. If there is anything our office can do, please contact us. If any information comes in, or you remember something, call us at once. I will begin to question some of your neighbors. There have been too many abductions in too short a time frame for no one to have not seen anything. Someone must have seen something unusual."

"Detective, I know we are not the first victims. There are some shady characters in this neighborhood, for example: that Steve Moore and Sandy Johnson couple. They're not married, they have two kids living in that trailer with them near the river. She's some kind of biker woman, and I've heard they're both big into drugs. My son, Nathan, had told me in the past that their kids would show up in school in clothes that smelled of cat urine, and the kids were dirty as if they never took baths. And that Selma Higgins lady, the widow, she's older, maybe senile? Maybe she hates children? They say that kids used to go there because she'd let them swim in her pond, and she gave them candy, too. I heard she did this because she is lonely, but what if she's crazy? What if she's got these children locked up in her canning cellar?"

"Well, I've also heard some things, too. That not only is Selma Higgins a patient of yours, doctor, but that your family has accepted invitations to dinner at her home, and that she is quite an outstanding baker. It would appear that she was a trusted friend of your family. No?" Detective Thompson inquired. "How could an old woman turn around so abruptly in her character, from a state of kindness, to one of terror and cruelty?"

"It's a crazy, up-side-down world detective, you tell me. My wife and I, we always thought she acted a little different."

"That does not qualify her as a suspect in these crimes. However, I will go and talk with her. I will be sure not to mention your changed view of her either, doctor. Panic does not solve crimes nor is it capable of aiding in the discovery any true source of a crime. It creates chaos and confusion. Being a professional man of medicine, you should already know that." The detective warned him. "Your neighbors, the Reynolds, they lost all three of their children this week. I don't see them pointing a finger at one of their own neighbors."

"Not yet detective. But isn't it true, that in profiling a serial killer, if it is one, that they usually reside very close to the area where they plunder their victims from?"

"Yes, it is a part of a profile, an aspect which figures in with several other consistent aspects, including, personality traits. You call me if you have any substantial information to give me, night or day."

And the doctor looked down, "yes, I will." He closed the front door and the officer drove back to the station, and the trooper followed Jeff Thompson back to his vehicle. "About those ceegars, detective." He eyed him with a toothless smile that was not a gesture of good will, but rather an expectation of something owed to him. The detective noted to himself that Blair probably always got just what he wanted in life, less the personal pride and victory in solving real crimes.

"I haven't forgotten Blair, I haven't forgotten," Jeff sighed. They walked over to the car, Jeff slid the report into his brief case and removed a fine looking cigar, holding it as if it were something precious."

"Ah, an illegal smoke?" He spied the cigar.

"No Blair, it's not from Cuba, just a very good cigar. Ya want it or what?"

"Sure, I wan' it." And the trooper took the cigar, slid it into his pocket, and stepped back. "Well, I'll be seeing you 'round. We've got search parties out, and above all, I'm out there searching for this freak, we'll get our man detective, and sooner than you think! Ya call on me if ya hear somethin,' right?" Blair pushed.

"Of course." Smiled Jeff, climbing into his car. He drove off in the opposite direction heading deeper into the neighborhood of Mangrove Lane. He watched in his rear-view mirror, as the trooper headed back towards town. His first interview was at the home of a one Daniel Schwartz, who, by virtue of being disabled and a bit odd, had somehow earned the nickname "Devil" Schwartz.

Jeff pulled his car into the long, narrow drive of Mr. Schwartz' home. He parked his vehicle, noting the condition of the home, and how forlorn it appeared to him. It brooded in a loneliness, a deep social isolation capable of existing only from the worst possible censure and humiliation society could exact. Old bicycles, lawn mowers and other assorted rusted, broken down equipment was piled near the front door, almost obstructing the walkway entirely, so that a person would have to walk around the accumulated junk, to get to the door. 'Perhaps insulating himself against the cruel company and words of other people,' thought Jeff. 'But, also feeding into their expectations of him, as well,' he pondered, knocking on the door. The front door was open, with the screen door the only barrier between himself, and the world of Mr. Schwartz. He knocked again, this time louder. "Hello! Hello in there; is anybody home?" Jeff implored. He had years ago dispensed with any fear of uncomely places and odd people, knowing that many underlying causes impel people to behave in different ways from the norms of socially acceptable actions. And certainly, these circumstances did not brand a person bad or good, it just was.

He watched as a figure came slowly down the hallway towards him. "Right there! I'll be right there. I'm commin'." The detective could see that Mr. Schwartz had a terrible limp, almost having to drag one leg, sort of, sliding along the floor. Mr. Schwartz opened the screen door, looking into Jeff's face. Jeff was suddenly shaken by the unnerving and uncomfortable condition of his crossed eye, however, quickly focused to compose himself and remain on track.

"May I come in Mr. Schwartz?" And he showed the man his badge. "I have some questions I'd like to ask you about the missing children in your neighborhood over the past week. I was wondering if you saw anything unusual; a different kind of car going by; anything at all."

"Yes, come in. I don't get much company; actually none really. You're the first visitor I've had in a long time. Come in."

And the detective entered the house, finding that it was neat and pleasant, and somewhat spacious on the inside. Mr. Schwartz bid him follow to a parlor area, where a coffee pot dripped with freshly made coffee, filling the air.

"Some coffee, detective?"

"No, thank you just the same." Jeff replied. But he really did want some coffee. He always wanted coffee. But, he was thinking about all the rumors he'd heard about, and considering the condition of the yard, the ominous appearance of the man, though surely by no fault of his own, he found himself harboring an unwanted pre-conceived disapproval or rejection of him. Perhaps the icing on the cake, he wondered, was the hunched gait of his dragging walk, and the scarred face and crossed eye, rendering a very poor demeanor of this disabled veterans' countenance. Maybe he had put something strange in the coffee? Maybe he was a very dirty person. Jeff sat down on a very comfortable, clean chair. It looked to be an antique, made from carved walnut. Mr.

Schwartz had an impressive collection of rocks and gems in a large lighted glass cabinet, just near his armchair.

It was a large Victorian house in excellent condition, restored, renovated and very well maintained. Jeff was surprised. In the foyer upon entering the house, massive crystal chandeliers hung delicately above, while a very old fashioned polished mahogany staircase wound upwards and out of sight, with an olive and grey paisleyed runner. "They sure don't build houses like this one anymore, Mr. Schwartz."

Mr. Schwartz poured himself a mug of coffee and sat down across from the detective. "No, they don't. My daddy left this to me in his Will. I have no other living kinfolk." Mr. Schwartz noticed the detective studying his rock and gem collection. "I have a much better rock collection in the cellar, if ya wanna see it? I have extra large specimens of smokey quartz with monazite crystals inside; I got emerald crystals; I got rutilated quartz with fine golden hair needles; I got me chunks of crystalized gold down below; why, you wouldn't believe what I've collected over the years. I travel to do my diggin' in North Carolina and other places about twice a year. It's good to get away from here, too," he reflected solemnly.

"No thank you, I don't wish to see your rock collection. Remember, if I see that still down there I can take you in for it!"

"Ah yes, well detective, how can I help you then?"

"As you've probably read in the paper, or have heard about, there are some missing children in this neighborhood in a specific, small radius that tends to very much highlight Mangrove Lane. Sir, do you know about or have you heard anything at all that would help to solve this mystery?"

"No. I sure ain't. I get got a paper two days ago, read all 'bout it. That's all I know, what I read. Ain't seen no different cars drive down the road neither that don't go there anyhow. And sure ain't seen no strangers in the area. But, ya know me, I don't go out much. Can't stand the town people. I keep to myself. Ya know, it ain't loneliness I know, it's peace. I got me a feeder in back for the birds, I like to watch birds ya know, I'm sort of an expert on birds," he confided, blushing; "and I've got chores to keep this house up that keep me right busy. In fact, I was working on my garden out in back when you drove up. Want to bring home some garden tomatoes and lettuces, Mr. Detective?"

"No thank you, Mr. Schwartz."

"Why, you can call me Danny."

"No thank you Danny."

"Those jerks in town, why they call me devil," and he leaned back, obviously comfortable in the deep worn, leather chair. "It's because of my eyes I think, devil eyes, they say. Got my beauty marks from 'Nam. Served over there for four years."

"I know."

"It don't bother me, why, when I get in the mood for company, I tap on ole' faithful, my still in the cellar. How'd ya know about it? I even have a name for her." He laughed in an odd, sort of hiccupping manner, sort of nervous from being unable to fit in socially for so many long years. A sort of adaptation, thought the detective. Or else a conditioned response, once again fulfilling other people's expectations of him. He had unconsciously believed everything that he had heard about himself being weird and different, maybe. Danny took another sip of his coffee. "Ya ain't gonna arrest me for my still, are ya?"

"No Danny, I wouldn't take that away from you. Plus, I have no evidence, do I? I've never seen it. And if the authorities went around arresting people in the states of Texas, Kentucky and Tennessee every time they found a whiskey still, nothing would ever get done in law enforcement."

85

"It's good, too. One forty proof, the good stuff; it'll put the shine on your boots, dust the lint off your shoulders, and is guaranteed to make you smile. Good music tappin' juice, too."

"Yes, I believe you Danny. I'm here today for a different reason."

"Ya don't drink then, do ya? Don't like houch."

"Why, I'll have a little sip of some bourbon once in a while. Off duty, of course." He coughed. "Let's get back to my questions. Okay?"

"Okay Mr. Detective."

"So from what you've told me," and Jeff began taking notes for himself, "that nothing out of the ordinary in any way, shape or form has occurred recently to your knowledge. Would that be an accurate statement?"

"Ya."

And the detective closed his notebook, placed it inside his briefcase and stood up. "Thank you Mr. Schwartz, you've been very cooperative."

"Sure ya don't want to take any tomatoes or carrots from my garden home with ya?"

"No thank you," but Jeff had secretly wished he could accept, but for his fear of the things he had heard, he again refused the kindness of this man. "Well then, I'll be off. I can find my way to the door, no need to get up." And Mr. Schwartz watched the detective leave, carefully walking around the obstructions near the front of the house, and over to his car. He watched him drive further down Mangrove Lane, the looping mosses sweeping the top of his car as he drove beneath a giant tree, then out of sight.

Jeff Thompson interviewed the majority of residents along Mangrove Lane, returning straight home from his last inquiry and not to the office, as was his customary destination after being out of the office during the day.

Mrs. Young awoke from her deep sleep. She got up and went to the phone, thumbing through the phone book. She called up Tom and Marilyn Reynolds, the people who had lost all three of their children this week. She needed to speak to someone who knew her pain.

"Hello?" Marilyn answered.

"Marilyn Reynolds? This is Meredith Young calling."

"Oh, hello Meredith. I'm so sorry to hear about your boy."

"Yes." And she took a moment to compose herself again. "And I'm sorry too, about your children. How are you? How do you make it through the day?"

"I don't know. I believe in God, I believe that God does everything for a purpose. Without my faith, I'd go insane, I'm sure. How are you faring Mrs. Young?"

"Not good Marilyn. I'm falling apart. I needed to talk to you, since you know how it feels. A detective was out today, and also a state trooper and the town officer. But, I don't feel any the better from their visit. They don't know anything at all. They don't have any clues, any leads. And it's true, what my husband says, that the profile of a serial killer, or kidnapper, is that he usually lives near or in the vicinity of his victims."

"What if it's not a he, and it's a she?" Inquired Mrs. Reynolds.

"True, true. We've always wondered why Selma Higgins acts so strange." Meredith confirmed, having stuck her foot in the door of some new possibility. Planting seeds of doubt and poison.

"Why what's so strange about her dear?" Marilyn asked, unconsciously bonding with her neighbor through their mutual grief. For the Reynolds and the Youngs had not typically associated with each other, nor had they ever held the same society. Dr. Young was an extremely accomplished physician, being a heart specialist. They vacationed to the islands every winter, and Europe in the summer. They drove a Mercedes, and their young son, Nathan, had his own Mazda RX7 sports car at the age of 16. Regarding their home, well, it was to the Reynolds like something from the pages of Architectural Digest Magazine. Utterly spectacular. Not a home, a mansion. It appeared from the outside, that they had nothing in common.

Tom and Marilyn Reynolds raised three children pulling together all of the financial resources they could to feed and otherwise support their family. They lived in an average-sized ranch-style home, and Tom worked at a newspaper as a writer, Marilyn a nurse. They worked long hours, and had alternating shifts, and therefore, did not always have the marital privilege of spending as much time together as she and her husband would have preferred, let alone the extra leisure time to vacation to Paris and Bermuda. Yet, the Reynold's modest lifestyle of hard work and in setting goals, and in knowing the value of a dollar by economizing their needs, and sometimes compromising their desires, made them very content people, not at all restless about life or the future. They were deeply spiritual people in their own eyes; which thus made them so. They did not envy the Youngs nor harbor any bitter resentment. Mrs. Reynolds, with all of her grief and pain, was as polite to Mrs. Young as if they had known each other commonly over the years. As if they had shopped and lunched together, had acquired shared memories; as if they had shared the same circle of friends and had existed in the same society. But they did not. What they did share, however, was a mutual affection for the country and for the wilderness. They had both placed a premium on a sense of privacy and self-control, which was the main feature of the neighborhood they both lived in. Besides, in town, the lots were not large enough to accommodate a house as large as Dr. Youngs.

Marilyn Reynolds loved nothing more than to sit out in her newly constructed and very beautiful back yard patio, overlooking the vast blooming fields and forests beyond, whose smoky hills rolled endlessly out of sight, while reading a good book with a tall glass of ice tea, spiked with a sprig of peppermint from her gardens, and a slice of lemon. That, for her, was contentment when she wasn't busy with her family, or at work. These were inner moments of deep peace. And sometimes, she had to steal these moments from the early hours of the day before work; or late at night, whereupon, the entire character of the vast world beyond her door took on a new and mysterious wilderness pitching her senses more alert than during the day, almost scaring her in a pleasing way with the echoing sounds of the animals at night. And at night, she felt almost as if the woods *were watching her.*

Marilyn Reynolds had been saving her money for years to have the patio and greenhouse constructed, and she herself had labored intensely over the plans, blueprints and gardens. Now that her dream had materialized into reality, she had a lovely place to enjoy some quiet time, with family, friends or alone.

The gardens of Dr. Young's estate rivaled her painstaking efforts, however. Mrs. Young's gardens were picturesque and remarkable: a sea of crimson tulips; heavily laden, intensely fragrant lilac trees; rivers of purple hyacinth to entice the senses with wonder; and the loveliest, largest roses one could ever imagine. Roses that created their very own breezes, fragrant and soothing. Every time Marilyn drove passed the Young's house, she knew that Mrs. Young always had fresh cut flowers on her table, and in her bathroom, and in their bedroom, too. But, Marilyn herself had a very beautiful garden, too, and was not lacking for want of floral beauty to grace the passing days. She was also more economical than the Youngs, in that aside from the flowers, she had an elaborate vegetable garden, and did all her own canning over the years. It seemed too, to be a common feature in the majority of homes built in this area, that large cellars were constructed. These cellars were cool in the summer months, and they also afforded the space for canning, as well as for hanging herbs and dried flowers. The cellars were ideal for storing collections of wine, and also beheld in their shadows and corners, memories stored from generations of family present and gone. Here too, from the floors of these dark cellars emerged stories and rumors of hauntings, and legends of murder, taking root in the foundation of family history and vining upwards into the light of day into everyone's living room. For people loved to talk. It didn't matter if it was at the local diner over a cup of coffee that had grown cold, nobody's name was sacred or spared, or if it was at the hairdresser's newsroom, the treble sounds of voices rising, rang like birds in cages, bunches of cages all in a row clanking together. And few people had a disdain for hearing about some misfortune that was not their own. For them, that was contentment, perhaps perverse, but nonetheless, quite real.

"Why," exclaimed Meredith, "she lives alone! She has no family to speak of. Her son and daughter do not keep in contact with her, and she's so old, one would have to wonder why?"

"Well," said Marilyn, "that doesn't make her too strange, really. Many families result in disparate lives from years and years of unresolved conflict. Maybe she dropped them from her Will."

"There's other strange things about her, too." Meredith Young confided to her. "All of the children who are missing, why they used to go to her home and play. They swam in her pond, she gave them candy! Now these children are all missing."

"But there are still children who go there who are *not* obviously missing, Meredith."

"Not yet. Perhaps she has them locked up in her cellar. The Good Lord can only imagine what she's done to them. Living alone can drive a person insane, I read that somewhere. She's not right, Marilyn. People start talking to themselves, they live in a world of imagination without contact with real people, without any objective feedback. They know no definitions or boarders of reality; perhaps not even right from wrong anymore. She may even speak with familiars, with spirits of the dead, chanting into mirrors, practicing candle magic, or even casting spells..." Meredith explained.

"But you and your husband have been dinner guests at her home in the past. I doubt you would have accepted the invitation, if you thought she may have been a witch. Witches tend to put strange things into their suppers, too," Marilyn smiled sarcastically. "Tell me dear, did she ever serve you up a hot bowl of newt stew?" She laughed. "I don't mean to be rude, Mrs. Young, but I believe at this point in time we need to look elsewhere for the source of our troubles, our joined tragedy."

"I think they're alive in Selma's basement cellar. I think the old woman is so lonely and bored, she keeps them around for company. Or maybe they are dead." Offered Meredith, staring blankly ahead.

"You mean she hangs out little children like flowers tied up and turned to dry?"

"Exactly." Meredith said.

"Meredith, I would think that a more likely suspect would be Mr. Devil, or Daniel Schwartz. I've heard he's about the weirdest person you could ever meet. I've never met him before, but gosh, nor would I want to. They say that if you look him in the eye, you're hexed for life! And his house, to see it from the outside, why, it's just horrible. Makes that big Victorian house behind Bate's Motel look like the Gingerbread House." Said Marilyn. "That place spooks me out every time I drive by. And I've never seen that freak outside of his house, not ever. Suppose some children got lost in the woods behind his house and he got to them! They'd be goners."

"You're right, but I still think Selma Higgins is into something bad. How can she keep her sanity all alone like that? What does she do with all her spare time? I mean, really, why even get out of bed when there's absolutely nothing on earth to look forward to?" Meredith insisted. "I intend to get to the bottom of this. I believe that my son is alive or lost somewhere. He knows better than to wander off into the woods. We didn't raise no dummy, Marilyn. Nathan is probably trying to outsmart his captor right now as we speak, ready for the right moment of escape to steal home! He can't be...dead, he just can't be. It's these strange people around here."

"I know you didn't raise any dummy," Marilyn assured her, the two of them forming a closer union of fear with the turning page of each new idea which they shared. Put simply, their imaginations had run wild with them like fires out of control, each fueled by the other. "I know I could never live alone, with no one to talk to, nothing to do, the same mundane routines day in and day out, endlessly boring, insidious, without relief. I suppose you are right, it could drive a person mad. Like listening to the same song over and over again, or water dripping on your forehead. Living alone sounds to me like torture. It is the culture of society that creates true solitude when we are alone, anything less, is isolation and unbearable loneliness." Marilyn pondered further.

"I mean, you know, older people can do strange things, she may be senile. Just because she's an elderly lady, doesn't free her from the perils and temptations of being human. She could have arsenic around her house. Maybe dead bodies keep her company. Maybe she doesn't feel so alone, even if it is someone who can't respond or talk to her, it's still someone that's there. She's not alone anymore. Maybe she talks to dead bodies and imagines that they actually talk back to her. I heard that when her husband passed away nine years ago, that she held a seance and tried to communicate with him. That alone, is pretty spooky stuff. And our children have been going there to swim in her pond and eat her baked goods and candy. I wonder if she has them playing with her Ouija Board? She's always inviting someone to come by and visit, trying to lure them inside!" Exclaimed Meredith with horror and conviction. "And, haven't you noticed, but she always wears black! Black satin, black taffeta, black chiffon, black lace, black velvet dresses. She could be into some kind of occult activity."

"Well Meredith, I still think that 'devil eyes' is a more apt candidate for criminal mischief. Exhibit "A": he's a bizarre loner, a recluse, and despises all people. Exhibit "B": he's got that rot-gut brewing in his cellar. Maybe it's driven him mad, it's been proven to cause brain damage, for sure." Marilyn informed her, "And I know about these things, I'm a nurse honey! That clear 180 proof rotgut can make people do crazy things, especially people who hate other people! I'm so glad we're not like that!"

"I'm going to call on Ms. Selma Higgins tonight. I'm going to call her throughout the night and hang up on her, so that she will know that someone is aware of what she's doing in that house of hers. That house of horrors. We could frighten her into releasing the children." Confided Meredith, as if embarking upon a brave cause. "And on top of that, I think the two of us should pay her a visit to her house tomorrow. See what she's up to, you know, just kind of snoop around a bit. See how she keeps her house up, what her mood is. Marilyn, I'm going to go for now, do some laundry. I'm glad I called you. I feel better now; this is all starting to make sense. We'll get our children back, and soon, too! It has to be someone in the neighborhood. It just has to be."

"Okay Meredith, we'll talk again tomorrow. Be sure you know what you're doing though, about calling up on Mrs. Higgins. You've really got to feel that she's involved in this whole thing. Think it over, dear. Be careful, and be sure. Bye for now." Ended Marilyn.

"Talk to you tomorrow, Marilyn," concluded Meredith. Vengeance began steeping her blood with the passing of every thought about Selma. And that night, after midnight, Meredith commenced with her campaign of hate against Mrs. Higgins. 'Old women always have arsenic around; why, something must be filling all that empty time she has on her hands. And all her invitations, why, I've even known her to invite total strangers over for tea. How absurd!' She thought. In fact, Meredith felt lucky that she was alone at home tonight, her husband being at the hospital on call, so she spent the entire evening telephoning and hanging up on Selma Higgins hoping to frighten her into surrendering to the truth. Meredith smiled with satisfaction, upon hearing her thin voice, weakened by fear, answering to nothing on the other end of the line. Meredith would hang up the phone and mock her, *"hello, who is this? Please stop calling me. Please stop this, you're frightening me! Please go away. Leave me alone."* The frightened voice would beg. She laughed in a mocking tone imitating Selma's words. At about 4:30 a.m., she fell morose and began grieving again for her lost son. She laid down in bed and slept until noon the next day. Her husband had apparently been home, and had left again, for he had set aside a tender note on the kitchen table, near a lovely vase of rubrum lilies.

At 1:30 in the afternoon, Meredith called upon Marilyn Reynolds once again. She agreed to ride over with Meredith and visit Mrs. Higgins, just in case, just to take a look around her house. Plus, they both agreed, it would be easy to get inside, for she was always inviting people over to visit with her anyways.

Selma's house was unremarkable in every way. It was not foreboding or scary in any way, nor was it extravagant or fancy or plush. It was a very old fashioned and tastefully decorated house. There was a gigantic, antique-looking grandfather clock chiming from down the hall. It smelled of old money. The rooms all bore a lived-in feeling, with worn, but clean, oriental rugs laid over polished oak floors. The rooms had a sanitary air to them, and blankets and towels in the house were all neatly folded with an ironed uniformity of order and taste. Her kitchen was replete with hanging tea cups in a lovely china cabinet, with beautiful plates displayed, and porcelain and crystal nick knacks decorating the shelves collected over the years. It was certainly a chef's kitchen, too. A large marble island beheld baking tools such as a rolling pin, a flour sifter, a dough scraper and other items which both ladies

94

were unfamiliar with in their scrutiny of Selma's home. Meredith even peeked into her oven, opening the door slowly as if a monster were going to jump out.

"Why Selma, what's that?" Meredith asked.

"It's a stone-cast oven, wood burning. Make's the best breads and pizzas." Mrs. Higgins replied, wondering why they were searching her home.

"Why is there a shot glass on the island?" Meredith persisted, trying to find fault with something.

"Because I throw in shots of water against the walls when the breads first go into the fires. It creates a steam that in turn produces a lovely crust." Selma answered her again, as if being interrogated.

"What do you keep in your basement?" Meredith asked the old woman intrusively.

"What does anyone keep in their basement, dear? Canned tomatoes, peaches, old letters, I may even have a nice old bottle of wine down there, if it hasn't turned to vinegar by now." Selma replied. "Oh, and probably some pretty elaborate spider webs to decorate a cellar proper." She laughed. "Ladies, your visit today is unexpected, may I offer you some tea? I have some lovely cinnamon rolls I baked yesterday, but have no one to eat them. Would you like one?" She pressed.

"No thank you Ms. Higgins." They both replied almost in unison. Normally, they would have loved a cup of tea and a fine, rich cinnamon roll. But thinking their host might be some kind of deranged murderer, they politely declined. The world for Meredith and Marilyn had been turned up-side-down, it was a topsy turvy world, a maddening carnival ride heading for horror, or whatever it was that they thought they would discover about their missing children.

"You look kind of tired, Ms. Higgins." Commented Meredith with a faint and knowing smile. "Not enough sleep last night?"

Selma trembled, suddenly turning pale, almost aging right before them. "No, no. There's nothing wrong at all. I'm fine. Just an old lady. I have my good days and I have my bad days. That's all it is." And she looked away sadly out the window, at a peaceful community of birds hopping together on a nearby branch. They looked bright and beautiful. It reminded her of her own life before her husband died, for her days were indeed lonely from time to time.

"Well, how 'bout a tour of the whole house? Maybe that bottle of rare old wine is good after all? Can we see the basement?" Asked Meredith plainly, almost insisting.

"No dear. I'm afraid not. It's a mess down there now, and I need to take a nap."

"So we can not take a look at your basement." Meredith persisted.

"Well, it can't be important, and it is a mess, some other time dearie. Some other time. Why don't you ladies let me take my nap now, I've grown tired suddenly." Selma asked, almost pleading with them to leave. To leave her alone. For she could feel that they were not stopping by for a friendly visit to inquire on her well-being, or to enjoy her company, but that they were genuinely snooping around. 'But for what?' She wondered. 'For what?'

"Well," huffed Meredith, puffing up like a bird; then I suppose we shall be leaving now. We'll see you again, and soon, too, Selma Higgins!" Declared Meredith, almost as if issuing a warning to her. A warning which Selma instantly observed.

"Good day, Mrs. Higgins," Marilyn said, leaving the house.

In the car the conversation was chaos. Meredith was convinced that some evil had taken place in the basement; while Marilyn felt that the orderly, neat and comfortable qualities of the quiet and well kept home indicated a very sane personality. Marilyn had mentioned something to Meredith which Meredith in her pathos obsession, did not hear. It was that Selma was truly a gentle and elderly lady, kind and harmless, even vulnerable. That Meredith should never call her again in the middle of the night, or at any other time, and hang up on the poor elderly lady. All this, Meredith missed in her preoccupation of continuing fears while she drove. And as they were driving, they passed Daniel the Devil Schwartz.

"The freak's out for a drive! I wonder where he's coming back from?"

"Did you see that! Did you see that!" Marilyn exclaimed.

"What?" Meredith asked, panicked.

"It was blood on the side of his car, near the door. It was as clear as day." Marilyn said, tearing up. Meredith pulled the car alongside the road. She turned the car around and followed Mr. Schwartz right up to his house. The women got out of the car and immediately surrounded his vehicle, examining every part.

"What in the name of Hop Barrel are you two women folk doing?" Danny asked.

"It's blood!" Marilyn exclaimed.

"Sure is," confirmed Meredith. "It sure is."

"I hit a deer yesterday. Didn't get all the blood off yet."

"You didn't go out anywhere yesterday, Mr. Schwartz!" Insisted Marilyn. "I would have noticed you driving by. At least you didn't go into town. That's for sure."

"I sure as hell *did* go in to town Mrs. Reynolds. And who are you to keep a check on all my activities? You ought to mind your own business!" He pointed at her in a conspicuous scowl of disgust. As if she were the deformed one, not he.

"Where are the missing children, Mr. Schwartz? Did you kill them? Do you have them hidden somewhere?" Asked Marilyn. "Where are they? Please, where are they? We can give you money."

"I don't know what you're talking about. You two women are out looking to stir up a good batch of trouble here. It's people like you that makes me want to *never* leave my house! Never, ya hear me! I dang regret it, too, each time I do leave." He scolded himself. "Wouldn't have met up with you two horses today."

"May we use your telephone, Mr. Schwartz?" Marilyn asked him calmly.

"No, you sure won't use my phone ya bitch hogs! I ain't got no phone to use! Who'd I call on anyways, meddlesome witchwomen like youz two? What a fun chat that'd be! You both git now! Go! Shew! Git off my property before I lose my temper!" He shouted at them.

The women ran back to the car, quickly making their way to the police station, telling their story. A squad car pulled up to Mr. Schwartzs' house about an hour later. The officer examined the car fully, finding no visible trace of blood on the exterior. Although, he had noted that a hose lay nearby and water was still running down the driveway, flushed across the yard. Mr. Schwartz came out and asked the officer what he was doing. Mr. Schwartz also explained to the officer that he had washed his car, because he had recently hit a deer.

Perhaps it was all the excitement generated by two hysterical women, perhaps it was the appearance of someone trying to cover up a crime scene, and perhaps also, that in this small town, it was the result of a lack of competent and thorough investigation by the police station, but just the same, Daniel Schwartz was handcuffed, read his rights, and escorted into the back seat of the squad car. With lights flashing the officer sped back to the station. The women sighed with relief, feeling that they could now get to the bottom of the entire situation which had held their lives in limbo.

Mr. Schwartz had requested an attorney, and being a Saturday, he would have to wait it out in jail until Monday morning to speak with one, or else come up with the bail money, which, of course, he did not have. Nor did he have any one single person he could call on to help him, so he waived his right to a call.

As word spread about the capture of Daniel Schwartz, also known as devil eyes, a riot began to form outside the jail. People marched with signs that read: "child killer burn in hell," and "murderer," and "justice finally met," and "devil eyes are dead eyes now" and on and on and on. Daniel Schwartz could not only hear the chanting outside the jail, but he could see it all from his window, the display of hatred for him, and the formidable atmosphere of sheer conviction which stood against him. With so many frightened, fearful, accusing people marching against him, the odds overwhelmingly against him now, how could an attorney set him free? He wondered. 'I must be the most hated person in this entire town.' He thought, sadly, never truly believing it before.

At the same time, Meredith persisted with her telephoning and hanging up on Selma Higgins. She was not entirely convinced that they had the right suspect behind bars. She was pretty sure, but not entirely convinced. Therefore, she spent the early evening for a couple hours, reminding Selma that someone knew about her and what she was doing. Meredith ended her telephoning when her husband came home around 11:00 p.m. 'After all,' she thought, 'he wouldn't understand. He might think I was crazy or something.' She switched her demeanor from tormentor to loving wife as quickly as changing a sweater.

Earlier, at 9:00 p.m., an officer had approached Daniel's cell to inform him that someone had burned down his beautiful house. The officer was straight-faced and apologetic, as if the poor man could still be met with a fair chance of a trial. A fair trial? How could it even go to trial? He had hit a deer. And that was the truth. Lots of people hit deer while driving. It was the politics of the entire situation that had already created a verdict of sorts, predetermining his fate. It was an actual demonstration of pure hatred. His house, with no insurance, was totally gone now. Where would he live? What would he do? No one would hire him, he'd never be accepted among society and find work, so he'd never be able to afford rent payments. He had no savings or money to speak of, and no relatives or friends. He lived from his disability checks, but they were not enough to support rent or a mortgage. He had owned his own house free and clear of any mortgage, provided for in his father's Will.

People had called him a "loser" and a "freak" over the years, and now he was discovering what damage they had really created, virtually digging him his own grave. He thought about how people had framed him to be someone he wasn't, and by doing so, they had collectively destroyed his life, even long before all this happened. They had dug his grave, and now had the leverage to push him in it. And each day thereafter that the label had been hung around his neck; much like the excruciating and searing hot branding of an Auschwitz number onto his arm, no one, certainly, would ever again be kind to him or give him a fair chance. So in the single act of his home being set ablaze and all of his life belongings destroyed; the bird houses he was building in the cellar, his rock and gem collection, his antique Victorian home which he defended from intruders by having created an offensive looking front yard or face, his life to him had now been completely ruined. They may as well have shot him or strung him up to a tree... And, he thought further, his deformities and eccentricities were the result of having once served this country and having defended these very people, who now persecuted him just for being alive.

At midnight, an officer went to check on Daniel Schwartz again, to see if he needed anything. And at midnight, they found Daniel the Devil Schwartz hung dead by the neck from his own belt, which he had fastened around a beam from the ceiling. His tongue extended, eyes bulging, his face almost a purple-black color, it was a sight to see for this officer who had only been on the job for almost a month now.

But for Mr. Daniel Schwartz, all his troubles were over. People cheered outside the jail. Finding the guilty party responsible for the arson job would be near impossible, in fact, it was the entire crowd that both burned down his home and hung him by the neck. But now, for the people, the child-killer was dead, and life could return to normal again in Lakeland, and especially, for the people who lived on Mangrove Lane. Such a feeling of victory was prevalent in the air, so much so that people held parties along Mangrove Lane; and the town bar was jam packed elbow to elbow with people celebrating the swift capture and just outcome of the murderer who had stalked their children. The doors of the saloon were open until daybreak.

Selma Higgins lay motionless in bed; mysteriously, she had suffered a heart attack at exactly the same time when Daniel Schwartz had hung himself. She could not reach her phone this time, and no more strange calls came in providing any final opportunity to scream for help, had she been able to knock it down on the floor. No one came by again to examine her home the following day, nor did anyone wish to inquire on the condition of her basement, with all the laundry she had hanging on clothes lines across the room, that she had wanted to fold and put away before allowing anyone to enter. Two days later after suffering all alone lying in bed waiting for someone to visit her, or at least call and become worried, lying there, unable to move, and staring at the ceiling praying to God, praying for help from anyone who would come by, Selma began choking, unable to breath. She shuttered for a moment in a deep chill, and passed into death quietly and peacefully, having spoken only one word just before she left: "Raymond," her husband. Her eyes looked not at the ceiling in prayer anymore, but were now cast upwards toward heaven beyond.

CHAPTER TWO: THE RIVER

On Monday Steve Moore was sitting as usual at the kitchen table surrounded by an overfilled ashtray, various magazines and books, dirty coffee mugs, as well as a hot mug in his hand. A cockroach scurried across the table, he raised an eyebrow from reading a magazine for a moment, as it dashed out of sight, and returned to the article. The trailer he and Sandy Johnson shared with their two children was certainly big enough, he thought, but sometimes when the kids were wild, it became claustrophobic. His daughter, Cathie, was 11, and suffered from emotional and psychological disorders, for which she took medication twice a day. His son, Andy, who was 10, was also recently diagnosed by their doctor with various disorders and trauma from a life spent growing up hard, from the mother doing drugs during the pregnancy, and from the condition of the mother being mentally ill.

Sandy sat up in bed rolling another joint, it was noon already. The kids would be off the bus from school in only 2 hours. "God dammit Steve, I'm almost out of pot again!" She yelled from the bedroom. "Ya fuckin' asshole, didn't ya hear me?"

"Ya, I heard ya," Steve answered, looking back down at the newspaper vacantly. "The welfare check ain't come in yet, you'll have to make do. If ya didn't smoke a joint every hour on the hour it might last longer." He bravely ventured.

"My ass you asshole!" She screamed, once again at war with him for want of her own self-hate. "I'm takin' the car out and goin' over to Sheila's, she's always got weed, and if she ain't got none, one of those assholes visiting her does."

"Bitch, you ain't takin' no car no place!" Replied Steve. "The kids have a doctor appointment today after school. I need the car. I was going to use the food stamps and pick up some pizzas on the way home, too. Kid's got nothin' to eat, why don't you ever git up off your ass and cook your kids some food, we're starving around here. I'm hungry. There's nothin' to eat. All you do all day long is sit in bed and smoke pot. Laundry ain't been washed in months now." He sighed. "There's a mountain of dirty laundry downstairs." He complained.

"The little bastards don't need nothin' but the clean dirty clothes they wear to school. They look just fine!" She screamed.

Sandy placed the joint in her breast pocket, put on a second flannel shirt, grabbed her purse and stormed out the door. "See ya fucker!"

"Where the hell you goin' in those tight pants and all?" He yelled.

"Fuck you ya prick!" She yelled out the window, tearing out of the drive and disappearing down the road toward Sheila's apartment.

At 2:15 the school bus stopped down the road and children spilled out from the door. Cathie and Andy ran towards their trailer, both reaching the door at the same time and fighting over who would enter first. "Ya dumbhead Cathie, get out of my way."

"Devil Doll!" She screamed at him, "I was here first."

Steve came to the door and they both squeezed inside at the same time. "Cathie told everyone at school that I'm on medication!"

"Did not ya little liar!"

"Ya, you sure did ya *s-h-I-t head*"

"Devil doll," she screamed in his face, in seemingly perfect defense. And with that the boy slugged her in the head and ran down the length of the trailer, throwing his school books on the floor; his hair messed, face pale, heart pounding. Cathie began stomping her feet harder and harder on the floor, crying, sobbing, then screaming in tears, "Andy hit me!"

"Alright you two, cut it out," was all their father said, not even looking up from his newspaper, lighting another cigarette.

"I'm hungry," Cathie whined.

"I ain't makin' no fuckin' meal. Go git a bowl of cereal."

"I don't want cereal. I hate cereal. I always eat cereal. I'm sick of cereal." She whined, crying like a two year old baby now, thinking that this would get her what she wanted.

"Shut up ya little brat!" Her brother yelled from down the hall. "Cathie needs her medicine."

"Ya Andy, and so do you ya little fart face, nipple dick..." she beckoned. And Andy came tearing down the hallway screaming fists forward, and rammed Cathie in the back of the head again, jumping on her.

"Dad! Dad!" She screamed, whining and crying.

"What," Steve replied without alarm.

"Andy keeps hitting me." She said.

"You two go outside and play, ya here me." He said, staring at the newspaper, oblivious of their rage.

Cathie kicked Andy hard in the groin, and he started screaming. "Okay, okay, you two, OUTSIDE right now!" Steve yelled at them.

"Don't we have a doctor appointment today!" Cathie told her father in a patronizing manner.

"No. I had to reschedule it. Your mother's taken the car again."

"Yeah, probably goin' to get p-o-t." She said. "Dad I'm hungry."

"You're supposed to eat at school. It's not my problem." Steve answered, unmoved.

"You can say it outloud, Cathie." Andy told her.

"Pot!" She said with an accusing finality.

"OUTSIDE NOW!!!!!" Their father screamed, standing up. And the children flew out the door disappearing down a trail and into the woods. The cockroaches returned, as if they had been hiding from the fury of the children's return from school. They scurried across the kitchen counter, stopping off at smears and bits of food pasted onto the countertop.

"We're not supposed to be here, ya dumbhead! Dad said we can't go further than this big ole' tree here Cathie! I'm telling mom!" He screamed, standing only an inch away from her face.

"So what. Let's go down to the river and swim. I'm hot!" She said in a teasing, sultry, adult manner for an eleven year old. "He doesn't care and mom's gone, let's go! Besides, they can't tell us what to do!" Cathie reminded him. " 'Common' *Devil Doll*!" She teased him.

"Okay, I'm gonna kill ya if we get into trouble again!" He yelled back in her face. The two children ran, following the trail which led to the sunny bank of the river. Back at the trailer their father sat, sipping on cold coffee, staring off at nothing, looking at the peeling walls in a dismal state of apathy, his cigarette ash now dropping on the floor. At Sheila's apartment, Sandy was fronted another bag of pot, but was presently thanking her generous friend in the privacy of the guestroom.

And in town, at Detective Jeff Thompson's office, Linda had taken the day off sick, while Jeff poured over files at his desk, his phones set on the answering machine. He was not at all satisfied that the person responsible for abducting all the missing children had been eliminated by virtue of the deaths of either Daniel Schwartz or Selma Higgins. And his gut instincts had always turned out to be true. He turned to his computer and researched old newspaper articles on missing persons within the past ten years; there were not many, plenty of domestic disputes, even domestic disputes ending in murder. His search landed at an article that was not quite what he was looking for, but he found himself reading it nonetheless. It was an article about a missing snake! A 20 foot pregnant reticulated python, and it's larger mate, which had both apparently pushed their heads, and he shivered at this detail, heads that were wider than a foot, through a basement window escaping from the room where they had been raised as young pets, and had, at the time of their escape, been feeding on chickens and pigs. 'How,' Jeff wondered, 'in the hell did the pet owner get the pigs in his house? And from where?' He laughed, thinking what a waste, as a pig roast was such a great way to celebrate with friends on a lazy Sunday afternoon; slowly turning 'round on a spit over a steady fire; and he was picky, too. The meat should never be overcooked so that it shredded, but rather should be carved out juicy and thick, smoky and richly delicious, almost oozing and sweating with its own glaze, half honied, half like maple syrup.

He returned now to the article, feeling hunger pains for lunch growing. He read further and wondered about why the owner had the nerve to place the event of the escaped snakes right into the missing persons column? Shouldn't this be in a different section of the paper, or in an article: 'pet owner of exotic animals fails to control two 20 plus foot pythons.' The article was dated five years ago exactly from today's date. What a coincidence, Jeff wondered, while he went into the supply room and opened the refrigerator door looking for something to eat. Yogurt, club soda, apples, diet Pepsi... He slammed the door fast, as if it were the refrigerator's fault. 'I know what I'll do,' he thought to himself. Back in his office, he dialed out to the local café to have the days' lunch special

107

delivered over to him: fried chicken, mashed potatoes, gravy, rolls, and coleslaw. They had the best fried chicken anywhere. It was never overcooked, and was always perfectly crispy and juicy. He returned to the bizarre article on the missing snakes. The original article had been responded to by an anonymous member of the community, who had informed the pet owner that he better find his snakes, because *if he* found them, he was going to blow their heads off with a shotgun. This article also pointed out to the incompetent pet owner that in certain towns in the state of Pennsylvania, all constricting snakes are outlawed as pets. He also inquired on where the pet owner had purchased the dangerous snakes, but Jeff found no article of reply. It seemed the pet owner simply wanted his snakes back.

Exactly five years ago from today's date. How strange. Jeff knew that in this semi-tropical portion of Texas, that such snakes would probably thrive quite easily, and there were plenty of rivers for them to live in, to support such heavy body weight. He began wondering how many residents in the community actually had missing dogs and cats. But, pursuing such a line of thought would derail him from his searches concerning the missing children. He felt for certain that it would happen again. And he knew about how Daniel Schwartz had been treated by the town people, the sort of 'iceberg welcome' and 'lynch mob goodbye,' and he had hoped that if any further unfortunate crime did turn up, therefore proving Daniel's innocense, that they would feel some kind of contrition or remorse for this poor man, for what they had done to him.

The phone rang and Meredith Young set down her cappuccino. "Hello?" There was no one on the other end. "Hello! Who is this?" Still, no answer. She sat back down, sipping her coffee, wondering if Selma Higgins had secretly stashed large sums of cash throughout her house, hidden in books, under carpets, inside drawers and vases. She wondered who would call her up and just listen to her voice on the other end of the line and then hang up. Only Marilyn Reynolds knew of her calling on Selma. 'It must be her,' she thought. It happened again. Returning to her coffee, she decided to get dressed and drive over to Marilyn's house to catch her in the act on the phone. She was out the door in minutes. She pulled up quietly at Marilyn's house. The garage door was shut, and there were no cars in the driveway. She walked up and looked inside the garage from the side garden windows, stepping in a knoll of Lily of the Valley flowers. There were no cars inside. 'Well, maybe they had car repairs made today,' she thought, walking up to the front door and knocking with a loud and accusing fist. No one came to the door. She walked around the house and found magazines lying on a beautiful glass patio table, all cooking magazines. She banged on the back door to the kitchen. Still, no answer. She looked around. The patio was a living waterfall of flowers. Cypress Vines and Moonflowers hung lazily in thick cascading showers from the trellis wall which spanned the entire length of the house; spires of lupine and delphinium stretched outwards in fields of indigo; and there was a large clay pot on the table of Evening Primrose clustered together, shaded by the umbrella of the table. Massive hedges of snow white and sunset peach Peonies framed the dark grey slate tiled patio area with striking contrast. 'What a lovely place,' Meredith thought. She spied through the windows at the vast and almost mathematically organized gardens with ripe hanging tomatoes; lettuces; thick patches of dark green basil and other herbs; carrots; green beans; and more... The vegetable gardens were protected within a beautifully designed greenhouse, so no wandering deer could come in and graze, and as no lock secured the door, she snuck inside gathering as many gorgeous fresh vegetables as she could hold in the loop of her shirt. She carefully ran back to her car, placing the vegetables inside an empty box, throwing a sweater over the top to cover it, and sighed with relief. 'Well, there's no one home,' she thought to herself. She wiped the afternoon sweat from her brow, and decided to go for a drive further down Mangrove Lane. For she too got lonely and bored during the long hours of her husband's absence at the hospital.

She backed out of Marilyn's driveway, heading down the road beneath the sweeping lace curtains of mosses and airplants which hung gracefully over the road. In less than a mile, she stopped before the secluded, broken down trailer of Steve Moore and

Sandy Johnson. There was no car in the driveway. 'White trash,' she thought to herself, 'white trash,' shaking her head. To the side of the trailer was a huge pile of garbage and old bed springs stacked high. There were toys, scooters and pieces of clothing scattered in the yard, indicating that no discipline dwelled here, that these children ran wild, that they were wide open, out of control. She thought about what horrible citizens these children would make once they grew up, what a detriment to the entire community they would be. She decided to pull up and have a look inside the front door. 'What if these people were responsible for the missing children? Why, their children were not missing, and why not? Their children ran the streets and woods like unkempt, mangy dogs that were not properly cared for, with tattered shirts and dirty faces. If any children should be missing, it would certainly do the community a favor if these kids were one of 'em,' she pondered. 'But no, *my* son is gone.' She frowned. '*My son.*'

She walked up to the trailer door, stepping around piles of cat food and a muddy Raggedy Ann doll missing an arm. She looked inside the door, assuming that no one was home, when an unshaven, wane face stared right back at her through the glass pane. She gasped stepping backwards, bracing herself. Steve opened the door, "hello?"

"Hello," said Meredith. Fumes of cat urine escaped from the trailer, and a dank, damp must that felt cold and black, even on this hot day, swirled all around her making her sneeze.

"You looking for someone?" Steve asked the woman.

"I'm sorry, I must be lost."

"You're Mrs. Young, aren't you?" He told her.

"Yes." She shivered.

"I'm sorry to hear 'bout your son and all."

110

"Yes, thank you."

"Must be a relief to have that Schwartz character gone now, we can all rest easier." He tried to comfort her.

"Well, I must be going. Sorry to have troubled you," she said, walking back to her car in haste, her heals sinking into the muddy yard. There was no actual driveway, just a sort of half-loop parking area.

"Awfully wet around here!" She complained to him, opening up her car door.

"River's just behind the house," he shouted.

She slammed the door as if escaping from something wholly offensive and bad, turning her car around and headed for home. She could smell the tomatoes and the greens from the back seat once the fresh wind came in through the windows. As she drove passed Marilyn's house, she noticed that her car was now home. She laughed to herself, "thank you Marilyn," she said, throwing a quick, arrogant wave at her house, zooming passed in her little red Mercedes roadster.

Marilyn had that unmistakable feeling one gets when someone's been inside your own private room or space. It was always her custom to walk the greenhouse and check on her vegetables each day. The door wasn't firmly shut and secured, either, and there were some torn leaves on the ground too, she noted. She wondered if this had something to do with her three missing children, if the killer had come back to the crime scene, if the killer had been here. The greenhouse had been constructed for the benefit of her children originally. With a big family to feed, canning was an economical and healthy way to eat, and she loved to cook. And her children were good kids, too. They liked carrots and onions, beets and tomatoes, fresh, crisp green beans and all the other wonderful lettuces she grew. She felt a melancholy shadow fall across her, while standing among the verdant vegetable garden,

111

with the sun blazing down through the screen-framed ceiling. She opened the windows and turned on the inside sprinkler system on her way out. She returned to her deep cushioned chair at the patio table, sipping on iced tea. She too, felt that the real person responsible for the disappearance of the children had not yet been caught. And even in her contempt for Mr. Schwartz, and his resulting death, she felt absolutely no guilt for having turned him in, in the first place, and for having started, together with Mrs. Young, all the deadly gossip about him threatening to get his gun and shoot them. For she knew he had never said that. And she knew also, that he never would have approached them with a gun. It was his theatrics, his repulsion to the whole situation of once again being accused of something he didn't do. She now felt certain that it was not him. Yet, not a tincture of guilt or sorrow for this poor man stirred inside of her. She felt, somehow, that this poor creature of a man was decidedly better off. She did, however, feel bad about Mrs. Higgin's death. And she firmly believed that Mrs. Higgins was indirectly murdered by her neighbor, the wealthy Meredith Young. She had scared her to death. The health of older people, she knew as a nurse, was frail and was a thing to be protected and nurtured. Not tortured. And certainly not tortured while all alone.

She wondered if she'd ever call on Mrs. Young again, with what she knew, for she swore to herself that she'd never tell another living soul what she knew Meredith had gotten away with. For the repercussions from the Young family would be endless, and who would believe her? This was a prominent doctor's wife. Most of the county went to his offices. They had an unblemished social record, and only associated with other rich, well-to-do members of society. And they held a rare and limited numbered key to the exquisite dining nightclub at the edge of town: where platters came out of the kitchen crowned with steamed whole Maine lobsters; veal and parmigiana tortelloni in a sauce of basil-alfredo; the thickest, most delicious cuts of prime rib and fillet and giant T-bones; why, the dinners were ethereal, they were events. Dr. Young was frequently in the newspaper, shining in some magnificent new achievement or contribution. The Youngs, realized Marilyn, would have the entire community turned against her and her family in a day, if she pointed a finger at Meredith Young in connection with the horrible and sad death of Selma Higgins. No, she better keep her mouth shut. It never happened.

She looked out across at the lovely dogwood and magnolia trees, so gigantic, way out at the end of the yard where the property line ended, where mystical doors opened into wild woods and fields beyond, waiting - beckoning her. Maybe if she changed into some shorts, brought a small jug of water with, and took a long walk out there, she'd return feeling better about everything. Better about the wrongful death of Mrs. Higgins, and how Meredith Young had terrorized poor old Selma late at night. And above all, she needed to find some solace from the emptiness she felt, from her children having suddenly been taken from her life. One of her last memories was of the children sitting at the kitchen table eating pancakes before school and rushing out the door to meet the bus. Then she remembered when they had come home, skipping off together to play down by the river. And after that, they were never seen again. Not one trace, nothing. Yes, perhaps a brisk walk into the woods would return a sense of vitality, quicken her blood, refresh her spirits. Perhaps even, it would help her on how to now behave with Mrs. Young, for she knew that any trace of blame in her eyes or in her voice, or in her mannerisms in the company of Meredith, would be enough to set off a chain reaction of retribution from that family, from the secrets and guilt bubbling like molten lava just beneath the surface appearance of things. And it always did start off with the small stuff at first, when a person's reputation gets destroyed: stuff is made up and rumors spread, escalating and rolling like a snowdrift tumbling down a precipitous mountain cliff gathering speed and volume and crashing finally in a total avalanche. The face in the mirror now distorted, unrecognizable, worse than any physical disfigurement, as it came from within and always changed. She cared not to be standing beneath the crushing weight of just such a predicament. She must cleanse her mind of everything, start anew, and keep hope that her children would turn up unharmed soon. She needed to somehow enjoy and like Meredith again.

She changed her clothes, put on her sunglasses, left a note for her husband, grabbed a water bottle and trekked out into the beautiful blooming forests beyond. But was she escaping from herself and what she knew, or truly returning to herself with a renewed sense of composure? For this, she didn't care: she simply forced herself to put one foot in front of the other and keep moving... she needed to stop thinking so much... everything would work out fine in the end... time would heal everything...

Detective Thompson printed off the articles about the snakes, and the only other two missing persons' articles from the past ten years. He threw his garbage from lunch into the trash can, wiping off his hands, and unlocked the desk drawer, pulling out the bottle of bourbon with an inverted water glass over the neck. He drank a neat three fingers, and returned the bottle back to its secret home, locking the drawer again. Placing the articles into his briefcase, he snapped it shut. He turned the walleye portrait around and combed his hair, leaving the office for home. He was stumped, now moreso than before. The death of Mr. Schwartz had affected him like some eerie nightmare carnival ride, some macabre funhouse with distorted mirrors bending and stretching reality. While driving home he thought that beneath all the cordial waves and smiles of his fellow neighbors and colleagues, that something as equally mysterious, perhaps even as deadly as the crimes themselves, had taken root here generations ago.

At four o'clock in the morning, Sandy Johnson staggered into the trailer smelling of beer, whiskey, cigarettes, pot, and God knows what else. She hadn't showered, so the affections from her friend who had fronted her the ounce of pot had dried on her legs and groin like pale cracked sewer mud. She walked like a man, strong, but not like the gait of a real man. She was what the towns' people referred to as a "biker chick": a hard-boiled, loud mouthed, foul mouthed, know-everything woman, with skull tatoos on her arms, and tight jeans studded with cheap rhinestones to flash warning to those higher evolved. Her makeup was harsh and indelicate, her demeanor raunchy and rebel, and her terms ruthless and uncompromising always. If she had been a bottle of wine, it

114

for certain would have been some jug of three dollar swill. Here was a mortal woman who would lie in the face of God, if he ever appeared before her. Steve was actually afraid of her, intimidated. If he had the nerve to ask her where she'd been, even though he already knew, she's go off on him like a Tommy gun, spraying him with insults and accusations. Her private whereabouts had become a living, breathing pandoras' box of evil. And he didn't want to open it. She came into their small bedroom in the awning lights of the new day, set her bag down, took off her shirt and pants, and slipped into a dirty pink robe, reeking of wild partying and wild men, and fell instantly to sleep. Steve could not sleep after this. It was not because he was a light sleeper, but because she stunk so bad. Usually when she was this drunk too, she had a tendency to piss on herself in bed. He wasn't in the mood. So he got up brewing a pot of coffee, sitting at the kitchen table, and lit a cigarette greedily. He hadn't eaten in two days, but almost wasn't interested. He had become thin, pale and ill over the years living with Sandy, his vitality having been sucked right out of him. At one time he had a good job, a fine income and was healthy, but he had caught her in bed with his boss, and the outcome was that he lost his job and got himself blacklisted in this community and others. There was no longer any hope or opportunity for work again around here for him. The lies about him had spread as quickly as wildfire, and he only stayed here now for his children, for he'd certainly never marry that woman, he hated her, and he hated himself for not doing anything about it to change his life for the better. The unemployment checks had worn out, and welfare played in next. And here he sat, watching the walls peeling and the cockroaches scurrying, and soon, the children would be shouting, hitting each other, crying, and otherwise battling war before heading off to wait for the school bus. 6:30 a.m. came and went, and no children stirred. He walked down the hall to their small rooms and found them to be gone. Not quite awake yet, no fear or concern pulled on him. He sat back down thinking. Apathy was like a hill of one's own personal mental and emotional garbage that needed to be pushed away by a big tractor and cleared, before one could focus on the present moment with any true sense of awareness or feeling.

After two cups of coffee, Steve became concerned. He looked back inside his bedroom, which stunk now, they were not there either. He searched every room of the trailer. He was alone. Even with Sandy back, he was alone. He stepped outside into the languid morning air, sweet and redolent with sweeping wisteria trembling in a faint breeze somewhere behind the house. They were not outside either. He walked down the road passing other trailer homes like his, the yards becoming nastier with windows looking out at him in a meaner tension. But, his kids were not to be found. He went back home and at 8:00 a.m. he called the school to see if his children were in class. They were not. It was then that Steven Moore called the police. And this time, the police immediately contacted Detective Thompson, circumventing the usual inquiries and routines.

"Linda, get me some more coffee," he yelled at her as she walked in the door with a fresh carafe of strong coffee. Starbucks. That was his favorite. 'She was a good secretary,' he thought. 'Kind of plain looking, almost looked dumb really, but she was no dummy,' he thought. "Linda!" He yelled again, never looking up from the report. She had been standing right beside him.

"Yes Mr. Thompson."

"Bring me the messages off the answering machine right now! Pronto!"

"Yes, Mr. Thompson, right away, sir." About ten minutes later she came in with a handful of pink slips, a box of doughnuts and a smile.

"You're an angel, now get the hell out of my office! I've work to do!" He scowled at her impatiently.

"Yes sir." She said, noticing that he smelled of a new cologne today. It was very nice too, she thought. 'It mingled with the sweat from his neck,' she thought, shutting the door behind her.

Jeff pulled the chain on the green glass desk lamp and studied the messages from yesterday and this morning. He stopped at the message about the two missing children from Mangrove Lane. He called the police station and they gave him the address for Steve Moore.

He stormed out of his office with his briefcase, "I'm leaving."

"I know," Linda replied.

At 9:00 a.m. Jeff arrived at Mr. Moore's trailer. The local police department was present, as well as Trooper Blair. They were all standing outside talking, except for Sandy Johnson, she was still passed out sleeping.

The detective walked right up to Mr. Moore and shook his hand, introducing himself. By now, Steve had become extremely worried about his children. They may have had a difficult life, not much money, but he still loved his kids. Even with all their problems and bad behavior, there was hope in him that someday, they would turn out right.

"Here's the report," the officer said.

"Good morning Detective Thompson!" Gloated Trooper Blair.

"Hi Don." He frowned, looking down at the report.

"Did you examine the house and check the yard?" Jeff asked Officer Truit.

"Yes sir."

"Mr. Moore, where and when was the last time you saw your children? Were they together?" Jeff asked him.

"They were together. They went out to the backyard to play yesterday after school. You know, they had a lot of energy, thought it best for them to get rid of it outside."

"What time did they come home from playing outside?"

"Well, I don't know. I suffered a leg injury in the past, and took some medication for the pain I was in and went to bed early yesterday, probably around 5:30 or 6:00 p.m. Thought their mother would be back by then, and make them some dinner. I was in awful pain Detective Thompson. Really."

"And what time did you wake up?" Detective Thompson inquired.

"When my girlfriend got home, at 4:00 this morning." Steve replied. "She's still sleeping now."

"You mean she doesn't know!" Asked Jeff.

"You go wake her up. I ain't doin' it!" He laughed.

"May I go inside your home, sir?" Jeff asked.

"You're welcome to it." Smiled Steve.

Jeff went inside and carefully examined the terrible living conditions of the home. He finally arrived at what appeared to be the parents bedroom. He opened the door all the way. It stunk of human urine, cat pee, alcohol and smoke - it was a rank miasma of neglect, mental illness, and poverty sweltering and hanging in the air like swamp gases. Jeff stood back for a moment gasping for a breath of air, then went back in wondering if she was dead or something. Maybe this was one of those violent domestic fights where the father kills the mother and the children. He approached the woman lying in the dirty pink robe, partially open. He couldn't help but notice what a homely woman she truly was, with her makeup running and smeared, hair a mess. He shook her arm gently. "Ms. Johnson, wake up. I'm Detective Thompson."

Slowly she emerged and surfaced to wakefulness. Jeff noticed the bag of pot on the dresser table. He couldn't believe that Officer Truit had missed it. He'd given up on the trooper a long time ago, amazed that he hadn't been replaced yet. "What are you wakin' me up for 'ya bastard." She growled, rolling over. Squinting, she rolled over and saw the very handsome man standing over her. "I'm sorry mister. What's goin' on?"

Detective Thompson showed her his badge, "I'm Detective Jeff Thompson."

"Is there a problem?" She asked, forgetting about the pot on the table.

"Yes. There seems to be. Your children are missing."

"That ain't no problem," she yelled with a raunchy, sarcastic laugh.

"I'm serious mam', they disappeared last night."

Sandy looked closer at what an incredibly handsome man the detective was. If she had cared, she would have looked at his left hand to check for a ring. She moved in such a way so that her entire robe opened completely in front, exposing her totally naked in front of the man. She looked up at him like a dog waiting for its master to feed him at dinner time. Jeff backed out of the room quickly, offended by this obvious manipulation. "I'll be waiting to speak with you outside, Ms. Johnson. Get dressed now." Jeff went back outside and spoke privately with Officer Truit, advising him to arrest the woman for the bag of pot once she came outside. The Detective had carefully removed the bag from the room and now handed it to the officer. "Do you know anything about this?" He asked Steve.

"About what?" Steve replied.

"About the dope?" Said Jeff.

"No. Never could control that woman."

Sandy came sauntering outside in a pair of incredibly tight faded blue jeans and a loose fitting halter top, so that if she turned or bent over her small breasts would be openly visible. Officer Truit read her her rights, handcuffed her, and walked her over to the backseat of his squad car.

"What the fuck is this shit all about!" And she screamed loud enough for distant neighbors to hear her.

"You are under arrest for possession of cannabis. The officer has the evidence now." Detective Thompson advised her.

"It ain't mine!" She yelled. "It's his, it's Steve's! He brought it into the house yesterday."

Jeff looked at Steve and Steve just shook his head. "I was home all day, the children saw me when they came home from school. Then I went to sleep after taking some pain killers for my injury. Sandy came home drunk about 4 o'clock in the morning. That's the truth, detective."

"Ya fuckin' prick! I'm gonna kick your ass when I get out, ya hear me dickhead!" She screamed at Steve.

"You be quiet Ms. Johnson, or I'll have the officer write you up for resisting arrest, too." The detective warned her.

"You fuckin' faggot, you don't know nothin'!" She screamed at the detective.

"Where'd you meet up with this specimen?" The detective asked Steve.

120

"Been so long, I don't remember. Felt sorry for her was all; and that was a long time ago. Now she's just about ruined my life. Where would I go? The kids are the only happiness I know."

"Officer Truit," Detective Thompson instructed, "I want you to write her up for resisting arrest as well. Hear me."

"Why yes sir!" Sandy was handcuffed from behind, sitting in the back seat of the squad car, and began kicking the door now.

"Alright, take her in to the station now officer, and I want both a breath and blood test done on her immediately. I want you to extract a confession on where she got the dope from, you hear me?" Jeff instructed him. "Cuff her ankles, too. Lock up the back seat area securely."

"Yes. Right away sir." And the officer ran to his car, struggling to cuff the ankles together, all the while the woman spitting on him. He secured the rear area, and drove back to the station, lights flashing, siren going. When he arrived at the station, there were two officers already waiting for him as he had previously radioed-in the information on the offender. The three officers carried the hysterical woman into a jail cell, pretty much just throwing her onto the cement floor much the same as unloading garbage from a can. She was screaming and spitting obscenities every second.

"Shut her up right now Officer Truit, I've got a throbbing headache!" yelled the chief.

"Yes chief." But Sandy did not respond to the instructions of the officer, so she was then carried into a sort of sound-proof holding tank, with one-way windows. An interrogation room that also doubled as a compartment for solitary confinement.

"Mr. Moore, I assure you that we will do everything possible to locate your two missing children." Advised Detective Thompson, sensing in some way that Steve's life depended on it.

"And what's that gonna be?" Whispered the trooper, "another lynching?" He smiled.

Jeff entirely ignored the trooper's comment, returning to his car and driving back to his office.

"Linda, these are all the files on the missing children. Prepare a cross-analysis for me on every single similarity between these cases. I wanna know where the children were last seen, how old they were, if they were alone, what day and time it was, and I want it in my office in one hour." He dropped the files on her desk and walked straight into his office slamming the door behind him. She quickly put away her nail polish, stacked the files in chronological order, and pulled up a blank comparative analysis chart on her computer. She entered the data and set it back on his desk in half an hour with a carafe of fresh, hot brewed coffee and a smile. "Bad day, sir?"

"Yes, very bad."

"Would ya like me to order out for a couple Italian Beef sandwiches with everything on them, and some pop for lunch?" She asked comfortingly, always trying to please him.

"Ya, order it from that Italian restaurant. They're expensive, but they've got great food."

"What would you like with that Jeff?" She asked.

"A murder suspect," he said dryly.

"No, I mean, onion rings, french fries, you know."

"Yes, yes, I know what you meant Linda. I don't care. Just order it and do it now." He scowled at her, twisting his moustache. She left his office shutting the door, finally understanding why there was no woman in his life. 'Of course,' she pondered further, 'love would soften him up quite a bit. Do him some good. This man is rusty and squeaky and ornery. He needs *it* bad.' She thought, smiling to herself. 'What a grouch. He needs to get all that tension out,' she pondered. But Linda never got any man in her life whom she really wanted, she got the leftovers, the users, the drifters and failures, the conmen and mentally infirm. They came to her as if she wore a magnet pulling them in, or as if some horrible curse hexed her life so that she'd never know any real happiness or love. Not ever. Cursed.

Jeff opened his door spying on her, watching her play with her hair, staring out the window; for he knew she was subject to occasional fantasies. About what, he didn't know. But one thing was for sure, he didn't care at all. When he was hungry, he wanted to eat. "What in the hell are you doing out here Linda? I come back from the crime scene and you're polishing your fingernails, now you're staring off in dreamland. What in the hell do I have to do to get some lunch around here? This is going to be one hell of a long day and I've plenty of work to do, and so do you! Snap out of it! I need your help. I want some food - I'm hungry!" He argued.

"I'm sorry sir," she said, almost like a spanked puppy. There was no manner harsh enough, no abrupt treatment that he could inflict upon her that she couldn't somehow justify or explain, or even revel in. If he couldn't give her sexual attention, she'd accept whatever other kind of attention he would give her. She was simply infatuated with him; obsessed with pleasing him. She'd often wondered if he had a secret girlfriend, for he was a very private man. But she dismissed this idea feeling sudden pangs of jealousy - there was no one, she was sure, he was married to his work.

The afternoon that little Andy and Cathie Moore ran down to the river seemed somewhat uneventful and usual. They were disobeying their father's wishes once again, which gave them a tremendous sense of freedom and control, a decided way to say "no" to the dark corners of their own lives, to blow the dark clouds away. They usually never went to the river though, generally preferring to swim at Selma Higgins pond, because, not only could

123

they swim there, but they could eat to their heart's content. There was seldom any food at their trailer, and their mother never cooked much: macaroni and cheese from a box; potatoes from a box; cheap frozen pizzas, whatever was easy and fast and cheap, so that Sandy could afford what was really important to her, smoking pot. But, over at Mrs. Higgin's house even with that funny smell of old skin leavening the air, saturating every room and indeed every object they touched, and the house always being as neat as a pin, there were always overtones of butter and cinnamon in the air hanging in invisible low clouds that they could taste. There were usually big baskets of cinnamon rolls stuffed with pecans; croissants so delicious and tender with thousands of layers of fine buttery dough, many times stuffed with chocolate and strawberries, or oozing at the tips with lemon curd. It was food from heaven like they'd never had before, so much better than what they had ever tasted from the local stores and restaurants; there were thick dimpled pizza breads with creamy cheeses, olive oil and red sauce melting down the sides. And she always had the very best homemade lemonade the kids had ever tasted. Selma had wire baskets with 5 tiers hanging from the ceiling that were always filled with fresh lemons. She had an herb garden out in back, too, with shaggy bushes of mint, and dark green fields of spearmint and peppermint interspersed with poppies. And they loved her iced tea, too, for it was always in keeping with the local custom, spiked with sprigs of mint or peppermint, and slices of lemon, with brown sugar stirred down into all the ice cubes.

One of the coolest things about going over to Mrs. Higgin's house to swim and eat and keep her company, was the gigantic old sweeping willow tree that hung over the large pond. Hanging from the giant willow was a tire swing, attached to an elbow in the tree. The willow, with its myriad branches so wide, was a kind of natural tree fort, so easy to climb and sit out on its sturdy limbs with their legs dangling down over the cool pond and its shirred sunlit waters reflecting the clouds and trees and worlds beyond. The pond was clear, deep and cool, with underground springs bubbling directly into it. It trickled off at ground level into a winding rocky creek channeling off any overflow of water away from the yard. And after a hard rainfall, the creek flowed fast creating sounds of waterfalls cascading all around them, with songbirds hopping along its edges. And the children always yelled if a little trout nipped at their legs while they swam. The pond was a place of discovery for the children, too, for there were turtles which came out to bask on the logs, and bullheads and crayfish and dragonflies all around, every day, and pretty leopard frogs. It was as if Selma woke before dawn sweeping a magic wand over the yard, beckoning whorling sundusts and spiritlight, and teal, pine-laden breezes to fill her large yard with the enchantments of a magic children's land, where no adults, save Selma herself, could enter. Selma's back yard alone had to have been more than ten acres. There were bright lemon fields of glowing buttercups, and hills of violets and shooting stars where the children would run in abandon, collapsing, laughing in the sweetly flowing flowers and butterflies as they lay watching the skies, spotting the moon during the day, telling tales, probably none of them true.

For they had suspected and preferred to believe that Mrs. Higgins was a witch, a good witch, as she always wore fancy black lace and satin dresses, and she bore that smell, too, that other people they knew did not have. A sort of lavender smell, mixed with the smell of old books. The children could never figure it out. It was very faint, yet quite real. And it was a smell of old skin, too.

She had always enjoyed the sounds of laughter in her yard as the children played. She took comfort and solace in it all, transported from her loneliness which she struggled with every day in living alone, and from the shadows cast by the memories of her departed husband. And she still sometimes talked to him, too, at night, bidding him goodnight as she turned down her lamp.

But now that Mrs. Higgins was dead, Andy and Cathie had no place else to go except the river. Many children had just recently, prior to her death, began going to the river to play because of the unkind rumors that flourished about Mrs. Higgins being strange, and perhaps even dangerous. The rumors started just before the children of the neighborhood began to disappear. Someone was jealous of her, or hated her. Perhaps it was some mother who could not give to her own child the love and magic that Mrs. Higgins served up on a daily basis. Someone got tired of hearing about all of the wonderful tales and adventures of their visits to her fairy-like gardens and forests, and the mysterious shimmering pond. And all the children bragged about what a wonderful cook old Mrs. Higgins was, sometimes even refusing to eat at home. Perhaps that was too much competition for one of the neighborhood mothers who slacked in many areas herself: in affection, and in passion. So, all in all, Selma had been rejected and boycotted by the children because of the gossip that had been struck like a match stick burning from house to house by their parents, with each rumor getting all the more twisted as they passed from each person to the next. That is, all except for little Andy and Cathie, who were perhaps compelled to continue in her company by the mere want of something to eat. They had grown up hard, too, and were a bit street-wise for their ages, so they knew in their bones and in their gut that Mrs. Higgins was no witch, nor was she a bad person. They knew it. And indeed, they were right. But ironically, they were not her favorite children to have come and visit, but as no one else would stop by anymore, and she had begun to throw away pizza breads and cinnamon rolls and the like, she gratefully accepted whatever company she could have. It wasn't until the day Meredith and Marilyn came by visiting, snooping around, asking questions, that she had any clue as to why the children stopped coming by. And then the phone calls...

So as Cathie and Andy ran down to the river to play, pulling each other back by the scruff of the shirt so that the other one would arrive first, they saw not what trouble awaited them. They swam in the river, which to them, compared with Mrs. Higgin's fresh flowing pond, seemed muddy and dirty. They could not see the bottom of the river when they stood in it. But, it didn't matter anymore, it was still a place to play. They splashed as he threw her up in the air, and pushed her underwater, why, they made so much noise they could have woke the dead. They laughed and screamed and splashed one another with violent release.

Tired, they both laid down on the riverbank which was half sandy and half muddy, in the dappling late afternoon lights. Their stomachs growled with hunger, but they accepted it now that Mrs. Higgins was gone, and fell into a restful deep sleep. So when the python slid in a straight silent movement coming up right out of the water, flicking its tongue, tasting the children, they were wholly unaware. They were sound asleep. With no one at home to discipline and watch them, they frequently stayed up late watching tv in their room, even on a school night. The python was an adult, and at 32 feet long, it was wider than a telephone pole. It was not a shy snake either. It was a reticulated python, the same one that had escaped only five years before. The python slid between the children, and began to coil its tail around the boy's hips.

"Cut it out Cathie!" He sat up screaming at her. "Ya dumbhead!" Cathie, still dazed from a deep dreaming sleep, slowly woke. She was used to him screaming at her about something. The boy, utterly awake now, stared in horror at the reticulated python which had entirely looped his body up to his chin, with its head now face to face with his own. The head of the snake was much, much wider than his own, making the snake look surreal, like a dragon. It actually looked into his eyes; its tongue was smooth, wet and hard, flipping against his face. Andy said nothing, he was in shock. Frozen stiff. Not dead, but in shock, for the snake had not yet constricted him, it had merely fitted itself tightly around him in a secure lock. It reminded Andy of the time he woke up while he was sleeping, but couldn't move. But this was much, much more frightening. Maybe he was dreaming, he wondered, tears running down his face. His lips were blue now, so the snake must have exerted some pressure around him. Yet still, they were face to face, eye to eye, in a hypnotic trance, Andy afraid to move. Next to him, his sister rolled over away from him and was asleep again, her face in the dirt. And all at once, it happened. The python, thinking its prey was dead because it had ceased all movement, opened and flexed its jaws as wide as they could get, even stretching some, to accommodate the girth of the boys head.
'It was like looking inside of the open jaws of a shark,' he thought. And in one single aggressive lunge forward the snake bit into the

boys face with its deep, sharp fangs, piercing the top of his head and his neck. At this point, the boy began shrieking so loud that birds scattered from nearby shrubs and trees.

Cathie sat up to see her brother being slid down the throat of the python, his arms pushing against the sides of the snake's head as the fangs bore down on him pushing him deeper inside. And Andy was small for a ten year old, thin from not having been well fed in life, for the most part. Cathie screamed and screamed. She could still hear her brother screaming, and it sounded as if his head was stuck inside a bucket. She grabbed what remained of him, his calves, trying to pull him back out. But there was no effort that this little girl could exert that even remotely affected the python.

The snake was as wide as two telephone poles, and her little brother simply disappeared while yet still shouting, down into the belly of the snake like a hot dog. Alas, his shoe fell off and he was gone. She could see the boys writhing movements inside the wet slimy digestive membranes of the python's stomach; then all of a sudden, he stopped. She could not hear him screaming from inside of the snake, nor were there any more movements of the webbed impressions of his hands pressing out from within, against the scales of the snake. And the snake didn't even look as if it had swallowed anything, for nothing bulged from its sides, there was only a little shoe that had dropped onto the ground near its head that spoke a tale of terror.

The snake now bore its hypnotic stare directly down into Cathie's eyes. She trembled, looking back at the snake, right into its eyes. It slid with elegant stealth right up to her, rising up off the ground to meet with her face to face, almost as if curious who this very brave little girl was who tried to save her brother. It lifted it's body up off the ground with seemingly extra miles of coils and body and tail all wound over the ground in a gigantic spread of snake. It's body was wider than her brothers, for they used to tackle each other both in play, and in fighting. Cathie felt as if she had just shrunk, it was the same feeling one gets after dismounting a horse from long hours of riding. That small feeling. The dragon dwarfed her, and it didn't need any arms to hold her still, she was standing-struck mesmerized as if by lightning. The python was in no hurry to eat this time. As it stared into her eyes, and she stared back into its eyes, stiff as a board in shock, and still thinking that she could hear her brother screaming and crying deep inside the coils of the pythons stomach, it began to move without her notice, to coil and loop upwards from her feet, stealthily approaching and winding around her hips, whereupon she suddenly looked down at her own waist and screamed. She had never screamed like that before. It was a sound that made the forests silent, an eerie deafening soundlessness, as if every living thing that flew and crawled and walked, was now watching this horrific spectacle and knew what was happening. Birds ruffed their feathers, not whistling, and looked on. Looking away from the snake now, breaking the sort of nightmare spell she was under, she tried to push the coils off of her, trying to push them down. It was a body lock that she had never experienced before, but she never thought for a moment that the snake would really kill her. She really wasn't even sure what death was. She was still thinking, therefore, she must be alive. Screaming and screaming and screaming. But, she was now way back in the woods where their father had forbidden them to go, practically a mile away from their trailer, and no one could hear her screaming except the animals of the woods and the river. This grisly scene of the girl standing with a 32 foot reticulated python coiled up her waist, and the snake having rose up to the same height as the girls face, head to head, her face round like a small reddish apple about to be plucked from the branch of its neck and crunched into, afforded the snake the time to further slide its previous appetizer deeper down into its belly. The snake began to constrict her, and her face grew redder. Her lips turned blue as she fainted. The snake, assuming this action to be the signal that she had been quickly extinguished, flexed open its jaws once again in a monstrous yawn, clicking its jaws open even wider now, and thrust forward biting into her head. The blood exploded from her crushed skull instantly foaming down her body, as if someone had just tipped a full bucket of red paint over her. Her feet jiggled and shook in terrific spasms, and she hit the sides of the python's head with her fists. She was choking now on her own blood and could no longer scream, but instead, struggled to breath. She coughed blood and began puking strange things she had never noticed before when she had been sick. Whitish fluids. The snake who had been in good temper previously, now became excited and angered at this girl. It chomped down on her head again with a heaving gulp that sucked her deeper inside the gullet, while she emitted a sort of howling sound, pulling in her beating arms. And like a straw the python sucked her up into the cavern of its belly, her body sliding upwards through the loosened coils of the snake and up to the cave of its enormous fangs, swallowing her whole, shoes and all. Mangled within, Cathie was still alive. Had she continued to squirm while on the outside of the snake, it would have constricted her until her heart ceased to beat. But since she fainted, like her brother, she observed a fate similar as he. It was dark inside, and burning juices surrounded her. Her arms were flushed down alongside her body, but she was able now to pull up an arm inside the snake and reach forward, touching her brothers bare foot. His foot twitched and jerked. She tried to call his name, but using her vocal chords only compressed her ability to speak into choking and sucking in the vile, smelly juices of the snake's stomach. She choked, feeling like she had just drown, washed ashore with waves pulling and pounding all around her in a surreal moving tunnel. Motions of waves that burned her skin like acid. She touched her brother's foot, and he gave a kick. As he did this, his skin slid off like melted candle wax. Their bodies, indeed, seemed like candles burning down in a stomach of acids dripping from solid to liquid, yet still, very much alive. "Cathie," Andy managed to gurgle. He was delirious, which was good, for it offered some insulation from the reality of the situation. "Get dad!" He whispered. And she cried now, choking on the deep piercing wounds the fangs had driven into her like knives. She continued to hold onto his dissolving foot like a vital link to reality. For in letting go, darkness and madness awaited her as surely did the ululating ribs of the snake.

The python was content and lying somewhat still along the lazy sunlit riverbank. Not completely still, though, for strange twitching and kneeing movements stretched outwards at its sides. The snake slid into the river, its head above water, and traveled downstream to its den. The sun reddened, too, finally sinking below the treeline, as the air filled with the clangorous echo of nightsounds.

And this is the story of what had happened on the afternoon that Andy and Cathie went down to the river to play. There was no telling now, after all these years, just how many adult reticulated pythons had made this very river their home. They grow rapidly, and breed successfully. But the thing was, they kept to this river, for it was wide and long and branched out in many different tributaries affording all kinds of area for the pythons to live in. Perhaps when the number of pythons outgrew the size of the branching rivers, they would explore new territory. Perhaps, too, that would be sooner than later.

The phone rang, "Hello," answered Marilyn.

"Marilyn, this is Meredith." She informed her, still convinced that it was her who had made the recent prank phone calls. She got a sudden chill wondering for a brief moment if Marilyn was actually innocent, and it had actually been the ghost of old Selma herself haunting her, calling her from the grave. Meredith had always believed in ghosts, and had experienced some unusual events as a little girl, but had never really talked to anyone about them before.

"Well hello Meredith, I haven't heard from you in a little while. How is everything?" She said.

"You sound out of breath, you staying out of trouble?" Meredith accused her.

"What? That's a funny thing to say? I just got back from a long walk in the woods. It was absolutely beautiful out. You'll have to come over and join me sometime. I'm a bit out of shape I guess, I'm pooped." Marilyn told her, hoping she'd never come over.

"Did you hear the news yet Marilyn?" Meredith questioned her.

"What news?"

"That lowlife couple lost their two kids," Meredith smiled.

"Who?"

"You know, Steve Moore and that Sandy Johnson woman. Those two. They lost their bastard children."

'Have a heart,' Marilyn thought to herself before answering. She collected herself; her hatred and fear of Meredith welling up within her rapidly, coming to her voice. "Oh my gosh, Meredith, you know what that means don't you!" Marilyn exclaimed.

"No. Just that those two loser kids are gone now too." Meredith spoke plainly.

"No dear. That Mr. Schwartz and Selma Higgins were both totally innocent the whole time. That's what that means. It also means that the killer is still loose. Still out there." Shivered Marilyn. "And I went out alone on that walk today!"

"Seems he prefers children dear, I'm sure you've nothing to worry about." Meredith stated coldly. "Well, I've got to start dinner now. I found some wonderful produce at the store today," she said, smiling to herself, almost laughing now at Marilyn.

"Okay Meredith. Thanks for calling me." She said, but didn't mean it.

"We'll be in touch." Meredith warned her, thinking that her phone better damn well never ring again with no one on the other end. She just hated that. Such a rude thing it was to do to another person. Really.

"Hope you enjoy your dinner, what are you making?" Marilyn asked, before hanging up.

"Well, I've some bell peppers, onions, garlic, fresh lovely sunny tomatoes, fresh basil..."

"You found fresh basil at the store?" Marilyn asked her, surprised.

"Why yes I did, today." Meredith answered her. "And I have some fine meats, think I'll make a special spaghetti sauce."

"That sounds nice. I'll talk to you soon Meredith." Marilyn said.

"Yes, yes we will. Goodbye Marilyn." Meredith said, almost with an ominous finality, hanging up the phone.

Marilyn shivered for a moment, hanging up her phone as well. She poured a tall glass of iced tea, and thought about going out to dinner tonight when her husband came home. Have some fun, take her mind off of things. She sat outside and relaxed, feeling spooked somehow from having spoken with Meredith Young. That one single phone call had totally ruined the pleasantly tired, and refreshed languid feeling that she had acquired from the beautiful hike in the woods. Now she felt restless, and perceived a sense of impending danger, she could not relax and could not feel content no matter what she did. She sat outside for a little while, then went to bed, thinking that a brief nap would change her whole outlook. "Damn that woman," she said to herself. And what haunted and scarred her deeply without any possibility of consolation, were her children. She kept having dreams about them where they would walk up to her and hug her, then just fade away to nothing. And that was it, that was the dream. She had resigned herself to the probable fact that her children were dead. She was already attending a counseling group for grieving people at their church. Her husband would not go, feeling that he was strong enough to handle whatever life and the Lord gave him. Mr.

133

Reynolds, in fact, observed the entire tragedy as a sort of test. He had begun to work later hours at the paper though, and came home with a sort of wandering Bob Cratchet emptiness, lost. 'Perhaps,' she thought, 'he hadn't accepted it yet; that for him, it really wasn't happening. Or maybe, he had simply lost all hope and felt that his children were dead.'

It was 5:00 p.m. and Detective Thompson poured over the similarities in the reports Linda had prepared on all the case files of the missing children. She walked into his office and threw his lunch wrappers away, emptied his ashtray, took away the dirty coffee mugs back to the sink in the supply room, and brought in a glass of water and another carafe of fresh brewed Starbucks coffee. "How do you ever get to sleep at night, detective?" She asked. "All that caffeine."

"I can't sleep without coffee. Shouldn't you be leaving now?" He looked up at her, annoyed; not noticing that his desk was now orderly and clean before him.

"Is there anything else you need before I go?" She asked. 'Gosh, he's so handsome,' she thought, 'even when he does act like a snapping turtle.'

"What am I doing tomorrow Linda?" He asked, not looking up.

She returned to his office with the appointment book and recited his appointments.

"Cancel all of them," he told her. "I've got to get to the bottom of this case. I'm not taking any phone calls tomorrow either; and don't let anyone passed that door, ya hear me?"

"Yes sir, I heard you." She said, closing the book and leaving. 'Just once,' she wondered, 'just once, he could be a little nice to me.'

And as if reading her very thoughts, or perhaps noticing her dejected gesture upon leaving, Jeff called out to her: "And Linda!"

She returned to his office, "yes sir."

"Thank you for all your hard work, if you think it goes unnoticed, you're wrong."

"Oh, thank you Mr. Thompson. I enjoy working for you so much....." She blushed, opening into a sort of thank you speech, continuing to elaborate.

He interrupted her, "now get the hell out of my office. I want you in to work an hour earlier tomorrow. Go home now," he said, smiling.

Linda drove home on clouds of excitement and anticipation. Jeff stood up and turned his walleye portrait around, combing his hair and his moustache, and turned the mirror back against the wall. He leaned back in his chair, unkeying the drawer with the bourbon in it, knee up against the desk, and had a small drink. *"The river,"* he said out loud. 'It has something to do with that river near Mangrove Lane. It's got to. The Reynold's children had last been seen leaving for it; Steve Moore's children lived close to it.' Jeff had never liked that river. It looked like the Amazon to him, wild, inaccessible for the most part, it flowed lazily in wide tributaries. Never the kind of place one would want to canoe or swim, really. And hard to get to it, kind of a place out of time, primeval. 'So how will I get there,' he thought, 'and where do I start?'

The following morning Linda arrived at the office early and Jeff was already gone. She rescheduled his appointments for the day, did some filing, cleaned the supply room, then pulled a book from her desk and read. It was one of those romance novels.

Jeff pulled up in Mr. Moore's yard. The car was gone, but he presumed that this was because his girlfriend was already out, or not yet returned from last night, so he walked up to the door and knocked. Sure enough, Steves face surfaced behind the plate glass of the door, looking back at him. Steve opened the door. "Hello detective. Any good news for me?" He asked, frowning.

"Well, I'd like to get to that river somehow. Is there some kind of access from your home to the river?" He asked him, still standing outside. Steve came outside and walked with him over to the entry of the trail. He pointed. That's it detective. That trail leads all the way down to the river. It's about a thirty minute walk down a twisting, hilly path that sometimes gets quite muddy; might have to hop over some fallen trees, too. I never go back there anymore. It's got a lonely feeling back there. Never allowed my kids to go passed a certain point in the trail, either. Don't think you'll find much except a big brown river detective."

"Much the same, I'm going to follow this trail to its end. See what I can see." The detective informed him. "I'll be back when I get back, Mr. Moore," and he disappeared down the curves of the trail. Steve Moore returned back to his chair at the kitchen table, staring at the walls with a deeper sense of detachment, a more fractured sense of apathy. Life had become a dull grey hallway that ended abruptly into a wall. It was 9:00 a.m. and he snapped open his third beer. He sat back down staring at the floor, his cigarette ashes falling to the ground. Nothing mattered anymore, although, nothing mattered much before that either. Sandy hadn't come home yet, but he didn't care. He figured the children had somehow walked into that mysterious Bermuda Triangle of missing persons with all the other children who had disappeared from the neighborhood.

Jeff couldn't believe the rugged terrain, almost discouraging further exploration. Some sections of the trail were pure sand, while other areas were rocky, and, traveling further, the trail became an obstacle course of deep pools of quick-mud. The kind of mud one doesn't want to walk in. It wasn't quick sand, but it would sink you down to your knees before the suction action stopped pulling, or its depth ceased to encase ones legs in a sort of cement-like muck. Jeff liked to fish, but in clear running streams without having to travel a labyrinth of forest to get there. This particular area had a distinct feeling as if no other human being had ever walked there before. Jeff was glad that Mr. Moore had warned his children not to hike out all the way down to the river. What a green tangled hell it was.

Suddenly the trail opened to a wide sunny clearing, like reaching the center of a storm. His heart beat quickened upon noticing a single shoe on the bank. He had brought long plastic bags with him in his pocket, and carefully picking up the shoe, dropped it into a bag. The area stunk. It was a strange smell, not quite like swamp mosses, rich green vegetation, and the decay from fallen trees, but something else. He could liken it only to the smell of an animal. Not a dead or decaying animal, but the odor of a living animal. Strange piles of muck dotted the waterline. He walked over to them. Using a long stick, he poked around the piles, and in the animal dung, found bones. He pulled out another bag from his pocket, and using a wide piece of a clay-colored rock, scooped it inside. Didn't look like animal bones, but it was very hard to tell at this point. The fecal remains would have to be examined at the lab, as well as the bones. Pulling out another bag, he placed the two bags inside the one and carried it back. He did not stand around the banks of the river for long, there was a very uneasy and vulnerable feeling cast along the harsh light of the shore with its almost sharp metallic reflection. Although he wasn't prone to fantasies or imaginings, he almost felt like he was being watched. He wondered if perhaps some wild derelict backwoods men lived out here, living off the land, or whatever. His walk back to Steve Moore's trailer was quickened by a very prominent sense of being ill at ease. A feeling that it was very possible to meet up with something or someone that was dangerous along the trail.

The detective knocked on Mr. Moore's door, jolting Steve from his lethargy as if he had been sleeping while awake. He stepped outside, "what ya got there detective?"

"Some possible evidence found at the riverbank. I'll be in touch with you if it turns out to be anything important." The detective told him, climbing into his car.

"You have a good day sir." Steve admonished him.

"Thank you, you too." Jeff replied.

"I will," Steve said mechanically, lighting up another cigarette and returning to the dead-end hallway of his trailer.

Meredith had always hated that. It was like being pulled in two different directions when the telephone and the doorbell rang at exactly the same time. She ran to the door: it was Marilyn. She told her to come in while she ran over to the phone assuming she wouldn't miss the call since it had only rung two times. Marilyn followed her. "Hello?" Meredith answered, out of breath. "Hello?" Nothing. "Who is this?" She asked. As she stood listening on the phone to silence, she looked over at Marilyn who had now found a comfortable chair to sit in, and realized that it had obviously not been her after all who'd been making the prank phone calls. "Hello, hello?" And she hung up the phone. "Strangest thing, it just started happening: someone will call and be on the other end of the line, but they never speak, they just hang up. Isn't that the most outrageously rude thing you've ever heard of?"

Marilyn said nothing. It reminded her of what Meredith had done to Mrs. Higgins. It would be best to refrain from getting embroiled in any commentary on this one. She didn't want to touch it. "Don't you have Caller ID?" She asked numbly.

"No. And every time I try and trace it, it skips back to the last real incoming phone call I had, as if it never happened. It started to occur after Selma passed away." Meredith confided in her, without any emotion or guilt as to what she had done to poor Mrs. Higgins. Rather, she spoke plainly, matter-of-fact, and emphasized the fact that she was being rudely and unfairly treated by someone. Perhaps even harassed. Maybe it was the killer, she offered. Meredith seldom had any real pangs about the disappearance of her son. He was more her trophy, than her son. She was more angry that he had been taken out of her life, than she was concerned if he was in any pain, or if he was even still alive. Which, she figured, he wasn't.

"What an unusual surprise to see you Marilyn." Meredith told her, feeling somewhat nervous and frayed.

"Well, I just wanted to stop by and say hello. Things have been kind of stressful lately, just wanted to see if you could use some company." Marilyn told her. Meredith walked her through the magnificent kitchen and out to the back screened-in porch with dark blue whicker furniture and thick, plush cushions. The room had beautiful ceramic tiled floors, with abstract patterns resembling the ghostly configurations of the Northern Lights. There was a thick blue and black oriental rug covering the area of the whicker couch, the two sitting chairs, and the center mahogani table with inlaid stained glass diamonds. A chandelier hung low, but it was not the usual sort of chandelier; it was a wrought iron medieval, multiple-tiered candle holder with long, dark blue tapering candles. Marilyn imagined that it must be stunning in the evening, with no other lights on. The room was further decorated with a full wet bar, seeming to also be made from mahogani or teakwood, with tall bamboo chairs. Antique lace curtains of midnight blue swept from ceiling to floor, which were pulled open now, affording a glimpse of the backyard with the in-ground swimming pool and tables.

'Wow,' Marilyn thought. She sat down in the comfortably deep, whicker sofa.

"Can I get you a drink Marilyn?" Meredith asked her. "I have wine, scotch, mineral waters, and a fresh batch of iced-tea."

"Meredith, I've got today and tomorrow off, and I'd sure love a glass of wine."

"What would you like honey?" Meredith asked.

"Do you have a cabernet?"

"Do I have a cabernet? I've got a whole wine cellar honey; you name it, I've got it. I know just what you'd love. I have an excellent collection of wines from the Alexander Valley. Let's open one of those first. I could use a little relaxation from all the crap that's been going on these days. I'll be right back Marilyn. Want some water with that too, honey?" Meredith asked her, genuinely warming up, enjoying the company.

"Please."

Meredith disappeared to the kitchen, and opened the basement door going down into the beautiful cellar with bricked archways and various corner wine tasting bars. She knew straight-away where to go, and returned back to the porch with the bottle and two crystal glasses. She immediately left again, returning with a pitcher of ice water with slices of lemons and limes in it, and two water glasses. "If you want any coffee later, let me know. I can make you an espresso or cappuccino, too, if you want one."

"I'm fine Meredith. This is perfect." Marilyn told her. She leaned back into the couch, as Meredith sat in one of the chairs, opening the wine and pouring.

"I'm so tired and unnerved," Marilyn confided in her, not really wanting to. But somehow, she didn't sense that feeling of danger and suspicion from Meredith anymore. Something had changed. She didn't know what, but their relationship was altered by some unknown circumstance. "Wish there was a spa in town, I could use a long massage," she sighed, taking a sip of wine.

"I have the number of a man who is outstanding. Just give him a call and he'll come out to your house. He does 1 hour full body massages, he can even do a facial. He doesn't talk much, so you can really relax. He uses citrus oils for the messages and they are so invigorating. Baby, if I wasn't married, I'd sure go for that man." Meredith said, instantly regretting it. "I'm kidding, you know how devoted I am to my husband - he's such a fine man."

"Yes, I know," Marilyn lied. "So you mean if I wanted this massage at my outside patio, he'd do it?"

"Absolutely."

"What does he charge and what kind of advanced notice do I need?" Marilyn inquired.

Meredith got up, went to the bar and wrote a name and number down on a piece of paper and handed it to her. "He's $70.00 an hour; and it's $65.00 for a full hour facial. I highly recommend them both."

"Wish we had a swimming pool. That's quite a pool you've got there. Marble, marble and more marble. Doesn't it get slippery?"

"I've got mats I put out when we use it. It's great at night, floating on your back, looking up at the stars. Used to be quite a romantic place, too, for Warren and I. But, he's so busy now at the hospital; I don't really see him that much. When our boy was first missing, he was home for me. But after a couple of days, everything went back to normal as if Nathan hadn't been missing at all. None of it seems real Marilyn. It's like a nightmare. Nathan was such an outstanding student and football player. Such promise for a fine future. We had hoped that he would become a lawyer. And he would have made it, too, if he had been given a regular chance. Nathan loved the pool. He swam in it every day, and Nathan also loved to explore the forests. He loved to take pictures. He was a sort of discoverer, an adventurer. On the walks we took together, Nathan was always turning over logs looking for snakes and other animals. When he was a little boy, he would explore ponds and lakes with his big net, bringing home catfish and turtles, and we'd have him just as quickly return them all back to the ponds and streams where he had found them."

"Nathan was sixteen?" Asked Marilyn, sipping on the wine.

"Was? Nathan *is* sixteen." Meredith corrected her. "Hell, I don't know. He's probably dead, but it's easier to pretend that he's just away on a school camping trip. Warren and I don't talk about it much anymore. We don't talk period, really. We pass each other like ships in the night now. Maybe it's his way of coping with this all. Maybe when he finds solid ground within himself again, he'll come home from hiding behind his work and reach out to me again." Meredith said, sighing, pouring herself another glass. You ready for one."

"No, not yet."

"How's Mark taking this all?" Meredith asked her?

"As well as I am. We talk about it, but it's the same conversations over and over again. We went out to dinner last night, just to get out of the house. Felt good, too."

"So you weren't home last night Marilyn?" Meredith asked her with interest.

"No, why?" Marilyn wondered.

"No reason dear. Things have been getting strange around here for me lately. Last night, for instance, I was reading when the light over my bed just went out. There I was sitting in the dark. I reached up and turned it off, then on again, and it worked just fine. We have excellent wiring in the house, everything is up to code, this house couldn't be more fine tuned and in better condition," Meredith said reassuringly. And this morning, I woke up and the faucet was running in the kitchen. Luckily the drain screen was loose or the sink would have flowed over! I know Warren didn't do it, because he never even came home last night."

"So you had your spaghetti dinner alone then?" Asked Marilyn.

"Yes. I'm so lonely here. It's like living alone, even though I'm married. Sometimes I wonder if the lifestyle is worth it. But, it's nice not to have to work. No offense. And I have hobbies that occupy my time. Swimming, going for rides in my car. I like to read, too, Marilyn. I read a lot. And my friends at the club. There was more to do when Nathan was here, with his polo meets."

"No offense taken Meredith. I love my work. I love being a nurse. I love helping other people, and especially now, it takes my mind off of myself and the children." Marilyn thought how Meredith had been recently criticizing Selma Higgins for her having lived alone, and that because she was all alone, it defined her as a strange, weird or unwanted person. Marilyn truly believed that living alone was unhealthy, but it certainly did not characterize or condemn that person as being unworthy of love, nor that such a person was at all unacceptable to other people. It did not identify an outcast; nor did a lone person represent a troubled person; for Marilyn believed that sometimes very exceptional people were cast away alone on the island of their own house, and many times these people were gravely misunderstood in their community and never given an equal chance to know happiness and love, simply because they were alone. 'They were made that way from having experienced some form of rejection, kept that way through reinforced gossip, and condemned for it by virtue of an original misunderstanding and prejudice generated probably, by jealousy.' Marilyn pondered. 'Poor Mrs. Higgins. She sure loved the children that flocked at her house like birds to a feeder. They were her friends. Without any friends, and with the strange phone calls at night, why that must have been what killed Mrs. Higgins. Something so simple as no one to bake for can be a devastating thing,' she thought. She began to feel uncomfortable accepting Meredith Young's hospitality. Marilyn took another sip of the remarkable wine, set the glass down almost emptied, and bid her goodbye.

143

"What's the hurry dear?" Meredith pressed.

"Oh, I've got some house cleaning I need to do." She said standing up.

Meredith walked with her to the door, "you have a couple days off from work now. You should relax." Meredith pleaded with her, wishing she would stay. "We could swim later, I don't believe that Warren will be home tonight. I could use the company Marilyn."

"No, thank you anyways. I need to get home. Thank you for the wine Meredith. Have a good day," she told her stepping out to her car, not looking back to wave.

The forensic reports came in from the lab on the fecal specimen and the bones, and Detective Jeff Thompson's heart beat hard when he heard the news. "Detective, what we have here is unbelievable. It's snake shit, Jeff."

"What?" He replied.

"It's human bones encased in snake waste." The technician told him. "Somebody got eaten by a snake. And it wasn't a garden snake either detective! I already forwarded this information on over to the zoological department and they informed me that it would have to be a giant of a snake, to eat a person. An anaconda or a python, probably. The bones were fragments of a crushed skull. Jeff? Are you still there?" Asked Mr. Sampson.

"Yes, Bob, I'm here. I just can't believe it, is all. I'm stunned. Fax me your reports and I'll contact the sheriff's office."

"It's on the way." The technician informed him.

"Chief Daniels please." Jeff said.

"I'm sorry, he's out of the office." Replied the officer. "Can I help you?"

"Truit, this is detective Jeff Thompson. I need to speak with the chief, now where is he?"

"He's over at the diner, sir."

"Right. Thanks." And Jeff hung up and went over to the fax machine that was inching out reports and photos. He looked at his watch, it was 3:30. He slipped the faxes into a folder, placed them in his briefcase and headed for the door."

"I'm leaving." He told Linda.

"I know." She replied.

Jeff walked into the café and slid into the booth with Chief Daniels. A waitress came over immediately, even though the café was packed, handing him a menu. "Just coffee, dear," he said.

"Okay detective," she said, suddenly perking up like a bird.

"Chief, I think I know what happened to all the missing children." Jeff told him. The chief looked up at him over his glasses from his plate.

"I'm all ears, Detective Thompson. Go on..."

And Jeff told him the story about his walk to the river and what he had found, and the lab results. He clicked open his briefcase and pulled out the reports and photos.

The chief looked over the materials, looked up at Detective Thompson, then glanced solemnly out the window. "Oh my Great God in heaven."

The detective had also pulled out the articles he had printed on the missing pythons, and the chief was now reading those as well.

"Like a perfectly fitted jigsaw puzzle. These are some excellent cross-analysis reports, Jeff. It all points to the river. Remember Jeff when those rumors came out on Mrs. Higgins being some kind of occult weirdo or witch? Well, my son used to go swimming and playing over at her house. Me and my wife saw no harm in it, until those rumors came out. It was after that, when the local children had to find a new place to swim that they began disappearing; and it seems word had passed among the kids that the river was the hot place to go. That's what Johnny told me. He said it was great because there were no adults around, lots of trees to climb and they could all yell and scream to their hearts content because no one was around to tell them otherwise, or tell them to be quiet. My God Jeff. Do you know what this means?"
The chief handed the documents back to Jeff and slid out of the booth, "common' let's go!" And they left with Jeff following the chief to the station. The chief stormed into the office, "Truit, get that Trooper Blair character out here on the double! Officer Merrick, get the Special Divisions Search Party organized. I'll only need four members tonight. Have them meet me at the end of Blackforest Road in one hour. And do it now. Please! Ann, I want you to make copies of Detective Thompson's reports and documents and put them in the current Mangrove Lane file on missing persons. Pronto girl. Jeff, this will take just a minute. When she's done, I want you to follow me out to the river."

"Chief, are you sure that Blackforest Road is the best route to take? Mr. Moores backyard trail led directly to the area where the snakes are feeding."

"If that article is right, there should be plenty out there after five years." He opened up a locker containing rubber boots that extended up higher than the knees. He threw a pair at Jeff. "Here, put these on," he said, sliding into a pair himself. Ann handed the detective back his documents. "Ann, when Special

Division calls in, tell them where to meet us and to bring appropriate river gear with and canoes."

"Yes chief." She said.

"Thompson. Let's go. I've got to hand it to you, you always solve these types of impossible crimes. Good work Jeff." Jeff climbed into one of the station's rugged Suburban Blazers, the chief following behind in an open air trail police jeep. Just as the two men were backing out, State Trooper Blair pulled up.

"What's all the fuss, boys?" He said, smiling with that mean-spirited toothless grin. "I'm busy today searching for the killer, this better be good."

"Trooper, you get your ass back in your vehicle and just follow us. You're wasting my time." The Trooper snarled back at him with great displeasure, backing up and following them, a glint of murder in his eyes.

Blackforest Road was a narrow gravel road lined by enormous living monuments of cypress trees on both sides, closely encroaching the road without any gaps between. In fact, the great branches of the trees actually entwined together at the tops and across the road, creating a sort of dark green roof of hanging mosses, vines and airplants, illuminated at night by apparitions of fireflies, wandering mists and swamp gases. It was a strange and bewitching road to walk down alone at night. It was straight, and perhaps three miles long, terminating abruptly at the river's edge, with no place to turn around; being a dead-end road.

At six o'clock everyone was parked in a line at the end of Blackforest Road: the chief, the detective, Special Divisions Searches', and Trooper Blair, who was by nature a very petty man, and who continued to eye the chief for the infraction of manner in which he had been treated back at the station.

"Just what in the name of Sam Hell are we doin' way out here in the middle of no where?" Boasted Blair, assuming that the meeting was a pointless waste of time, and trying to make the chief look like a fool.

The members all gathered around the chief, awaiting instruction.

"I brought you all out here today, because Detective Thompson has provided me with sufficient evidence to support the theory that there are some rather gigantic snakes on the loose, snakes that were once pets that escaped approximately five years ago and are now probably living and reproducing in this very river. It is our opinion that these snakes are responsible for the disappearances of the missing children from Mangrove Lane. Mangrove Lane runs parallel with the river, and at some points is only a half mile through the woods. This will be our first recorded point of investigation."

Trooper Blair interrupted, "so it's a pet snake eating people?" He laughed in a menacing gesture of feigned disbelief.

"Trooper Blair, did I ask you to open up your yap again?" Scowled the chief.

"No sir." Blair replied.

"Then shut the fuck up!" Screamed the chief. For he believed that this was the best and only manner in which to handle Trooper Blair, as Blair was a sort of Pit Bull of a man, needing to fight and confront in order to feel balanced. He required strong discipline and structuring. But now Blair was raging and storming within like a wild sea, wanting to capsize this chief who had humiliated him in front of the team of people. Blair stared unblinking at the chief, silent.

"Now, can we get back to business?" The chief admonished the team.

"Ya, but there's one thing chief." Said the detective.

"And what's that Thompson?" Asked the chief, puzzled, looking tired.

"You probably just scared all the snakes away!" Jeff said, everyone except Blair laughing. He had created a sense of unity in the team with his humor, extinguishing the flame of hate which had struck fire between the chief and Trooper Blair. It was like a pilot light of hatred dimly trembling in a thin blue flame, ever-present, fused between them. And sometimes it flared up wild like incendiary spots on the sun.

"Okay. I want two members of the search team to travel south down the river, Parker and Smith, go now and dispatch your canoe. I want everyone to meet back in two hours exactly. Let's synchronize our watches. I've got 6:15. I want the other two search members to travel in a northerly direction up the river. I want observational reports made, I don't want any heros. If you see one of these giants, do not, and I repeat, do not try and bring it in, kill it or otherwise restrain it at that location. We don't have the expertise nor the equipment to do so at this point in time. And furthermore, I don't want any one of you to end up getting yourself eaten for dinner tonight. These pythons, they are called Reticulated Pythons, grow to an adult length of 32 feet. Ya hear me everybody!"

"What'd ya want me to do? Just stand here all night?" Smiled Blair, intensely annoyed, fully steeped in a menacing posture. He had instantly alternated his many faces from one of compromise and cooperation from only a moment ago for purposes of conforming, to his former stance of animosity and spite.

"I'm gonna get to that State Trooper Don Blair, if ya'd just give me the time of day to do it!" The chief answered him, noticing Blair's darkening hostility. A formidable attitude struck the countenance of his face, an impulsive, indulging arrogance that made him look, for the moment, like he was capable of doing anything.   But the chief didn't flinch.

"Why don't ya go wash the chief's car!" Laughed the detective, holding his stomach.

The chief busted out laughing, too. Everyone could sense that Blair was getting hotter and hotter by the second. Trooper Blair was at his boiling point; a sort of chancy, breakneck, impulsively explosive rage that was contained by either the greatest reserve of composure they'd yet seen in him, or the worst thinly stretched and worn restraint possible, pushing a new limit. He looked like his head was about to explode: his cherry face, burning beady eyes, with a condensation of sweat now accumulating over his angry brow. Something invisible now inhabited the air around them. It was a decided feeling of imminent danger which they all immediately dismissed, simply because Blair was always fuming off about one thing or another. Everything pissed him off.

"You kill me," laughed the chief, looking at Jeff. The chief sighed, still laughing with that kind of uncontrollable hilarious laughter that is forbidden like when one is in a library. The chief looked at Blair. "Blair," and he continued to laugh, wiping a tear from his eyes, "I would like you to walk the south shore and search for evidence. And Thompson," he said as he looked up at him again now, sighing, trying too hard to stop laughing, and upon noticing the comical grin on Jeff's face still mocking Blair, a hilarious smirk made without even turning his head so as to avoid Blair's notice, the chief suddenly lost control busting out in a generous howl of laughter that he just let go of, dropping his clipboard.

"It's somethin' they put in the soup over at Nellie's Café," Jeff winked at Blair. "He'll be alright."

The chief composed himself, sensing a deepening danger and gloom issuing from the unstable Trooper Blair. "Jeff you just get your ass down the river, go north, and be back by eight!"

Blair took off stomping along the river in a southerly direction.

The detective and chief looked at each other. "What an arrogant asshole?" Jeff said.

"I know, he's always been like that. He actually seems to soften and get nicer whenever somebody gets killed around here, like a load was just taken off his shoulders. That guy scares me, Jeff. You better be careful now joking around with him. He's not right. I'll make a couple calls on him soon and take a look into his background, see if all his parts were sewn in together right." The chief told him.

"Maybe Egor dropped the good jar, and they ended up putting in the wrong brain?" Laughed Jeff.

"I'm serious, adopt a new attitude on this guy. He's a loaded cannon swingin' 'round. Maybe his mommie made him wear dresses when he was a little boy or somethin.' I don't know." The chief pondered solemnly. "But somethin' sure ain't right about him. Never could pin-point it. He almost scares me. He's always got to bust a nut over some trivial issue; always creating problems and conflicts between people. The other troopers can't stand him. They always make him ride alone."

"Maybe he's wearin' dresses when he's not in uniform," Jeff added. "He lives alone, ya know. Never's had any girlfriend that I've heard about."

With this the chief busted out laughing again. "Man that's an image I can see. I can actually see him at night doin' somethin' like that, ya know, dancin' around the house at night in women's dresses."

Blair had stopped only several yards down the south bank of the river, stepping into the woods, hidden by forest. He stood listening to the two men making fun of him.

151

"I wonder how a blundering, angry Frankenstein of a man like that ever got to be a trooper?" Wondered Jeff.

"Don't ya remember? His dad was judge, and a damn good one too, before he passed away 'bout four years ago. He's related to his job."

"How come he ain't got no smarts then?" Pressed Jeff.

"Sometimes it happens that way. And maybe, just maybe, his momma got binked by the postman?" The chief snickered. "Oh well," he yawned, exhausted from laughing so hard, "I'm going to watch our post here. I grabbed a textbook on snakes from the office, I'm going to read it now. You go, Jeff, and be careful. Come back early and let me know what you see, okay?" The chief told him.

Jeff smiled, laughing. "Yes sir, I will." And Jeff headed north along the bank of river with the quieting lights of evening slanting down in streaks and beams of orange and blue. He didn't notice anything unusual, no piles of snake droppings, and moreover, no snakes. But, this did not mean that there were no snakes. He had recently obtained proof that in fact, there were large snakes inhabiting this river. He instinctively felt that traveling south down the bank would have been more conclusive, but he continued with his instructions.

Blair crept through the woods like an animal, coming up closer behind the chief's car. He poured the chloroform onto a handkerchief, and slowly, very slowly, crouching down behind the car, approaching the chief from behind, reaching through the open windows of the car, gagged him in an intense arm lock around his neck. The chief slumped over dropping his book and coffee, releasing it slowly, as if he had just fallen into a deep sleep. 'Frankenstein,' Blair thought. 'I'm no monster. My pets were monsters though. Glad I don't have to feed those bastards anymore.' This giant of a man slumped the chief's body up over his shoulder, grabbing tent stakes and another sack from his car, and carried him to an area along the south bank of the river. He duck-taped his mouth, and tied up both his wrists and ankles, pulling up the knot and tying them together, so that he would be unable to independently kick out his legs, or move his arms outwards either. The chief was immobilized. He lay in a deep, baked, dry ditch along the riverbank that almost resembled a giant coiled space for a resting adult python. Piles of snake waste dotted the edge of the river and progressed even further into the woods. 'Leaving him here tonight, vulnerable, why no one would ever see him again. That is,' he smiled, 'except in bits and pieces in a pile of black muck where he belongs.'

Detective Thompson returned from his search along the north bank and walked over to the chief's car. It looked empty from a distance. He looked around as he walked, feeling spooked. For some reason, the hairs stood up on the back of his neck. As he approached the car, he could see that the chief was lying down in the front of the car, probably taking a little nap. He sighed with relief, moving his shoulders around to loosen the tension he could not understand.

"Chief, I found more piles of snake waste along the bank." He spoke as he walked up to the car. "We'll need to come back tomorrow and take samples again and intensify the search; we'll probably even need to start capturing and relocating or exterminating these snakes...." he said, leaning into the window of the car. He instantly recognized the man lying in the car not to be the chief, as the cloth was shoved over his face popping him in the nose like a baseball. Blair had delivered a sort of punch to the face while rubbing in the chloroform. Blair extended his head and arms out through the window, holding Jeff against the car, the cloth against his face. Jeff struggled for a moment, then became limp, falling to the ground like a stately felled tree.

Blair probably hated Detective Jeff Thompson the most. He had been a very successful detective, he was the best in solving crimes, and had, in fact, an unblemished record. The detective's talent combined with his excellent personal reputation in that he led such a private and clean personal life, made him irreproachable. For there was no censure to be found in a person who is married to his work. For if he doesn't have a family, then he isn't ignoring or hurting anyone. Blair dragged him by his arm down the south bank where the chief lay. He bound up Thompson in the same manner. The chief watched in horror as he saw the drugged detective getting bound up and duck-taped like himself.

Blair kicked the detective in the back, but he was still unconscious. He waved at the chief now: "bye bye. Have a nice evening, *you're both dead meat now!*" He had been sure to place their bodies in a deep, low ditch so that they would both be below ground level when the canoe team paddled passed. And even worse, he had staked them down together into the ground with a tent spike he had taken from his car, so they couldn't even roll out. 'All they could do,' he thought, 'was lay there and wait. Well, they can look at each other, but their filthy mouths are shut now, that's one thing that's for sure. And they can watch each other get eaten, too,' he thought smiling. And that, he liked.

He pondered the situation: 'I know these snakes can swallow a deer, and although children can be easily swallowed whole, these men should also be able to be completely eaten, as well. And hopefully,' he thought further, 'they would be digested quick enough, or else the snake would regurgitate the bodies back out, if they started to rot inside the stomach.' Blair felt troubled for a moment looking at them, thinking that it would be bad if they only rotted. Or would it?

He wondered if this whole thing would work. He had not planned on any of this happening today, it had taken on a life of its own, made even easier by the certain and unusual supplies he had always kept in his car. It was a macabre play with each new moment turning another page of events. The play had been set into motion by the way they talked to him; by the way they had been humiliating him over the years. It was everyone's constant rejection of him with no hope of ever being accepted or having a friend who understood or cared about him, which had become a source of uncomfortable daily agitation to him, leaving him utterly vulnerable to new and old pain, and keeping him unfocused on more important things. And everyone at the station treated him exactly the same way. It started when he was in school, but it never ended in his adult life, as he thought it would have. He knew he was a little different, being oddly sized and all. But it seemed to him that they should have given him an equal chance, and he loathed being called Frankenstein. He couldn't remember always feeling this mean inside. And yet, he still wondered if this whole situation would work, for there was still time to free them and undo the process he had started. But considering what he had already done to them, even if perhaps during a moment of temporary insanity, there was certainly no turning back now. They would torture him for his remaining days if he released them at this point, even asking for their forgiveness. They would destroy his life with a hurricane vengeance, and so too would the whole community, who had over the years only been waiting and holding back for such an opportunity to hear *anything* bad about him so they could draw in close and attack. 'No, I've got to see this thing through. If I order that the search be put off for now, for a month or two, with no other leads turning up, I can then resume pursuing the snake theory later, after things settle down a bit. Then I can be the hero, and people will like me and think I'm a smart guy.' His mind was racing while he walked back to the post. He laughed nervously at the fate of the men and what kind of evening awaited them.

He connected a tow chain between the cars, set the chief's car in neutral, driving Jeff's car backwards down the narrow road which had taken on a solemn darkness that sort of crept all around him like dry ice. He reached the road quicker than he thought he would, adrenaline pumping through him, and he became amused by how easy it was. He thought further on the whole matter, for he had never before harmed a person in his life, this was a new experience for him unequaled by any other. It was exhilarating. All the anger, humiliation, pain, the guilt, tortured memories and unbearable censure that he had absorbed into the very cells of his being from everyone over the years, now flowed out from him like water busting open a dam, and he found release in this one single terrible act. He had always secretly taken pleasure in the crimes that had taken place during the course of his job. And it was also true that he hated children and didn't care at all that they had been turning up missing. He only searched for them so that he could wear the credit for having solved the crimes, taking Detective Thompson down several notches. And he knew about the snakes, too, for they were his pets only five years ago. He was glad when they escaped, because they were simply getting way too large to take care of anymore. Especially that one pregnant python. And boy, they sure had dispositions like living demons. They were fierce and aggressive and as mean as could be. They acted possessed, demonic, always hissing and lunging at him with their snapping fangs.

Trooper Blair had always hated the way the community had treated him, it was the same way that they had treated Daniel Schwartz, but they had to be civil to him only because of his position and his family. He'd certainly never intended for the children to get hurt, but much the same, it sure didn't bother him not one bit. In fact, the whole situation of the missing children and the escaped pythons had given him the idea of how to get rid of his constant tormentors, even if the detective wasn't his boss, he still had to work with him and look at him. He just thought he'd never really do it.

Sometimes in this world, evil people get very lucky and are given many opportunities and unworthy praise, where the good man fails by virtue of his spiritual test to be so. So when Blair pulled the cars off of Blackforest Road and onto the main road, he looked down the road, and found that less than a quarter mile away was Stricklin's Swamp. It was once a deep lake that had eventually, over many years, begun to fill in with forest growth. Blair counted on the depth of this swamp. He reversed the cars, climbing back into the detective's vehicle, and drove towards the swamp, which fortunately again for him, there existed a sufficient decline in the ground, a hill of sorts, to aid in the momentum needed to dispense with both cars.

He smiled to himself when he thought about how their cars had been chained together, and how the two men were both bound up together sitting on the bank now, Jeff probably just waking up. Positioning the first car, he drove the second car right up behind it and pulled in on the slack of the chain. He placed a large rock on the accelerator of the first vehicle pointed at the deep swamp, and pulled the shift from park to drive. The suburban took off so fast it almost took his arm with it. It spun in the mud as it drove into the swamp pulling the jeep with it. The beauty of this swamp was the extraordinary drop off in which there was a steep rocky cliff immediately at the shoreline. The suburban began to nosedive downwards, but could not because it was chained up to the jeep. And then both cars simply sank down into an oily black morass of bubbles like fated ships at sea. Blair was pleased with himself.

Watching the last paint on the roofs of the cars submerge, he brushed off his uniform and ran back to the post. And he ran and ran. Owls hooted from nearby trees. Sounds rustled in the darkness, as if the forest had been sleeping during the day and was now wide awake, eyes blinking everywhere.

He made it back before the two search parties returned. He looked at his watch, it was 9:45. He sat in his car and lit a cigarette, and after having smoked three in a row in a mindless daze, the two canoes paddled up virtually at the same time in the thick darkness, pulling up to shore. He heard their voices, then watched them loading their vehicles and trailers with equipment and canoes. They walked toward him now.

Blair greeted them almost with an air of hospitality, like he was hosting a party. He explained that they were late and that the chief and detective had already left, having found nothing. They too, admitted that it had been a poor time of the day to start such a search and that it was indeed difficult to see, and suggested that tomorrow morning would obviously be a much better time. In fact, the search members almost seemed pissed off. They accepted the trooper's instructions without question. Perhaps something had scared them, and they didn't like it; canoeing down that python

157

riddled river in the black of night. They could feel and hear the danger all around them, maybe even smell it, but they could never see it. Blair advised them that the chief had called off the river search for now, and that the chief would be in contact with them in the near future. Blair thought for a moment how surprised he was that they had even returned alive.

The two teams thought no more about this, for they had resigned in a mutual air of disappointment, fatigue and anger, and left without further comment. When all the cars pulled out from Blackforest Road onto the main road, they drove in the opposite direction of Stricklin's Swamp to get back to town, so they didn't even have to pass it, even though it was dark and it wouldn't have mattered. Blair, therefore, didn't have to further suffer any ill feelings or doubt about what he had done today, there was no challenge of guilt upon driving passed the sunken cars, and this helped to further wall off the entire event into nonexistence. 'It never happened,' he thought with political flair. He was amazed at the ease in which it had all been accomplished. He walled the two men up alive brick by brick, thought after thought. He thought about them staked into the ditch, bound up uncomfortably tight, unable to speak, smelling of sweat and fear in the blank space of night. He couldn't believe he had actually done it. It was so easy. Now with the detective gone, as well as the chief, who he knew also despised him, he could go further up the ladder. He would not have to travel and drive so much, his ship had come in, he could now be the big-shot in town, the leader. He could dispel the communities' inherent disdain for him by following up and killing the snakes in two months. For surely after two months, they'd both be eaten and all evidence would be gone. He would even have time to return and remove the tent stake and any other incriminating articles prior to calling back the search. All evidence would be gone, or at least, all blame. The only trace of evidence that could ever exist, would inhabit his conscience, and therefore, it was a closed case.

"Marilyn?" Meredith said.

"Yes."

"Did you see the news tonight?" Meredith pressed.

"No." Marilyn answered.

"The chief of police and the detective are both missing now!" Meredith informed her.

"Too many strange things are going on around here," Marilyn replied vacantly. Marilyn had recently sunk into a deep depression about the loss of her children; the untimely death of Mrs. Higgins and how she had been tortured or indirectly murdered by Meredith; and she had also come to certain terms with herself about the manner in which she and others had always treated Mr. Schwartz. She felt absolutely guilty. For even she had hit a deer before. The only difference was that no one threw her in jail for it accusing her of murder, nor had they burned down her house, all in the same day. And these dark events happened so fast, without a chance for him to think clearly, without the benefit of any kind of defense which was his social and constitutional right. She understood her part in his death and truly grieved for this poor man. She wondered about his interests and likes, and what his days had been like; if he had been happy with solitude, or miserable in isolation. She thought that perhaps she should visit his grave, which was not located in a Christian cemetery because he had committed suicide, but was instead set in an old overgrown and neglected graveyard outside of town.

She remembered the day when she and Meredith had stormed up to his house accusing him of multiple murders, and everyone believed them. The wildfires of gossip they had lit together blazed high in town, insidiously entangling him in a public guilt from which he could not free himself. Of course, even though she felt responsible for having indirectly murdered him, it would always be an impossible fact to prove, but *she knew* she had a hand in it, just the same. She helped him fasten his belt to the ceiling. Oddly enough, she had begun to unconsciously wash her hands throughout the day not realizing it, but had she, she probably never would have understood why. She had become immobile with depression, and her gardens became neglected and overwrought with weeds, ultimately dying or disappearing within sticker bushes.

Marilyn had also believed, and perhaps out of desperation, that Meredith had been somehow inexplicably wronged by Mrs. Higgins, and so she was guilty also now, to a certain degree, of aiding Meredith in her campaign of hate and ignorance.

And over the years the people of Mangrove Lane forgot about the terrible incidents that had occurred. They made it through their days as if everything had always been the same. For they didn't like change, they liked the same thing the same way each and every normal day. They accepted and coped with the tragedy that had occurred in their town, and the subsequent extermination of the dangerous pythons. And they had a new detective now, too. His name was Detective Donald Blair. They had given him a nickname, because of his triumphant victory in solving the mystery of the missing persons: "Hero Blair with a Flair." For he had single-handedly solved the ultimate crime in the history of their town. And from that time onward, the sale of pet constricting snakes had become outlawed. No more children went missing like ships into a Great Lakes' November storm. Detective Blair went on to even marry, and had a good life.

Meredith continued to see and hear strange things that would happen around her house that she could not explain. Doors closed mysteriously by themselves. And at night, lights would suddenly shut off. The smell of baking bread loomed in the early twilight hours of the morning, yet her husband could never smell it. Nor did he hear the sound of footsteps walking in the house that she complained of, so she no longer mentioned it. But, as always, she was able to find an explanation, an excuse or reason, a rejection of all that was real before her.

A CREATURE IN THE WOODS

A CREATURE IN THE WOODS

A GREY AND SOMBRE WOOD
I

I had always been afraid of this stretch of road. Even during the day, trees blinked and creeks whispered through the hills. And at night, all was alive. I even memorized the particular locations of certain trees as a child growing up in this big, wooded country, so that should they come together at night, hands entwined, moving 'round great pumpkin fires or creeping up into the open fields to bath in yellow moondust and zenith fire, I would know that they had moved.

Perhaps a witches hut boring into tree and rock, with an old stone chimney piping plumes of smoke, was hidden deep within the shadows of the wood. A stone hut covered with lichen and weeping vines and upon whose roof soft mosses grew to bed the doves. A hut guarded by owls and spider webs, where magic brews were stirred and thunderstorms conjured by the rigid twirl of a finger. A very secret place, surely, whose stories were so highly coveted that if it needed to in an instant, the whole house could disappear and in its place stand only a toppling crop of mushrooms in a grey veil of mist.

These are the woods of my childhood and they have not changed at all. The massive trunk of an oak tree broken at the top by a stroke of lightning, stood barren like a sharp pencil stuck in the ground. Eagles had always favored to perch upon its narrow mount.

I could not remember from any of my travels, an accumulation of more unique trees all gathered together in a single area. A perfect lobster-claw bend in a dead Elm seemed the most comfortable home for an owl.

Bats began to drop and scatter in the air and a solemn, brooding loneliness overwhelmed me. I felt like I had died: yet still continued to walk alone down this strange road apart from the rest of the world which lived up above and beyond my sullen grave. Lichen and mosses hung in dank lime curtains, sheer and fragile, emitting a rich earth smell of decay and wet green growth.

This road tonight, with all its subtle elements of perfumes rank and sweet; and dense, powdery blooms; of the tremulous drumming of grouse upon the ground and the sweet night air rinsing through the heads of the trees like waves crashing in the forest, all these separate and same elements of sky and ground tempered a fire-essence of magic which struck the air around me.

I had a two mile walk back to my house. Behind me, my car had broken down and I had left it pushed off to the side. I would have felt comfortable anywhere else *but here*, for it to have died. I turned around looking back down the narrow road which cut straight through the woods for half a mile, then turned out of sight.

The sun melted red over the hills as crescent bands of purple, then indigo, rose in the sky; then a thrilling, deepening blackness, reaching beyond the outer limits of the sky, shimmered, densely enfolding all that I could see.   The boughs of the trees creaked like the masts of great ships. And suddenly behind me, there grew the steady and increasing pace of footsteps.

I stopped and listened.

Nothing.

I continued onward with renewed zeal to reach the warm yellow beacon lights of my home tucked away safely in all this darkness. I began to notice my own breathing as I walked faster.

It started again. Branches snapped in a creeping path towards the road: the broad, heavy weight of something pushing straight through, and not around, thick bushes, echoing against the woods.

Closer and closer it came. I stopped and turned around: "Who's there?" I offered the dark. One moment it sounded as if it was right behind me on the road, and then the sounds of something squeezing through dense forest suddenly drew in, coming nearer and nearer, as if it could smell or hear me, steadily following my movements. When I stopped walking, it stopped too, and all became quiet. A sickening, unearthly silence rose all around me in a fog, issuing forth as if my life were some fire smouldering in the night giving direction to The Thing which watched and followed me carefully. I became uneasy standing still, waiting to hear some kind of movement or sound. Even if I could determine the location and nature of the sound I doubt that it would have been any comfort to me anyways, but every steady thought I had was in itself a brace against the maddening fear which now filled me.

Waves of horror washed beneath my feet. My legs felt weak from fright. I stood waiting for the thing to pounce upon me, to devour me alive. I imagined some wet, bristling winged demon with grinning bat face and long spindly legs, the clop of hoofed feet quickly hopping behind me. I imagined that some bargain for my soul awaited the table of his chase. No, perhaps it was a skeleton, iridescent blue as if assembled by the alchemy of mere moonlight alone, with clattering bones like empty cups. A skeleton running to surround me in a swirl of surreal, chattering skulls, glowing skeletons dancing around me. Maybe a rotten corpse animated by a soulless, mindless hunger for something warm, *perhaps warm meat,* dragging itself in lazy, decomposed gestures, having wandered up from some underground labyrinth of caves, where nightmares and shadows dwell and frequent, and putrescent mists crawl in glowing foul brooks thinly over the ground; across the walls like moving spectres, and beneath the ceilings of the caves *passing through* stalactites and clusters of hanging bats like subterranean ghosts.

But just as The Thing seemed to approach me within arms reach, did it entirely and suddenly disappear. I stopped and looked completely around me. An owl hooted from the woods, whose melancholy call sunk into the background of a deep and endless silence, a motionless fury of unseen activity looming all around me, brimming in a vast soundlessness, as if I were trapped inside a giant drum about to bang and go wild.

I ran until I could no longer move. I stopped completely out of breath bending forward and holding my knees. I became overwhelmed by the uncanny presence of other worlds whose infinite doors opened all around me like orbs spinning in surreal tangents around my every thought and move.

NOT OF THIS WORLD
II

Suddenly without any advance a wild storm stirred the woods. All around me, trees blew whistling wildly in a macabre and phantastic frenzy; up and down went their arms, sweeping, blowing 'round. Leaves scattered across the ground running towards me, exploding at my feet and surrounding me in a flurry of wet bats. The road behind me actually darkened, deepening in folding capes of sable like some great curtain about to part. An abyss, some boundless, fathomless chasm like the deep of a great ocean stroked and rustled the curtain of folding purple and sable space.

I walked forward as if involuntarily ushered along a taut and precipitous tightrope pulled across this world, to some other. The curtain trembled and stars shook. Should I falter only for a moment in my concentration on my narrow course, I would fall endlessly into a deep pit, a phantasmagoria of infinite geometries and dimensions, boundless and forever reaching. Falling and falling among the blazing fires and brilliant lights of crystal starscapes whose furthermost shores scintillated like billions of crushed diamonds scattered across an infinity of space - falling and falling and falling, not up, not down, traveling in a never ending tangent through a space which existed only if I suddenly departed from the last remaining remnant of this world, the road.

I stood still not knowing whether or not I remained on the visible course of this world. I looked around to see if I was real: Before me, the road continued and I could see off in the distance the yellow lights of my windows guiding me home like a lighthouse in a wild sea. Behind me, the mesmerizing black and purple rippling folds of fluid darkness trembled, waiting. The woods were alive. Wooden fingers clenched and stretched. Lakes, ponds, rivers and creeks became living wells upon whose silver watercaps blinked millions of eyes as each stroke of lightning trembled.

I was filled with the sensation of numbing, sickening vertigo, as if I were precariously walking along some narrow course, an invisible skyscraper ledge: *'don't leave the road,' 'don't leave the road!'* I thought to myself with a chill. 'Look steadfast at the warming lights of home, and don't turn around. Whatever you do, don't turn around.' I said to myself. Reality melted away from me in rivulets and pools seeping underground and out of sight. I began to talk outloud to keep from going mad: "Happy is the man who is home; happy is the man who is home; happy is the man who is home..." I said, over and over again, to steady my sails against the solar gails which assailed me. Suddenly as if delivered from some kind of dream-state the world came into focus, and the road and the world seemed real again. All fear was lifted from me. I laughed, hitting the road with the tip of my shoe just to hear myself in all the dark, as well as to give my fears a bit of a kick, when suddenly, the beast lumbered out before me issuing a loud and horrible shriek, wailing and tossing its head like a giant bear. It's tail swung over the road, eyes burning red in the dark. And in an instant, it sprinted towards me.

Delirious with fright, *I ran off the road* and into the woods to escape the glinting fangs which hung before me. My eyes watered and hands sweat, I grabbed onto tree limbs which quickly withdrew, shaking me off in a whorling fury of shrill piercing winds. I stopped at the entrance of an underground cavern hidden behind a cropping of boulders, I called inside and my voice echoed eerily back to me from a mazework of tunnels. It was a cave I didn't want to enter.

I kept running and The Creature behind me shrieked wildly, drawing in closer and closer behind me, reaching for me with its long fingers. Reaching and reaching. I ran hard. In a horrific blur, the knives of its fangs sank into me and its red mouth tore open my back and I fell to the ground. I looked up at dancing red eyes burning over my face as The Creature swooped me up off the ground in a frenzy of blood and foam. Strips of wriggling muscle and tissue were ripped off like clothing, piling carnage to my side. Levitated by the savage hunger of the beast, the pain numbed to nothing, and I looked upwards *for the last time* at the merciless skies. And upon me sleep fell: a dreamless, soundless peace. Death picked me up in its knowing embrace and we flew away. Beneath me, my chest and head fed The Thing, and my deathbed, a red tangle of wood, faded, as we flew upwards, higher and higher, further away...

HAPPY IS THE MAN WHO IS HOME
III

       I awoke from the sudden jolt of having fallen off a cliff, spilling the coffee from my cup over my lap. 'Wow, what a nightmare,' I thought to myself, stretching off the couch. I looked at my watch. I was late again. Late for the town meeting, and I sure wanted those property taxes lowered. In fact, there were three things that I absolutely hated in life: taxes, gossip, and cold coffee. And I would certainly go out of my way to cure or avoid any one of these human ailments.

I combed my hair, grabbed my keys and hopped into the car. Trailing down the long forest road my car suddenly lost power. I steered it off the road. I sat for many minutes trying to restart my vehicle with no success. Funny, I hadn't had any problems with the car recently? I got out and looked down the road, and then back again towards home. Both points seemed suddenly to stretch out and away from me in the gathering darkness.

I had always been afraid of this stretch of road. Even during the day, trees blinked and creeks whispered through the hills. And at night, all was alive. I even memorized the particular locations of certain trees as a child growing up in this big, wooded country, so that should they come together at night, hands entwined, moving 'round great pumpkin fires or creeping up into the open fields to bath in yellow moondust and zenith fire, I would know that they had moved...

SILENCED SCREAMS STILL SCREAMING

CHAPTER ONE: SMOKE, LEAVES
AND PUMPKINS

Creamy blue smoke rose up among the bare oak trees, streaming in long, wavering beams like lights shooting down through the windows of a cathedral. Dried copper, rust and cranberry leaves blew across the yard in a sudden whirlwind of air. It was Halloween day, Saturday, and the sounds of rakes combing the yard, children's laughter, and the snapping, popping embers from the firepit filled the air. A large shiny black crow flew over them, squawking, and landed in an oak tree gazing down upon the children playing. Melissa came out of the house with a tray of popcorn balls, cotton candy and caramel dipped apples rolled in crushed nuts. She also brought out a bowl of candied wax teeth and giant sweet tarts shaped like skulls.

A crowd of pumpkins with grinning, eerie expressions, two, three and four feet tall, were gathered in a corner of the patio watching the children play. Pumpkins who had cast their magic spell the night before as the children slept, having flown into their rooms in wisps of orange flowing moons with greenbrier faces, now gathered silently, watching as the dreams they had sprinkled in sparkling stardust over their sleeping heads now flowered in bursts of laughter and mystery, the enchantment rising high around them in fast whipping flames from the firepit, and by the spilt ruby clouds of the setting sun.

Samuel and Aurora reached their arms up onto the trays, pulling down treats to eat, and sat around the wild crackling bonfire. *Leaves spiraled above their heads, stirred down in the sky by the hands of invisible witches.* The air whorled softly, magically, with the spiral dusts of autumn spices. The dried and powdered skins of leaves, as well as drying mosses, grasses, and brisk rattling weeds all puffed, waved and fanned their tannic musk to the capturing winds which rode the trees like crashing waves, billowing and blowing the dried herbs of summer dreams among the

172

warming, drowsy and enchanted dappling lights of a final summer day.

"Mom? Can I bring my gypsy cards with to Uncle Joe's house tonight?"

"Why, of course you can. Why don't you two go inside and put on your costumes? It's starting to get dark out and we should go Trick or Treating soon." And with that, the children disappeared into the house, and returning in their place was a ghost and a mummy.

"Did you pack your overnight bags?"

"Yes, mommy, Oooooooooooooohhhhh," teased Aurora, holding her arms up in the air, walking toward her mother. "Boooooooooooooo!!!!! I'm a ghostiepoo...Oooooooooooooh," she wailed, sailing around the patio. A pumpkin blinked, grinning with a worn patina of ancient October lore and legend.

"Aaahhhhhhooooooooooooo, to you too, little ones, get your bags and your pumpkin baskets, mommies' having a little party tonight. It's time to go Trick or Treating, then off to Uncle Joe's for a special Halloween dinner."

"And what's Uncle Joe gonna make us?" Pressed Samuel, hungrily.

"How about big soft, crusty Italian Beef sandwiches with lots of dipping juice; and ravioli; and key lime pie with a fluffy meringue topping. And pumpkin pie, too, sweethearts."

"Sounds like mom brought some food over!" Declared Samuel, laughing. "Uncle Joe doesn't know how to cook, remember that 4th of July barbecue this year mommy? That's why you've been baking the past two days." He laughed.

"Yes my little detective, now you cut that out: your uncle wants you to have the best Halloween slumber party ever! You should be sure to tell him how much you love supper and thank him as well! You will, won't you? And you too, Miss Aurora!"

"Yeah," replied Samuel.

"Oh Yes!" Exclaimed Aurora. "I'm already hungry!"

"And you be good, too! Listen to what your uncle tells you. And I don't want you up too late tonight, either. Listen to your Uncle Joe now. Ask your uncle if you can listen to your Edgar Allan Poe album, and your Tales of Mystery and Suspense, with Vincent Price, album. And look," she said, stuffing a cassette into the boy's dufflebag, "here's a tape of Arch Obler's Lights Out! stories. Be sure to shut the lights off when you play these."

"Oh boy!" Exclaimed Samuel, rubbing his hands together.

And with this, Melissa rounded up the children into the Cutlass Convertible and took them around the block Trick or Treating. She parked the car along the curb before the old Crooker house, rumored to be haunted. Old creaky shutters swung in the wind. Coal black darkness leered at them from a broken window.

"Okay, I'll be waiting right here for you guys," she said, winking at Samuel.

"Common' lets go!" Said Samuel, grabbing his little sister's hand, climbing out of the car.

"No, no, I'm not going up there!" Aurora protested.

He pulled her up to the front step holding her little hand, and knocked on the front door. Little Aurora looked up expectantly at her brother, then back again at the door. His knock echoed throughout the big house and in a moment, the door creaked open very slowly. Long, blue tapered fingers suddenly clasped the edge of the open door, which was suddenly thrown wide open! The eyes of the fiend glared red at them, sunken into the wrinkled pasty bleached flesh of the cadaverous face of the monster. The monster, staring down now at Aurora who stood frozen like a board, shrieked suddenly like a wild cat extending a long red tongue. He touched his face with his long fingernails, turning his head back, laughing in a cackling, maniacal abandon, as Aurora screamed and screamed, and ran back to the car. She dropped her candy basket and flew into the back seat of the car. Samuel popped a quick 'thumbs up' to his uncle, picked up his sisters basket and skipped merrily back to the car, giggling in his tight ribbons.

"Start the car, go!" Aurora cried. And mother squealed away from the curb, tooting the horn, and the monster waved at them as they left.

CHAPTER TWO: THE PARTY

Patting their heads, their pumpkin baskets brimming with multi-colored candies, they opened the screened door and went inside Uncle Joe's kitchen. "Sure smells good in here," said the mummy.

"Ah huh. Oh, what a Halloween we've had!" Beamed the ghost. "Where's Uncle Joe?"

"He'll be back soon. He's running on some errands at the store now. Here, look, there's a good show on TV. Common'. Look, it's *Night of the Living Dead,* and after this, much later tonight, if you're good and you don't drop any toads down your sister's shirt at the dinner table, you can watch *The Haunting, The Time Machine, The Legend of Hell House* or *Salem's Lot.* Lots of good shows to watch tonight. "Look here guys! *The Legend of Sleepy Hollow.* Now that's a great show!"

"They're coming to get you Aurora..." said the mummy, walking stiffly with his arms out toward his sister's neck. And the scene on the television screen mirrored his movements. The mummy extended its hands, placing them around the girl's throat and began tickling her wildly. She screamed and jumped up on the couch. Mother turned off the lights, except for a dim light over the stove, as Uncle Joe walked in with an armful of presents all wrapped in paper witches, graveyards and ghosts.

"Oh boy!" The children exclaimed.

"Okay, I'll be back by noon tomorrow, be good!" She said, leaving with a handful of roasted pumpkin seeds.

Melissa had engineered a most uncommon party. She had invited Keith, who was a psychiatrist and a hypnotist, a trusted and old friend, and Estelle, a gentle lady in her late sixties, who worked at the town library and was a historian of certain merit. She

176

considered both Keith and Estelle to be her best friends: for they were wise, compassionate, and dedicated individuals whose love of life was infectious. And especially Keith, with his outrageous sense of humor.

Glowing, life-sized rubber skeletons hung in the doorway, and cobwebs and orange and black streamers decorated the ceiling. Halloween was indeed a day for adults, too. Dramatic carved jack 0' lanterns with flames for eyes and needles for teeth glared wildly, flickering hard from candles lit within.

They sat at the ornate, long oak table, sipping on a sparkling cranberry champagne punch brewed with lots of peppermint leaves and pieces of lemon swirling in the icy cold, bubbling bowl. They talked quietly, as if the veil between the visible world that we can see, and the unknown, would later part just at the stroke of midnight. Melissa passed around small plates of homemade pumpkin pie for dessert, and it was the first time that she had ever made them fresh, and felt so proud with how beautifully they turned out. The orange lights cast by the fireplace animated the room in a gentle spirit of crackling, burning wood, and a warm, fragrant oak punk punctuated the air, as the billowing, twisting smoke rose up the long chimney and out among fields of stars blossoming beyond. Several vases stuffed with plump, dewy marigolds decorated the dining room, and sweet fresh aromas of crisp autumn days and rich earth bewitched the air.

"It smells like morning sunlight in here, so many flowers together," said Estelle, sampling the pumpkin pie, as Melissa eyed her for a response. "How absolutely delicious, this Melissa, is the very best pumpkin pie I have ever tasted, dear. Truly amazing." She told her.

Relieved, Melissa took a sip of the punch and smiled.

"What an absolutely lovely dinner this was tonight, Melissa. Thank you," Keith said. Your appetizer of oyster's on the half shell with that icy wine, what was that?"

"John Jos Prum." She smiled.

"...yes, and the pheasant consomme you served right afterward was ethereal, what a perfect compliment to fresh oysters," he added. "We couldn't have eaten better if we all went out. And your main course was excellent too, such a huge, juicy, perfectly cooked prime rib, served on a platter surrounded by asparagus and mushrooms, it could have been a portrait Melissa. Such passion! Why, I'm ready to move in!" Keith winked. "Of course, even if you couldn't cook...."

"All right Keith, behave yourself..." Cautioned Estelle. "She *always* spoils us, Keith!" Estelle told him. "Living alone, I seldom cook any special dinners for myself. Meatloaf, sometimes shrimp, but lots of sandwiches, dear. This was a rare treat. I enjoyed the basket you served along with the prime rib of beef, filled with those tender, golden, homemade rolls, they were exceptional, dear, each roll came out so tall and delicate, smelling of yeast and butter. You'll have to share that recipe with me."

"Well, thank you. I'm glad you're both here. We need to do this more often. I've absolutely enjoyed myself, and the evening's not over yet! How 'bout if I put on a pot of coffee?"

"Sounds wonderful," Keith said, comfortable and deeply content, savoring the moment. He watched the warm flickering ruby shadows of the room cast by the fireplace, like rippling facets of gems shivering along the walls and the dark patterned carpets. He thought for a moment how it felt as if an enchantment now covered the room, cast by the tranquility of the sweet fragrant marigolds; and the sounds and smells whirling in the air from the burning, crackling oak fire. Keith's face was flushed with roses from the brisk vitality of the punch; and from the rich spices and creamy taste of the pie, reminiscent of autumn harvest and Thanksgiving. He wrapped himself up in this timeless moment of contentment, a quiet moment of secret rapture, his senses saturated in textures, tastes, and aromas, and in the deep peace of simple and beautiful things. He felt languid, as if resting in a warm sunlight. It was a decidedly masculine reprieval he experienced. He was now unbound from the distractions of convention and the hurry of work. And yet it was a freedom imparted upon him by virtue of an esthetic alchemy of feminine creativity, by the poetry expressed in the foods, and in the quiet atmosphere of the room.

Melissa went into the kitchen and in a moment the quiet steaming sounds from the coffee pot, with its rich aroma, filled the air. She reached up in her china cabinet for her delicate sunflower china cups. They sat around the table remembering old adventures growing up, and especially bringing to tale those mysterious evenings growing up as children together, walking passed the old graveyard coming home from the movie theater late at night, then passed the dark lake and the spillway, and all the other wondrous, magical nights when the world was an open door to all that was possible, where dreams waited just beyond.

Trick or Treaters came to the door in a flurry of pirates, vampires and devils, and Keith could not resist the fun in scaring them. After all, *it was Halloween*. So he put on a large, oversized shirt, stuffing it with hay, pulling the hay out at the wrists, and put on a mask. He fitted a pipe comfortably in his mouth, lighting the rich tobacco. A little tobacco, he thought, to create rapport and conclusion to the wonderful pie and champagne punch. He sat in a chair next to the haystack near the front door, with a large bowl of candy on his lap. Lined up along the sidewalk were burning jack-o-lanterns, eerily beckoning the children to come near.

Melissa placed a green light bulb over the front door, which cast an eerie glow over the slumped monster in the chair and the flickering pumpkins. She put on a steady stream of perfect Halloween music: first was Mike Olfield's *'Tubular Bells,'* then she played Bach's *'Toccata & Fugue in D Minor,'* and Berlioz' *'Symphony Fantastique - March to the Scaffold,'* and Dukas' *'The Sorcerer's Apprentice,'* all this solemn, melancholy music filling the open forested yard, with the drifting leaves and balmy, warm breezes, and black clouds streaking across a full, ivory moon like witches stealing away to deep wood firedances, where kettles simmered

179

over flames with mysterious brews that were sipped in abandon. 'Such a perfect Halloween night,' thought Keith, smoking his pipe. Even the bats were out flapping around quickly, squeaking in the dark. 'How very perfect,' he thought.

The sounds of shuffling feet scurried up the sidewalk towards the house. Melissa and Estelle hid behind the curtains, watching outside. One by one the children walked up to the monster "prop" with the candy bowl, all taking big handfuls, as no one, they thought, was watching. An owl hooted from a gigantic, towering oak tree. Upon the advance of the last child in line, dressed up as the Tin Man from the 'Wizard of Oz,' Keith leapt to his feet and shouted "BOOOOOOOO!!!!!" With arms held up high in the air, Keith chased the Tin Man across the yard. Children scattered and screamed into the shiny black street, and Keith took off his mask, laughing, smoking his pipe.

About an hour later, the Trick or Treaters thinned out, until no more flowing gowns appeared from the road and silence fell upon West Oakwood Drive. The music played low, and the candy had been picked over like seed from a birdfeeder that had withstood an assault from the frenzy and flurry of flapping wings and darting beaks.

Inside, the fire still crackled, and Keith, Estelle and Melissa listened to old radio albums of *'The Shadow,'* *'Lights Out!'* and *'Tales of Mystery and Suspense,'* with Vincent Price, by the dim wavering shadows cast by the fireplace. Macabre shadows began to creep out from unseen places, flushed against the walls - hiding. The arm of the turntable lifted up and carried back to its cradled position.

"Shall we begin now?" Melissa asked them.

"Yes, I'm rested and ready," motioned Keith, relighting his pipe.

"I think it's that perfect witching hour, where the veil between the world of the supernatural and the natural is the thinnest, like a mist. Your house has grown so silent, Melissa. A kind of crypt-like soundlessness. I think it's perfectly spooky enough to start." Added Estelle.

They gathered around the dining room table. Melissa lit candles in the center of the table and then set out the Ouija board. They placed their finger tips just in the air suspended above the dial, and became quiet.

"Go ahead, Estelle." Advised Melissa.

"Oh Frank, if your spirit is here with us now," she spoke, please tell me. I've been so lonely without you. Tell me our hearts still beat as one," and Estelle began softly crying. "I'm so lonely without you, dear Frank. Are you here with us now?" And the candle flames rose high. The dial began scraping towards the yes, pointing clearly at the word.

"Frank, what does the future hold?" Estelle asked him.

And the dial carefully scraped over to the letters spelling the word: BEWARE.

"Frank, can you be more specific?" She insisted. Again, the dial scraped over to the letters and spelled, very clearly, one right after the other, the word: DEATH.

"Who will die?" Asked Estelle.

"Estelle, we shouldn't ask this type of question. We aren't even sure it's your Frank that we're talking to now." Melissa told her.

"You guys are moving the dial on me, I can feel it." Laughed Keith, breaking the chain and taking a sip of the punch, which by now had lost most of its vitality.

"Put your fingers back up," scolded Estelle.

And without hesitation, the dial scraped once again sweeping from letter to letter, and spelled the name: MELISSA.

Melissa broke her hands from the dial. "This is nonsense. I'm so cold. Did someone turn the heat down?" She asked, getting up and reaching for a sweater. "It's freezing in here. There must be an open window."

Like the wet, silent, infinite air within a mausoleum, the air became soundless and still, yet steeping in something unknown, as if someone or something was watching them now. Red embers snapped from the fireplace. The candles flickered and stretched, rising higher and higher, rippling brightly, shearing from side to side. The silence *felt* as though it were about to explode.

Suddenly a rapid banging shook from a room upstairs and quickly stopped. They looked at each other. It sounded as if someone had pounded their fists against a wall.

"Well, if this isn't the most spooky Halloween ever." Added Keith. "Who set that one up, you Estelle?"

"No, there's no props or tricks in the house, Keith. I know you appreciate that we take these matters very seriously. You're just scared yourself, and too afraid to admit it. Why don't you go upstairs and have a look?" She challenged him.

"Why should I? Why waste my time? There's nothing there! How can you take something not founded on scientific principle and act on it?" Keith asked her. "That banging, for example, probably the timbers of the house expanding and contracting with the cold. But no, you guys gotta think that it's a monster upstairs, or that it's your deceased husband giving us a secret message, Estelle. Why can't you *just for once* think that there is a logical explanation for things? I'll tell you why ladies, because it would make life less fun, less exciting for you!" He advised them.

"We made a mistake somewhere." Said Estelle. "You weren't concentrating Keith!" She scolded him. "That's why we received a confused message from the board. Life isn't one bit logical, Keith. I don't think, anyways."

"Then let's try again," said Melissa, not frightened by the ominous omen of the talking board. "In fact," she said, "*let me* ask the next question!"

And they all solemnly placed their fingers back over the board. "How will Melissa die?" Melissa asked the board.

Nothing. The dial remained still.

"How will Melissa die?" She begged.

And again, the dial began to slowly scrape from one letter to the next, spelling out two words, this time: BURIED ALIVE.

"What?" And Melissa broke out laughing. "That's absolutely ridiculous. That will be the last time I ever use this board again." She said, as she instantly withdrew her arms to her sides, sipping her drink. Suddenly there came the murmuring of many voices from outside the window. "Keith, you go see what that is! Oh, what a night this has been!"

Keith got up and went to the door, looking along the side of the house near the windows, but no one was there. He came back in and tossed two more logs in the fireplace, rubbing his hands together. "Sure did get cold fast in here. There's no one out there," he said in an air of comical disgust. "I didn't hear anything except the wind rattling against the door. You two women are playing tricks on me: Trick or Treat! Ha ha you guys, very funny stuff; two little funnywomen, that's what you are: be sure to buz my office when the two of you grow up someday!" He sighed, filling his pipe. "We should try something scientific, like hypnosis. Melissa, you said that tonight you would be interested in getting hypnotized. How 'bout it, might take your mind off this gloomy

Ouija Board, and the ghoulish voices outside the windows that nobody can hear except you! You guys kill me!" he laughed, shaking his head, relighting his pipe.

"And the banging upstairs *obviously* didn't happen either, Keith!" Estelle said sharply. "I heard the voices outside the house, Melissa dear - honey - I sure did," She said, trying to comfort her.
"Now woman, I'm doing my best here. Don't take such offense. I told you what I thought about Ouija Boards. I think you tap into your own worst unconscious fears. The board only mirrors what you already know, but refuse to face, and it reflects that information back to you in a language as obscure as deciphering dreams. Okay? What's a man got to do to get some more coffee around here? Drive down to Columbia himself? 'Common' let's all get in the car and get some coffee... Common, let's go..," Keith said, raising an eyebrow comically looking around. Now Melissa, you're not too afraid to go into your own kitchen, are you? Think the cabinets will start banging open and closed?" He laughed, pleased with his own logic and his ability to distract Melissa.

"No, Keith, I think I can handle it, Mr. 'Know Everything.' "

"Then you'll drop your preoccupation with the message from the board right here and now, 'cause I can see it's eating you up!" He scolded her kindly.

"Yes."   She smiled, pulling her sweater closer around her. Suddenly she turned her head toward the windows again, and there it was again: the steady murmuring of many voices, solemn, almost funeral. 'They can't hear it,' she thought, looking at them both now, feeling suddenly very isolated and oppressed.

She went into the kitchen and made another pot of coffee, bringing out a tray with a carafe of coffee and a bottle of brandy with large snifter glasses, and sat down. The entire time she was in the kitchen she had that unmistakable feeling that she was being watched, that something was following her every movement. That she was not alone. Thinking that they had all unwittingly conjured spirits from beyond the grave, or from beyond the realm of what is good and virtuous and safe in life, she poured neat shots into the snifters, serving the coffee.

"Well. Don't you want to hypnotize me now?" She said. "I want to be taken back into another lifetime."

"Well," Keith said, let me finish this and relax, and yes, we will. You need to unwind a bit so you can relax well enough to be hypnotized. Drink your brandy, girl." He pointed.

The candles continued to flicker hard on the table. Suddenly, as if slipping out from the door of some parallel dimension, an enormous black shadow, blacker than the darkness outside, suddenly stood before them, the reflection crossing angles of the ceiling. They looked at each other in horror.

"Whose here! I demand to know who is here! Who are you?" Keith asked with a seriousness that frightened the women, sensing his fear. Keith stood up and tried to turn on the lights. The power was out. "Must have a short here, Melissa." And instantly, just as he said that, the black shadow disappeared just as quickly as it had first appeared. It was like the immediacy of seeing a comet. But now, the cold grew colder in the room. Melissa finished her brandy and cup of coffee and moved over to a chair beside the fireplace. Silent. Not saying a word to anyone.

"Well, if you two ladies don't have me scared senseless tonight, thought I saw the shadow of a giant man wearing a hood standing over us! Thank God for the brandy dear, I need it tonight! I'll be right there. Your house feels weird now, different somehow. You've got my nerves all unstrung. Think I'll help myself to some more brandy... Here Keith," he said to himself, "why don't you have some more brandy? Don't mind if I do." He answered himself, pouring a big shot. "Put that damn board away Estelle." He said, walking over to Melissa nervously, hitting his shin hard against a chair. "Ouch I think I'm sober again, that really hurt!"

"But it was just starting to respond." She pleaded.

"Put it away." He said, firmly, without option. "Can't you see she is upset?"

"I'm sorry Keith, I just thought that I could talk to Frank some more..."

"Fine, you talk to your dead husband while I hypnotize Melissa back into another lifetime. I don't believe in *any* of this crap! You two are nuts! Melissa, why don't I hypnotize you to help you stop smoking? Why'd ya have to pick such an abstract subject?"

"But you promised me, and it's Halloween night!" Melissa pleaded with him, looking up at him with a longing that was almost romantic, sweetly teasing him. "Oh Pleeeeease Keith, just for me?"

Estelle sat on the nearby sofa, pulling a thick blanket over herself, and watched the fire. She held her coffee cup as if it actually gave her the only warmth she could feel in the room.

Keith finished his brandy in a quick gulp, and held his palm over Melissa's forehead: "now I want you to relax. See the room with your eyes shut. Totally relax. See and relax your head, your neck, light pouring into your shoulders now, down your arms, see and feel your fingers. Down your chest and waist now. See and feel and relax your hips, both legs, and slowly, down to your feet, see your feet. Relax, take a very slow, deep breath. See the room again, but don't open your eyes. The fire is burning, vases of marigolds are placed all over the room, see them now..." And Keith paused a moment, so that she could look around the room, with her eyes shut.

"You are floating upwards, out of your body... You are weightless, like a feather, like a wisp of perfume you're drifting upwards, like the smoke drifting up the chimney, go with the cream glare of the twisting smoke rising up the chimney and out into the open skies above the house. Follow the smoke as if it were your spirit... Glide gently upwards, you can fly, you can float, you are drifting upwards... You are the smoke and are now above the house. It's cooler outside now, isn't it?"

"Cooler." She said in a voice without expression.

"You're glowing in a white light, it is like the smoke which glides upwards towards the stars. Look down now at the roof of your house. See the chimney where you came from. Know that we are down inside that house. You're flying upwards, drifting upwards still in an effortless motion, swimming in a current that is taking you away, far away now..."

Estelle looked up, and returned her gaze back to the fire.

"You are five years old now, what do you see?"

"The Christmas tree, bright lights, my music!" She giggled, holding her fists up to her mouth.

"Yes...and now, Melissa, you are two years old. Where are you?"

"Beach!" She exclaimed happily.

"Are you playing with your mommy at the beach, Melissa?"

"Mommy, over there!" She exclaimed, moving her hands in the air.

"And now Melissa, I'm going to take you back even further now. Back, back Melissa, further back now... You're two months old."

Melissa made silly infantile whimpering sounds, head rolling, looking all around the room. Eyes widening. A prevalent sense of wonderment filling her face.

"...Melissa, listen to me dear. We're going to go backwards now, *before you were born.* Go back, go back Melissa... leave this

187

place, flow back to the other side... go back in time now... ...the door is open for you Melissa, walk through it, go beyond the open door, see the door opening... I want you to go back through many lifetimes, through the pain and discomfort of being born many times, through the fear of the unknown when you've died before, and the ease with which you moved on afterwards... Keep going, further... let go.... doors will open, each door will represent a different lifetime, walk through each door as they appear before you... they will keep appearing before you Melissa, keep moving through them, notice what you see, but don't stop anywhere... just keep going, pass through as if a current were pulling you, like swimming, you are at the turn of the century now, go back, way back, it's now 1789...where are you Melissa? Where are you? I'm calling you Melissa, follow my voice and nothing else... no matter what you see... follow my voice only... Where are you? What do you see?"

"It's *sooooooo coold in here!*" She spoke in a grave and desolate tone.

"Where are you Melissa?" He insisted. Estelle now watching intently. Captivated.

"I don't know....   I'm moving through walls now, ooooooooooooohhhhhhhh."

"Are you in a house, Melissa? Your house, your home?"

"I'm home in this castle. This *is* my house. I can't walk. What's happened to me? I'm floating down the hallway, over carpets, down the staircase, *aaooooooohhhhh......*" she whispered eerily, her voice echoing as if it were rising up from the bottom of a wet, dripping well.

"Who are you Melissa," Keith directed her.

"I'm Rebecca, I'm a young woman. My body has form, but it's not matter. I'm air, etheric. My father..."

"Yes, Melissa, tell me..."

"My father murdered me right here where I'm standing now. He chased me to this staircase with an axe. My sister was away in Austria, she never knew what happened. I fell right here on this staircase, screaming for my life. What had I done to deserve this?" She asked in an eerie, departed voice.

"Keep telling me about this situation, Melissa, ... or I mean, Rebecca...." Urged Keith.

"The axe rose and fell in a horrific blur of steel and scalp. I remembered thinking that somehow it was raining in the house, but it was my blood splattering over me. Up and down went the steel of the blade, and his face, his features so imputed with iniquity and hate, every expression as he swung mocked at my own terror, it was his face that scared me the most, he didn't look like himself anymore, he looked possessed. I couldn't really feel the blade after the first time, just numbness, the horror of it all was so surreal, as if it were happening to someone else, and not to me. A profligacy of depraved enjoyment in what he was doing overtook him, he was very excited. He looked as if he had been conjured up from the depths of the netherworld, demonic hell, with his hideous laughter grating on me while he swung, chopping me to death. It's right here where I'm standing now. This is the place." She whispered. "And all of a sudden it just stopped. Everything became cold and wet and dark. No sounds. No screaming. No more could I see that horrible face. I didn't know where I was, but suddenly the whole scene disappeared as if an angel had taken me away."

"Where are you now, Rebecca?" Keith asked.

"I'm drifting now, flowing, he's over there! *Oooooooooohhhhhh, fathir, why did you kill me? How can you just sit there when my body is over there, beneath the floor! Oooooooooohhhhhh Faatthher... help me father, my spirit cannot rest... pull me up from beneath the floor boards and bury me in a grave...I'll never leave you alone, father, murderer! Can you not feel me now? I'm*

189

moving through you, ooohhhh your heart is soooooo cold, your black soul. Ahhhhh, can you not feel me? I'm much more than a chill....father....."

Keith and Estelle stared at one another, faces frozen. "This has never happened before!" He whispered to her.

"Bring her back, bring her back this instant!" Whispered Estelle.

"Aaaaahhhhhhhh, yes, father..." Rebecca moaned. I'm behind the draperies now, dear murderer. Can't you see me? Over here father! Ooooooohhhhhhh, my whole life was before me...I was in love father. You stole my life from this world, now I am forever bound to wander this house. What happened to Jonathan? Did you kill him too? Did he remarry? Did he think that I ran away from him, that I didn't love him? Did he marry my sister? I'm inside the curtains murderer! Can't you see me?" The ghost asked him, moving toward the man in the chair. The spirit swirled around him, the light in his lantern flickered high and hard. The apparition flowed before the fireplace. "Ooooooh, ffffffffaaaathir, please help me... bury my body at the graveyard. Oooooohhhh, it's sooo cold down here. Rats, faaathhir!" The spirit moved through the wall and disappeared down a hallway, trembling chandeliers as she passed.

"Melissa! I order you to come back! Return to your body now! It is 1994. You are a young woman. I want you to move forward now through many lifetimes, go through the doors until there are no more, do not stop dear Melissa. Open the doors, find your home on West Oakwood Drive. You are thirty two years old. Come back, come back now Melissa. Come home to your children who love you!"

Silence. An unearthly silence loomed all around them in the shadowy room. Her eyes moved rapidly beneath thin lids. Her fingers stretched and closed. Estelle stood up, "why isn't she responding Keith? Keith, I'm frightened. Bring her back right now!"

"I don't know what's happening, something's wrong."

"Ooooooohhhh faaathir, you killed me."

"Melissa, it's Keith, your friend, we grew up together. You are under hypnosis and you can will your mind to return to this very room where you sit. Come back to your home, you're alive dear! *You're not a ghost!* Come back to us! Can't you see the roof of your house yet? Your body is getting heavy now, not light, not floating, you can not fly, you can not float. I command you to return to your body. Look at the living room, the fire still burns! We are waiting for you Melissa!" Keith implored, feeling desperate and powerless, as if something had come over all of them this evening, something that was way beyond their own control.

"Funny, Keith, did you hear that? I thought I heard the sound of pigs chortling in the walls. Must be the brandy. Keith, did you hear it, too?" Estelle asked him.

"No." He said, scarcely listening to her at all. "I mean, yes, I think so. But this night has been one hell of a carnival ride anyways, nothing makes any sense."

Melissa slumped forward, hands loose. Keith carried her off the chair and laid her down on the floor before the fireplace. "Try the lights, see if the power's back yet!"

"No Keith, nothing." Estelle told him, her voice noticeably frightened. She ran to the phone, but the phone was disconnected, or not working somehow, either. "If we ever make it through this night I'm gonna kill you Keith," she said half humorously, half desperately, losing her patience. "What do we do now? What are we going to do!"

"Let her lay here by the warmth of the fire. She's only under hypnosis. She's lost or something. I'll just have to keep admonishing to her."

"Take her to a hospital, honey, I'm scared."

He placed his head against her heart, and felt her wrist. "She's alive Estelle. I bet she'll be sitting up within 5 minutes. She's breathing just fine. Maybe she's playing a trick on us!"

CHAPTER THREE: TO WAKE UP DEAD

The great courtyard of the Hampton House of Northern England lay silent. A steady, gentle rain misted down upon the brickwork. Solemn, grey doves scattered in the air and neglected rose bushes overgrown with weeds struggled against the steep, straight walls, staring blankly at the sky. The towers of the house were invisible among the low clouds, and Mr. Ashbury Hampton left the castle for his rounds of ale at the Dolphin Pub, his car trailing until gone, down the narrow, winding, forest road, from her view in the attic walls.

Rebecca watched his car, and then the misting empty road. Grey rain fell steadily upon the courtyard in musical, mesmerizing showers, looming up into dull clouds of fog that rolled across the meadows and beyond. *"It's soooo green,"* she whispered to herself.

She looked out across the bright, lime-colored, emerald meadows, framed by dense forests that were filled with shadows, one of them hers. The forests watched Rebecca inside the lonely chamber, as she watched the moving forests. Rebecca's darkness loomed within the long windows of the castle, *the forest shadows* lurked among the gnarled, creeping root systems which ripped up and above the ground in macabre, wooden forest steps. Vining staircases of wooden roots twisted up hills and above the valleys in pathways overlooking waterfalls; twisting roots like frozen lightning that stretched out from the trunks of the great trees like fingers clutching earth and sky. She was staring out into the gloom, when suddenly, a box slid against the floor behind her. Rebecca turned and in a moment recognized the person standing before her, to be her sister.

"Rebecca!" Moaned the ghost.

"Anna!" Rebecca answered.

They moved towards each other among the dim shadows of the attic. Upon trying to embrace, an auroral light flashed between their forms, as their bodies passed through each other. Rebecca had walked through her, and stopping, disappointed, turned now to regard her sister again.

"This is hard to get used to," Rebecca confided in her.

"Yes it is!" Laughed Anna. "I want you to know that he murdered me only a year after he took your life. He thought I was going to tell. But what can a person tell, when they know nothing? He said that he had forbidden you to marry Jonathan, and so you ran off. And I believed him. I'm so sorry Rebecca. It was his guilt which compelled him to murder me, it haunted him. It shadowed his days. I really didn't know anything about it at all. I had no clue. I had believed him."

"Can he see us?" Rebecca wondered.

"I don't know. Perhaps he thinks these strange occurrences to be his imagination? Maybe his conscience speaking to him. Images of guilt."

"Evil knows no guilt, sister." Rebecca whispered.

They stood in the light of the massive, long window.

"Ooooooohhhhh, Anna, I'm below the floorboards."

"And I've nourished the weeds, dear sister. He buried me in the rose bed. No roses have ever grown there since." Anna moaned ghoulishly.

And the two sisters sat among the shadows of the attic, around a small, circular, wooden table, abating each others' loneliness, narrating tales from their troubled sleep.

"And where have you been, Rebecca?" Asked Anna. "I've been walking these halls alone for so long."

"I can't really answer that Anna, I remember some other place, it seemed so real, but now, I don't know, it seems more like I dreamed it. I don't know where I was, but something brought me back here and we are reunited."

"Tea? My poor sister." Smiled the ghost.

"Up here? Can we taste it?" Rebecca asked, as if she had forgotten what it felt like to be pure spirit.

"Watch this," Anna said, disappearing beyond a wall and reappearing some time later with a tray holding a teapot and cups. Anna set the pot on the table and poured.

"Ooooh, it's warm. It's good," Rebecca told her. "Oranges," she sighed. "I love oranges."

"Some people can see us, and some can not." Anna informed her.

"Can father?" Asked Rebecca.

"*Oooooooooooohhhhhh Noooooooooooooo,*" the ghost sighed. "*Poooouuurr meeee some more....*" Said Anna.

"Well, do you always have to sound so eerie and morbid?" Asked Rebecca.

"*I am* a ghost, you know." Whispered Anna, laughing, faintly disappearing, then reappearing again in her chair.

"Melissa! Let go, you're getting heavy. Come back to your home, we're waiting for you..." Keith implored her. "You are no longer under hypnosis, you are back in your home now, coming back now, look around Melissa."

Estelle looked up at Keith, and Keith again felt Melissa's wrist for a pulse. Nothing now! The grandfather clock chimed three times from the hallway. He quickly pushed her chest and bending down, blew air into her mouth. "She was just fine a minute ago Estelle, I swear on my own life she was!" Keith held her in his arms for a moment, then picked her up and raced to the hospital where the emergency crew worked vigorously to revive her. An aneurysm had apparently extinguished her life in an instant. But she didn't look dead, Keith and Estelle later agreed. She looked like she was only sleeping, or at the very worst, in a coma.

And in the cold, bleached corridor of the hospital, she lay covered, tag jiggling from her toe. And from the final request set forth in her Will, that no artificial devices be employed to preserve her life, and most unusual, that no embalming fluids be administered pursuant to her corporeal demise, that a speedy funeral was thus set. No one understood this request, but it was indeed honored. There are many eccentric final requests, the morticians laughed.

Her family, together with friends, all stood in the falling rain, black umbrellas dotting the graveyard. Wide black umbrellas blooming beneath the pattering gloom, the grim monolith of headstones, the patulous, exploring fingers of the bare trees and the dancing mist, all this up above the ground, and below, only darkness. Skeletons lay sleeping, their skulls crumbling upon pillows, arms against their sides, and their dust, the powder from their bones, their very essence was sealed within. Church bells tolled across the yard. Long ropes lowered Melissa's coffin down into her deep grave, squeaking along the pulleys. A handful of wet earth was thrown over the lid of the casket. Sobbing burst like rain clouds. And one by one, group by group, the people left. She was all alone now. Thunder rolled and faded, and the world became black.

CHAPTER FOUR: THE HAUNTING OF HAMPTON COURT

"Let's scare him to death!"

"Indeed, dear sister, a fine plan. But still my body would feed the climbing vines and weeds. *To free ourselves*, is our goal." Anna said, sipping on tea. "There *is* a way to make him see us."

"What?" Rebecca asked, their cups moving in thin air.

And that evening, upon Ashbury's return, Anna and Rebecca conjured the patrons of Conscience and Truth upon their father's head. As he sat before the fireplace, they wove their ghostly magic summoning hooded spectres and headless ghouls who moaned and wailed in terrible cries of agony, dragging the memories of their tormented lives in heavy chains behind them in a wake of clanking irons. The phantoms now walked the corridors of the great house with Anna and Rebecca in a surreal parade of clattering skeletons, pallid revenants, macabre shadows, and leering demons tiptoeing and hopping with cloven foot and vulture wings, wings blinking with millions of dark eyes imprisoned by the feathers and folds of its nefarious vest.

Rebecca laughed with a bloody smile, standing just behind him, as she conjured her heart to begin beating from beneath the floor boards before him. She remembered her brutal death, and her sweet, stolen life, whose river was now barren. And she began to hate him again. No more would fear thwart her living soul. The sword had been tempered and drawn, and it was time now to plunge her revenge deep into the heart of this man whose vile deeds had delivered her into this endless nightmare. It was time now to rip out the black heart and feed her vultures. Her murderer was hers now, and she was going to make him know and feel the curse of her wandering spirit, and the sweet loss of her very life, and the love that she had lost forever.

The sound of Rebecca's heart pounding from beneath the floor grew louder and louder, until he set his book aside and stared in horror at the floor. Legions of monsters cast from the depravity of his own shadow flew from him, like thousands of bats scattering from a cave, climbing upon the walls of the castle, trembling the vast hanging tapestries and creaking open all the doors. Spectre's swung their sharp harvest blades, their deep, black hoods swaying. Cobwebs blew and vast organ pipes roared insane, chilling and deafening in a profane and lunatic chorus. The huge French windows blew open and the fire burned wild. And crawling in upon her vines, Anna vied and wound, little tendrils touching walls, growing fast across the floor. Each rosebud grew to bare her face, as she crested 'round in waves of twig, leaf and velvet red, petals configured by eyes long dead. Inch by inch she crawled, creeping towards his feet. All this their father saw, as the subtle veil between worlds which surround us always lifted swiftly like a curtain, an illusion, and he stood staring now, trembling, watching blood dripping down the walls. He held his hands over his ears to stop the maddening funereal organ music which played in horrific chords over and over again. "Dear God help me!" he cried out. "Stop it! Stop it!"

Triumphant with their deeds, their father ran out screaming and turned himself in to the police. He confessed his crimes and was ordered by a court to spend the rest of his days in an asylum set within walls even thicker than at home. He identified the location of his murdered daughters, and their bodies were blessed and buried in sacred graves up on a hill, where sunlight washed over them, cleansing them new again from a lifetime of such tragedy.

"And now to part, dear sister," spoke Anna. "Our spirits finally free from this terrible house."

Rebecca and Anna bid goodbye, drifting apart. Rebecca watched as Anna's form dissipated into the bookcase, disappearing behind it. And Rebecca, floating backwards, too, drifted also through the wall, passing beyond a lovely portrait of herself as a child.

198

CHAPTER FIVE: SILENCED SCREAMS STILL SCREAMING

Melissa moved upwards through layers of memories, rising up and unwinding lifetime after lifetime like a movie reel, finally remembering her children, her home. The Halloween Party? She was having a party! She felt heavier and heavier, until at last Melissa saw the open sky and her rooftop below, but no smoke curled atop the chimney. Over there, her street! There's children playing! But something was wrong.

Like waking suddenly from a deep dream, she abruptly opened her eyes. "What. Where am I? Keith, Estelle, this isn't funny!"

The living room was black, pitch black, against her straining eyes. 'I must have fallen asleep,' she thought. 'Everyone's gone. The house is *soooooo dark*!' Melissa moved her arms up hitting a solid object immediately. She was not sitting anymore, but lying. She swung her arms upwards and her fists struck against cold steel that was close before her. "No! No!" *Her voice died*, trembling, as delirious waves of horror washed over her upon realizing where she really was. Her existence had been like a delicate crystal glass which held full a joyous life, and now shattered, mere shards from a broken window over time, each piece reflecting a different view of things past, she stared wildly out into the darkness. "The talking board, the board that talks, I must make this coffin walk..." She chanted over and over. 'My throat is so dry,' she thought. 'I need a drink. The wine's over on the table.'

Leaves spiraled above, stirred down in the sky by the hands of invisible witches. "Oh dear God," she cried: and open were the gates of Hell, as she began to scream.

THE MYSTERIOUS GUEST

THE MYSTERIOUS GUEST

CHAPTER ONE: HALLOWEEN DAY

A distant drum of thunder rolled in his mind and he awoke. He watched the chalk-white seagulls flipping and turning in tight flocks against a pale turquoise sky. Waves rinsed against a polished agate shoreline and the grey, melancholy cry of seagulls filled the air with its haunting sound.

Nathan McGregor leaned back against the oak tree, closed his eyes in the warm baking sunlight, and breathed in the intoxicating fresh air. The rake slipped out of his hands as he dozed off. Copper, pumpkin, vivid yellow and leaves veined with blood gently spiraled and tumbled down from the trees all around him. Glowering embers, snapping and crackling from the pile of burning leaves, sparked upwards. A cirrus of smoke loomed in the air with its gentle spell of incense, flowing down and across the beach and over the rocky shoreline. Hands of smoke, curving and caressing the still air, touched his face, his hair, the rush of marigolds and sunflowers and was gone again, as tender yellow lights filled the world.

His aunt Maggie, whom he lived with, was inside cooking and decorating for their Halloween party tonight. Nathan looked around the yard appreciatively at the raked piles of leaves, and went inside the house. Black candles flickered hard with menacing intent. Pumpkins, forlorn and sinister, flickered from teethy grins and widening eyes. Black and orange streamers looped and twisted down from the ceiling, with cobwebs in the corners. A life-sized skeleton hung from the front porch, creaking slowly round. Pictures of witches and ghosts, and monsters and demons were taped to the windows and walls, summoning the mysterious worlds just beyond our reach to now join us, to come and pull up a chair and sit at our table tonight, to fill us with wonder, to make us jump with that sudden tap behind our shoulder or that chill at the back of our neck as if some demon stood leering, awakened by our tales.

"Sure smells good in here!   Aunt Maggie."

Nathan walked into the kitchen. "Come in and sit with me a while," she offered, setting small glasses of wine down, its exotic mysteries and notes shining in deep purple-red moons of ruby light, soft pools of violet petals which mirrored their faces with each solitary sip they took.

The tall hickory bakers' rack was filled with large rounds of bread crackling upon its inlaid wire racks. Pumpkin pies cooled, flaky butter croissants oozed at their tips with lemon curd, and on the third tier a braided brioche bread stuffed with apricots, dates and golden raisins, and brushed with an orange liqueur sighed and vented, with invisible rings of cinnamon and butter curling in the air.   At the corner of the kitchen counter near the long window was a sturdy wicker basket stuffed with baguettes of bread: some were stuffed with garlic; some with herbs; and some with nuts, his aunt explained, and some were filled with Italian hams and cheese. And the baguettes that were more narrow and slender were simply jeweled in pieces of salt.

She sat down at the long, wooden table with him and raised her glass to her nephew. A delicious smokey, steamy haze rose in the air, reaching the high, hammered-tin ceiling.

"To our party tonight."

"And to your beautiful cooking, dear Maggie."

And they clinked glasses drinking a careful sip as if wanting to capture the flavors and notes of the wine as long as possible, never wanting to say goodbye.

"What time will everyone be here?"   She asked.

"Probably another hour or two," he gestured, reaching for the bottle.   "And with all this simmering, bubbling and roasting hospitality no less than the greatest ghost stories shall meet our table tonight! What a Halloween party it will be." He smiled, pouring one more afternoon repose into their dreams and glasses. "So what's for dinner?   ...what treasures await our friends from their long journeys?"

Maggie walked over to the wood-fired oven and pulled out a prime-rib roast smeared with herbs and stuffed with garlic cloves, surrounded by a mote of vegetables. She basted it with a very dark, almost black-looking wine, and slid it back into the steady fires within.   On the sideboard was a tray of quails stuffed with chopped plums, the delicate meat soaking up the wet fruit. These she was going to grill over the flames of the top burner, just before serving. Another tray lay beside it covered by an inverted plastic container, of rising dinner rolls. Delicate, stretching, webbing white dough to be brushed later with egg and roasted dark golden. Rolls that would soon emerge from the oven in earthy aromas of yeast and butter, with razor thin crusts and soft, fluffy, snowy-white interiors, to mop up bits of beef juice and pools of grilled plum drippings from the quails.

Maggie walked over to the refrigerator and opened it, almost as if she had forgotten what lay within.   "And we have mussels and clams for the pasta dish; delicious cheeses to go with dessert, these I think I'll pull out now..." she said to herself, "and a Chocolate Truffle Cake as tender as pudding...."

"Can I help with anything?"   Nathan offered.

"Well, I suppose everyone can lend a hand and make themselves at home once they get here.   I have everything mostly done now," she said, wiping her hands upon her apron.

Nathan poured another spell of the wine, passing her glass over as she sat down.

"To the family, bless their souls! We are the last remaining members, you know."

"Unless you get married Nathan."

"Ha! That's a joke, never again! I'm much too busy with my writing anyways, and tending to our home. Besides, I have some friends in town, dear auntie. I usually stop and have a cold one when I get to town for groceries."

And she smiled at him, understanding his need to be free. She had planned on leaving the entire estate to him in her Will anyways, for no one else was around to take care of her, and she certainly couldn't get everything done alone. She indeed appreciated his fine company very much, and all of his hard work. After all, she had been so close to his mother, her sister, and understood how such a wonderful friendship between Abigail's son and herself, would make the ending years of her life so richly pleasurable. As if it had been a parting gift bestowed upon her by her sister. She had read somewhere that living alone was actually unhealthy, that it could either create or sustain illness.

They sat relaxing in the kitchen, as the shadows lengthened, crawling macabre and cold across the yard, now reaching for the house.

CHAPTER TWO: THE PARTY

Red wax ran down the candlestick and pooled like a spot of blood on the table. Nathan left the table and returned to their friends with another bottle of wine. Lights flickered from the candles, as well as from the jack-o-lanterns. The heat from the small candles inside the pumpkins changed the expressions of the carved faces, which now bore watchful leering glances, whose bright lurid faces changed with sharpening teeth, grinning eerily in muted, fluttering orange shadows.

Nathan smiled at Maggie, who was seated down the table next to Bill. They were both tired from the days' preparations of yard work, cooking and from cleaning the rooms of the house for their friends' weekend stay. Maggie watched the deep purple wine flow into her glass and back up to her cheeks in a warm glow of cheerful abandon.

Outside, pipelines of Lake Superior crashed against the cragged peninsulas and the precipitous forest cliffs. The wind blew in a shrill chorus of falling voices against the screens. The immensely vast forests which rolled freely across Michigan's Upper Peninsula were now covered in a sightless, grave-black night of piercing wind, lightning, and ominously cracking thunder which vibrated the floor boards beneath them. Root systems of lightning flashed from sky to ground with a simultaneous loud crack of thunder. Instantly the power went out. The infinitely gentle, enchanting spell of Beethoven's *Adagio Un Poco Mosso,* and the crystal lights of the chandelier with its shivering jewels sparkling over the table were suddenly gone, both sight and sound extinguished suddenly like a flame. A flame whose curling sulfurous smoke once extinguished, drew into itself a sheer black darkness: deep colors of the grave and of wet raining nights in a lonely wood. A surreal black loomed all around the candles and pumpkins in moving shadows, lifting up its spectral arms, creeping 'round. A deep, chilling silence settled in, broken only by the sound of thunder, surrounding them in mysterious waves, its mephitic, moldy catacomb eeriness deafening.

Orange faces flickered hard in delicious fear and weird waterfalls of wax trembled down the length of the candlesticks sending black shadows dancing against the walls and ceiling as these night spirits gathered in close, watching them.

Maggie closed the window near the table as a downpour of rain deafened the conversation and the frenzied, spectral flashes of lightning and cracking thunder charged their collective mood with a mysterious excitement. Eyes flashed like liquid candle flames and big, nervous smiles rode their faces.

"Such music," exclaimed Helen.

"There used to be so much *magic* in life," Bill said, saddened by his eminent truth. "As we all grew up together, there were so many things: music concerts, in fact, remember <u>Genesis, Selling England By The Pound</u> and <u>The Lamb Lies Down on Broadway</u> at the Auditorium theater? *That*, was magic! And it was theatrical, not just music. But a doorway to another world."

"Yes, I remember that one song, *The Musical Box*, I'll never forget it." Nathan said.

"There were conversations and storytelling at your kitchen counter, Nathan, remember?" Bill said. "Your mom was an angel, too! I remember that there was always a candle burning on the counter, it was fitted atop an old, round Italian wine bottle, one candle atop another. And it seemed as if the burning candles sort of kept score of our conversations and stories, by the volumes and thick layers of its dripping wax. And I remember this too," he reflected, "that your mom always had a pot of Irish stew simmering on the stove, hazing the room. You could taste lamb and beef in the air, and turnips and potatoes brewing. I always knew I'd be asked for dinner, too." He laughed. "We had conversations that changed and moved us, that inspired new thinking. I remember being so absorbed in conversations that I felt like we had all journeyed far beyond the walls of the room, to places around the world, far away from the commonplace, mediocre, three dimensional world of our lives. And the music you used to play, how beautiful and sad it was. It was Debussy, wasn't it?"

"Yes," said Nathan, "what an excellent memory you have!"

"And your mom used to play the piano, some haunting melody which she had composed herself. ...and there was a fire burning bright in the fireplace..."

"Yes, Bill, you are certainly opening up windows from the past. What wonderful, simple, loving days those were." Said Nathan. "My dear mom.."

"I remember when we used to take walks around the lake at night, talking about the stars, about life and death, about our dreams and nightmares. I remember the one night when we brought along a bottle of champagne and your best glasses!" Bill added. "We sat on the fence by the spillway, looking up at the big yellow moon reflecting the dark lake in vast skies, wondering what the future held."

Nathan added: "and we hiked the local forests during the day, those vast, beautiful oak forests with secret lakes, forests that are no longer there because of all the development, and that horrible golf course they put in."

"Yes, now there's condos, subdivisions, apartments, strip malls, sidewalks, million dollar pre-fab houses built over swampland, the noise and fumes from cars traveling where deer once ran. It's all gone now." Sighed Helen, holding a deep reprieve from her cigarette. "All gone. What days those were. I remember when we all went skinny dipping at one of those forest lakes, and someone stole Don's shorts! I think you had to wait until dark to get home, didn't you?"

"Yes, love, I did." Don scowled at her.

"Well, I guess it's why we moved to the Northwoods." Said aunt Maggie. "To recapture that special peace, that sense of pure energy and vitality one feels when living in the country. I love watching the Northern Lights, the stars at night, hearing the lonely howling of a solitary wolf, I feel grounded here. I love my gardens, I love the smell of bread baking from the wood stove. I love to cook and read books. All simple pleasures, I assure you. And I am an old woman, and this is how I wish to spend the rest of my days. Now Nathan, he could go out again into the world, he could find a more lucrative job, a woman, maybe even marry again. But he chooses to stay here with me and write articles for the magazines he has contracts with. We aren't rich, but every single bill gets paid on time, and we are happy. I feel grounded here, I feel whole and alive. I sometimes wonder if Nathan is lonely for a bride, but I'd imagine that if he was, he'd leave, at least for a while. And this house is certainly big enough for the both of us to follow our own daily interests without getting in each others' way. That's the beauty of it all."

"Big enough?" Asked Bruce, "why it's a Victorian mansion. I've never seen anything like it before! They simply don't build houses like this one anymore."

The sounds of wine pouring and crusts tearing, soups sipped, and the transporting flavors of tortelloni stuffed with clams and mussels, in a broth of garlic, tomatoes, wine and herbs, imparted bliss upon its unwary explorers and kept the table humming just beneath the high treble notes of conversation. The drumming of the hard rainfall and the sharp, cracking thunder filled them with excitement.

"I would think," asked Bill, that people around here place more of an emphasis on your spiritual and creative worth as an individual, as opposed to being judged by what kind of car you drive or what kind of watch you wear, or how much your oversized house cost.... am I right?"

"But people are still *just people*," Don interrupted. "Remember that quote: 'we are poised somewhere midway between the beasts and the Gods.' I think people behave more closely like animals, than like Gods or saints. I think that there is no such thing as perfect sanity, that all people have problems, flaws, inconsistencies and weaknesses. I would think that small town living would actually be suffocating and backwards, and that these people would take advantage of this simple human reality, the normal human condition of somehow being flawed as we all surely are to some degree, turning it into some kind of drama and blame. I'd rather have the big house and the sports car, over country living and the prospects of having too much empty time to do nothing. I don't want to live in poverty. I don't want my life to revolve around the latest cheap gossip over who left their poka dot shorts out on the line." Don said.

"The absence of material things does not spell poverty, Don. What do you mean you wouldn't like a small town?" Asked Aunt M.

"The endless gossip, neighbors with their noses constantly up your ass, ya' know. Always *assuming things* before knowing any real facts, or even having the intelligence and interest to inquire about what the real facts may be. But, if it was their life, their reputation on the line, things would be very different - they would back and support each other. They'd be given a normal chance. And a normal chance to live their life. You, however, would always remain an outsider.

"You'd have no privacy! They'd be lookin' out their window watchin' to see what you were wearin' and what you were doin'. They don't look for respectable, common causes in situations. How could a person defend their innocense against such social corruption and unscrupulous paranoia? Could drive a person insane, it could. And if you made a common human mistake, *like they do all the time*, you'd probably get to live with it forever - it becomes who you are. Condemned, judged and branded for life by some trivial, petty thing, regardless of whether or not it was even true, *it would be what they want to think*, and that human mistake or issue would become your identity, and how you would be understood from that point on. I think that small towns are cruel! They'll have you believing you're stupid, crazy or inferior in a heart beat, and if a woman alone in this world, then a slut, it's whatever slot they wanna throw you into that would best destroy your credibility, integrity and personal sense of well-being. You'd be isolated, become a social leper. And I think this would be especially true if you ever accidently or unintentionally crossed someone, in other words, if there was a common human misunderstanding. I wouldn't want to live my life being misunderstood by everybody on a day-to-day basis, always having to defend trivial issues, constantly splitting hairs over nothing. Life is too short for that! They probably do a check too, on your personal and work history and where you come from, and your life is then in the hands of old enemies who'd love to ruin your chance to be happy in a new place, or a place where you thought you could live your dreams. Lots of things happen in a workplace that are unfair and dishonest, I believe, but how would this person ever be able to defend the truth of a situation, where he had been wrongfully slandered out of sheer spite and hate from an old rival at work? And they'd believe it; eat it up like dessert. It'd be your last supper; so to speak, and you'd have to accept that you'd be tortured for the remainder of your life if you stayed, as if your life didn't matter and had no worth, fated to live in cruel isolation for the rest of your days from being misunderstood and hated for no real reason at all. And on top of this, the thing that burns my blood, is that there really are sick people out in this world: raping, murdering, lying, cheating and the like, yet these people fit into society with graceful ease and acceptance."

"Don, I'm sure it isn't like that at all. Sounds like you've been reading some pretty heavy mystery novels lately? There are good people and the bad everywhere you go. It isn't just located in either the city or the country or any place in between. Country people aren't like that at all. You just need to get to know them; and let them get to know you back. You've never even lived in the country before, so how would you know? Some people are cut out for it, the slower pace, the quiet, and some people enjoy the city, so why do you have to create a heated political battle over it, where someone has to be right and someone has to be wrong? It's what it is." Helen told him. "People are different everywhere, it's a big world we live in. You're just jealous. What's the problem?"

"Because Nathan thinks he's Thoreau now," Don answered, "like he's escaped a terrible fate by leaving his old neighborhood. Which, I have to admit, is quite overpopulated and overbuilt now. I agree it's unfortunate, all the commercialism and greed. Even the forest preserve is crowded!" He laughed. "I can't tell you of a more stressful place to go, than the local forest preserve. ...and ain't that somethin.' "

"So Donald, then what's so bad about the country?" Asked Aunt M. "So far the point of living in the country for us is the solitude. We keep to ourselves here, don't know that many people really. There isn't a neighbor here for miles, and the nearest town is 29 miles away. I suppose that some of the things you say could be true, but then again, it would depend on a person's lifestyle. Hanging around in a bar all the time would be unfortunate, in terms of a person's happiness. But if a person worked, had good friends and a wholesome lifestyle, I don't see how that would attract the type of people I think you're referring to here. I'm not defending country people or city people, nor putting them down. Live and let live. Nathan and I love the wilderness. And actually, we have friends that come in from town once in a while to visit, and they are excellent people! They live their values. Why else do you think that country living is so bad?" Aunt Maggie asked him, curious, angered by his remarks. For she had grown to love living in the country, and had found true friends, as well. She was proud of where they now lived.

"Well, one would think of things like nepotism, the rejection of new ideas and new people, cliquish social groups, and a sort of lawlessness that only thrives in the obscurity of a remote, small town because they can get away with it. That's what I mean." Don laughed, twisting open another beer.

"Don, I find some of your comments shocking! You are so cynical, so sarcastic. You don't believe in the decency of people, nor in love, or in the mysteries of the universe which Nathan and Bill are talking about here. A real neanderthal! Mr. Cromagnum Man." Helen laughed at him. "It's like you just lumbered out from a cave with a club in your hand. And look at you... ...you look like you haven't shaved in two weeks."

"I haven't," he smiled nonchalantly, lighting up a cigar in a smug and complacent air. "Quit raggin' on me ya bitch," he laughed nervously, looking up at her to see if he'd gone too far, if he had survived his own remark.

Helen's face burned red, and suddenly, a cluster of lightning exploded, striking something nearby.

"Look! Look at that!" Helen exclaimed, having completely forgotten her insult.

"What is it? Oh My!" And aunt Maggie moved over towards the window, looking out into the wild darkness. "There's glowing blue lightning branching over the ground."

Nathan could hear the urgency in her voice, mixed with the excitement that had been rising in them all.

Everyone gathered at the window. The lightning spread over the ground in fast moving electric blue currents flushing into the woods and beyond in glowing, branching carpets that traveled out of sight.

"St. Elmos fire?" Nathan wondered, looking at Bill.

"Some kind of Ball Lightning, possibly," said Bill. "It's very rare."

"It's a damn thunderstorm you guys, where's the beer Helen, get me a beer."

Helen slid a beer towards Don, and they all sat back down.

Bill tried to resurrect his point again: *"There was* magic in life when we were all growing up. I believe that we live in such a vast and mysterious universe: a universe of pure mind, a universe all around us in the world we live in, and the universe which houses the living worlds beyond our solar system, that to assume we are randomly born without any purpose and then die to sleep in an endless night of death is certainly more absurd than any efforts to establish the spiritual nature of mankind and his absolute relation to all living things. When we were growing up, we had lives that opened the doors to this kind of excitement and wonder. And it's like it's all dead now. We live in such a processed world, people are processed, seldom understood. Seldom is there any emphasis placed on the magic of learning, the odyssey of self discovery and spiritual growth. The unknown."

"Well now Bill..." Don said plainly. "You and Nathan always go off on these superman tangents. You talk to me like I'm stupid or somethin'. You sound like you're reading from a text book Bill! Brothers, it's just life: you eat and sleep, and pay your bills and taxes on time. I keep it simple. The city is civilization, and this place is uncivilized, and if Nathan wants to sit in a flower patch and watch the stars, he can go philosophize all the way down the unemployment line. Time is money, you guys. Whose gonna pay my bills if I don't think and talk *the way they think and talk*, if I don't conform with popular activities. I'll be branded a freak, I won't have any friends. I like to snap a few cans at the ginmill, I like to shop for things I want, and I sure would love to be able to afford a corvette...get more broads that way, too..." laughed Don. "I've got friggin' Thoreau and Emerson idling here, but neither one of you has a financial worry in the world. Me, if I don't punch in at the mill on time, it's my ass.... Whose gonna pay my bills?"

Nathan took a sip of wine, "You always make me feel like I'm speaking in a foreign language, or that my words fall on deaf ears. I find many of your opinions offensive Don. You've never lived in the country like Helen pointed out - you don't know what you're talking about. I realize that all people are entitled to their opinions. But what Bill is talking about, or trying to get through

214

to you, is about the magic of the human mind, the boundless realm of the imagination, and that an altered state of mind is merely a normal experience of evolving intelligence and spirit; a furthering and birthing of our true self from out the wet, dark chrysalis of human potential."

"That's heavy." Said Don. "You, my friend, *need* another drink." And Don reached over pouring Nathan a full glass of a dark, ruby wine that shimmered in the candlelight.

"Let me put it to you this way," continued Nathan, ignoring Don's sarcasm: "I believe that the evolution of human consciousness is an insidious, tedious, process, smote full of pain and suffering, yet behind it all lies the Greater Mind, our connection to God, which is what Bill was trying to say that we used to be more aware of. What lies beyond the surface appearance of our life is our divine connection with the infinite and to all living things. What I'm talking about is community harmony and a general social conscience and compassion, not rebellion. Original thought creates great works of literature and art, composes music which transforms people's souls, it impels people to *seek to live* their highest dreams, and encourages that indescribable sensation of really feeling alive in the present moment, the doors of our senses finally open. From the day we are born we are subtly conditioned to ignore and deny the higher sensibilities which dwell within, our connection with the eternal and the divine. Now how is this concept hard for you to understand? This is the mystery, the magic, that Bill refers to." Nathan said, pausing. "The primeval urgings of an evolutionary push forward in the development of the person toward wholeness is upon us now. It is the same primordial urging which time and adaptation brought about to the fish, as they specialized and eventually crawled out of the waters. And in terms of human awareness and intelligence, it is a process whereby the intellectual, emotional, spiritual and physical elements of the person seek integration, seek actualization of its very presence within. The acorn has burst. I believe that we all possess an inner genius, it is our ultimate birthright potential."

215

Don laughed, looking around the table at everyone to be sure he had their attention: "Nathan thinks I'm a genius!" He smiled, taking a hard pull off his cigar.

"No, not quite." Replied aunt M. "I don't think that's what he meant, dear."

"Nathan," Don replied, "I'm sorry if *my opinions* offend you, but I'm a regular working man. I like the city, the excitement, I would be bored to death living out here. I loved growing up with everyone here, and all the fun, the great talks in your kitchen, all the parties and the kegs of good beer, not to mention the food, ...but realism, not idealism, dominates my thinking. I don't feel 'magical,' Nathan. And I would get bored living in the country. Period. ...This is outstanding beef, by the way, you're an excellent cook Maggie. I've never had a meal like this in a restaurant. You're lucky Nathan, you see, you live in your own little world here. It's true that I don't know much about Monet or Emerson or Beethoven, but I work hard, and I know that there are good people out there not livin' high and mighty, who I can talk to without having to move off to the ends of the world to reach. Maybe their lives seem boring to you. But life has been reduced to this level somewhat: a repetitious ritual of working, eating, sleeping, paying bills and doing it all over again. Life *has* lost some of its romance. But we've grown up, we're adults now. We have responsibilities now, bills to pay."

"You've *never* looked at life deeply," Helen rode him, tapping her cigarette in the ashtray. "Look at the time you tried to outrace a train in your pickup truck and lost, you got a totaled vehicle and somehow lived to walk away and joke about it like you're some kinda' daredevil comedian, utterly invincible simply because *you're you*. You're lucky to be sitting here at all with us tonight," she informed him. "And what about the time you shot arrows off in your yard in the winter, and dug up your dad's rose garden trying to find them. Or the time you shot yourself in the foot lying in bed. And all the dope you've smoked! Why, I remember that one Christmas Eve night when you went ice skating down at the lake with just a santa clause hat on," she wagged her finger at him. "And you were drunk from that homemade still you had in your parent's basement."

"I'm not getting a fair trial here, aunt M," Don frowned.

"You've always taken whatever life has dropped on your lap or whatever was easiest," continued Helen. "Everything's a joke to you! I remember when we had that party out in the big yard at Palatine. We had a bonfire burning bright. And all of a sudden from no where comes Don," she said laughing, looking around the table. "He rides a bicycle right through the fire and snaps open a beer."

Aunt M looked at Don in dismay. "Honey, Nathan is referring to human consciousness evolving into a state of sacred intention. He is saying that people are becoming mindful and conscious of their actions, as well as the consequences of those actions, and that right and wrong have become a community concern, and that a single community voice can now be heard. That violence *and pornography*, hatred and pride, dishonesty and theft, and all the other dark aspects of human nature are being tempered by virtue of their constant failure and the resulting unhappiness and personal torment which these types of actions bring into peoples' lives. They don't work, and, they never will!"

Helen pointed at him, taking a long draw from her cigarette. "Listen to this lady, she's right!"

"And that," Aunt M concluded, "is real human magic. So it does really still exist Bill, maybe not along the lines of your ideals, but it's there within people."

Helen jumped on the opportunity to attack Don. "Don is just so dumb or drunk or something that he can't grasp the meaning and spiritual quality of country living, nor the culture of city living. Life is one big crotch to you, Don!" She challenged him. "Don't even try and talk about mystery with him." Helen frowned.

"You're trying to flatter me...." Don winked at her.

"Nathan and Bill are trying to discuss the interrelatedness of all living things. That there exists a living, vital connection, a life force which flows throughout all living things, and as we evolve, a complex soul develops, a soul which reverberates with the grace of God, a soul that knows that all life is sacred, and is one and the same." Aunt M added. "...Don, you should have gone to college, dear, like the boys did. Or church. Or you should read more, life is so short you know! Maybe you should be more like Bruce, here. He never says nothin', 'till he's hungry. They say a quiet man is a smart man, unless you know better. And Helen dear, you know I believe that the ultimate good in man *must* develop into a sort of regular everyday, conscious way of living. *It must happen.* For if it doesn't, the planet which is our house, will be destroyed. There will be no future for mankind. Mmmmmm, I did do a nice job on the pasta, I think. Fresh basil from the garden really makes a difference. You know they say that if you *really can* do something well, then it's not bragging," she blushed. "Sure wish I could lose some weight, though. Honey, pour your auntie a little more wine, just a little bit more, okay?"

Bruce, who had been silent and eating with abandon, and from the expression on his face one could tell that he hadn't heard a word of the entire conversation until now, leaned over and poured Mrs. McGregor some wine.

"Thank you, honey."

"You're welcome," he said, returning to a plate of crispy, tender quails, picking up the whole bird and eating it, with pieces of plums falling back into the sauce.

"I read." Don defended himself. "I'm a smart guy."

"Yeah, Playboy, Penthouse, Sports Illustrated once a year...." Helen said, disgusted. "You've spied every stupid slut whose sold

218

her soul for money and vanity that's ever been published in a peek magazine!"

"No. You've got me figured wrong."

Helen finished her glass of wine and looked around stretching. "That was the best meal I have ever eaten in my life! An appetizer of delicious grilled quails stuffed with ripe plums; your tortelloni stuffed with mussels, sorrel and cheeses; and a thick cut of perfectly cooked prime rib glazed with your port wine peppercorn sauce; not to mention the different homemade Italian breads and your baked onion soup. Wow, I'm impressed! You must've been cooking for days! I'm gonna clear some of these plates and see what's in the kitchen for dessert for later, aunt M," Helen said. "You know, you've always been like everybody's aunt. You're Nathan's aunt, so we've all just called you auntie, too. The love in your heart shines through your hands in your cooking." She said, collecting empty plates and disappearing into the kitchen.

"Thank you sweetie. I'm experimenting on all of you tomorrow night."

"How's that?" inquired Bruce.

"Well, I've been thinking about this dish I'd like to make. One of you could take me down to the market for fresh live lobsters tomorrow morning."

"Ya, and what dish is this?" He persisted. "Lobster, sounds wonderful!"

"A flaky, buttery pastry dough risen in a hundred delicate layers, with a just-cooked-through lobster tail in a creamy sauce within. I think it would work, but I could be wrong."

Don raised his hand as if in a classroom, smiling, the cigar dangling from his lip.

"What are you doing Don?" Asked Helen, still annoyed with him - wanting to be annoyed with him.

"Volunteering to take Aunt M to the grocery store tomorrow morning. I need to pick up more beer in town anyways. Maybe stop off at that museum bar, the one with all the hunting mounts and bears, and snakeskins on the walls, and," he said, eyeing Helen for her reaction, "those big-breasted country girls," he laughed. "Nope, the more I think about it, I need to go!" Don said. "I'd be glad to help with groceries." He could see the veins in Helen's temples throbbing, and he laughed to himself with this. Her neck was all red, too, he noticed. 'I wonder if she loves me,' he thought to himself amused.

"Oh, what a Halloween night this has been," sighed aunt Maggie. "You just relax now Donald, we may not be going anywhere tomorrow, if the road is washed out tonight."

"You mean we could all be stranded here together for days and days?"

"It's happened," she said, smiling at him, watching him look over at Helen with teasing eyes. "Anything's possible..."

"Just like the good ole' days," laughed Don. "I love you guys, gezzz, it's been a long time since we've all been together. Too long. Bruce, good man, say something for Pete's sake!"

"I wish something would happen tonight." Bruce said, sounding disappointed, as if his wish would certainly never come true.

"What do you mean?" Asked Helen.

"I wish something would happen tonight: Like what we always talked about: UFO's, telepathy, life after death; ghosts; the universal mind... I wish that something would happen tonight that would prove the existence of the paranormal, and all the mysterious and unknown things we've always talked about, so that we could know for sure that they're real." Bruce clarified.

"You mean," commented Nathan, "about the universal mind, when a person through meditation or mental discipline can reach a zenith of pure mind, pure consciousness, that instantly transforms or renders the person at that single moment into infinite dimensions, pure energy, antimatter? Is this what you meant by universal mind?" Nathan asked. "You always were a hard-core science buff."

"Bruce has been watching too many Star Trek episodes." Scowled Don. "Beam me another beer Helen!" He winked.

"Yes Nathan," Bruce replied, ignoring Don, "and I'm not a poetic person, but it could be described like comets of pure mind traveling passed suns and moons and planets in a never-ending, infinite tangent through the space-time continuum. I believe this represents the ultimate pinnacle of evolution, non-matter, beings that exist solely in etheric manifestations of consciousness, traversing the universe with the momentum and immediacy of sheer thought alone, transmutable living minds." Said Bruce. "It's hard to grasp, but fun to think about. Like stargates and wormholes. You would exist exactly in the space you imagined."

"How would one get back?" Asked Nathan.

"How does one revert to the genesis of fish and monkeys?"

"Good point," laughed Bill.

"What?" Don asked.

"Well," said Bruce, "that's what I meant, that I wish something would happen to us tonight that would prove the ultimate postulations of scientific *and* philosophical inquiries, and beyond."

"Bruce," said Don, "I'm grateful you've been quiet all night long. Otherwise, I'd be suffering one hell of a headache right now. The only headache *I've got*, is the one *Helen* gave me," he said, laughing. "But, she doesn't love me anyways. So I sit here alone in my sadness with my beer."

"Not quite, the evening's not over, and the doorway to another world could come crashing open on us..." Warned Nathan. "These types of conversations, I believe, attract a certain energy field, infinite parallel realities that simultaneously co-exists with three-dimensional reality all the time. And being that we are all the way out here tonight, in the middle of no where, surrounded by hundreds of miles of vast forest, a climate similar to a sort of deciduous Amazon, with all this primaeval, sacred and natural energy surrounding us, and with our childlike wonder, *something strange* just might happen tonight!" Nathan smiled, knowing that he was beginning to spook Don.

"What is it that you wished would happen? What would you like to see Bruce? Would you like to see a ghost or an alien, maybe the wolfman tonight," laughed Don, looking at him in feigned disbelief. "I don't think that a thunderstorm and annoying conversations out in the middle of no where, are enough to create supernatural activity. But who knows?...... You guys always think I'm wrong anyways. Why argue with you. It's like talking to a fence post. I'd rather talk to a fence post sometimes."

"You know what I want Don?" Paused Bruce, "I want to see you scared to death! That's what I want! I want those conventional illusions to come crashing down on you, so you don't know what's real, or which way is up or down."

Don looked out the window, his face washed silent, and made no reply.

CHAPTER THREE: GHOST STORIES

Lightning struck the ground outside the window, quickly illuminating the crashing waves of Lake Superior. "It's a perfect night for a ghost story!" Baited Nathan, looking over at Bill.

Nathan had always enjoyed Bill's special company. He was a writer also, as well as a scuba diving instructor who enjoyed exploring sunken ships. His intelligence, coupled with his sparkling loyalty as a friend, and original, unique personality had always made his families' parties fun, as well as serious and a little bit magical. Bill was still a little boy who loved thunderstorms, storytelling, new ideas, the smell of crackling fires and the conviviality of good food. He took Halloween seriously and always endeavored to lift it beyond the cocktails and food level, into the mysterious and creative realm of ghosts and graveyards, of intelligent conversations transporting the group into parallel dimensions where all time stops, as if they had all actually left the room and traveled faraway, only to return once again, with the passports of their hearts stamped with some foreign emblem or memory. And then, upon their return, it was always time for an Irish coffee. Everyone liked Bill and sensed a genuine common bond with him. Bill cleared his throat, as he did habitually, and smiling, poured himself more wine.

"Before we commence with the stories, can I make anyone a scotch first?" Bruce offered as he stood up, stretching and gathering a couple plates and bowls. "Aunt M? Nathan, Helen, Don, hey Don over there, wake up buddy! Bill, looks like you've got some wine going on?"

"I'll have a little nightcap with our ghost stories tonight," Helen gestured lazily.

"Hey, I'm not sleepin'! Don said. "Just tryin' to keep my mouth shut for a little while and stay out of trouble. I'll take another beer, though.   Grab me a Rolling Rock, Bruce. You're a good man."

"Nothing for me!"   Laughed aunt Maggie, "I'm so full I can't move."

"Me either. I'm all set," said Bill. "How 'bout some coffee?"

"Ya dumbhead Bill - the power's out!" Snapped Don. "He's so fuckin' smart he's stupid!"

"Oh yeah, I forgot," he laughed, clearing his throat.   "Maybe I'll have another glass of wine. Just one more. And some water, too." Bill went over to his brief case and pulled out a manuscript.

Orange lights poured in from around the corners of the door from the wall candles in the kitchen, as Bruce returned with a tray of drinks and settled into his chair waiting to be transported to another world, or at least, scared out of his mind.

And Bill began, holding his manuscript like some precious sea scroll. He cleared his throat as if signaling to his unconscious mind that his storytelling voice now emerge, as well as to prime the attention of his listeners.

Bill looked at his friends all gathered together tonight from afar: 'What a fun group of people,' he thought, 'they are my real family.' He took a deep drink of wine, which by now had opened up nicely, and wrapped himself up in the warm, comfortable blanket of storytelling, casting mood, images, sounds and smells from another time into this dark room. Indeed, the air was charged with the sweet anticipation of being scared, safely scared in the warm circle of flickering lights in the theatre of the dining room. Long, hollow thunder rolled and shook close by with skeletons branching in sporadic plumes of rippling light, and he began reading...

"This story is about an abandoned manor house in Barrington Hills. I heard about it from some friends at work and

was informed that the mansion was vacant and unlocked, and absolutely haunted," He laughed.

"The first time I went to the house, which was more like a castle, was at night on my way home from a party, about one in the morning. There I was, standing in the driveway of this medieval manor house looking up at steepled rooftops melting into the blackest, overcast night sky. A numinous explosion of silhouettes moved in bouncing clouds around the bathouse at the top of the silo. It felt as if the house was waiting for me. Turrets glistened in the darkness. Long, smooth window panes blinked liked wolves waiting to jump out at me in a patina of malevolent anticipation. Frozen and hunched, the house lay silent as I held my breath walking to the front door. Inside, the light revealed an interior devoid of furnishings, except the scattering of strange, yellowed game pieces from some other time period. Neglect inhaled and exhaled all around me, slowly, taking in a long apterous breath and releasing its unclean and foreboding dim air. Before me to the right was the kitchen, and to the left, a large living room with a massive stone fireplace which was at least five feet high. To the right of the fireplace was an old piano which seemed as though it would start playing by itself at any time now. The floor in the living room was oak and there was a large dark stain in front of the fireplace near the pokers. Aside from the piano, there was no other furniture in this room. A hallway filled with shadows beckoned at the opposite end of the living room, so I followed it," he laughed nervously, taking a sip of wine, and continued.

"At this point, no more lights worked in the house. I turned on my flashlight and followed the cavelike hall. The walls of the cave were constructed of cobblestone and the hallway was at no point ever straight. It twisted and turned like a deep cave echoing my movements within, replete with the sensation of squeaking bats and dripping stalactites. The yellow beam of the flashlight discovered a room to the left, again unfurnished except for a chair positioned in front of a set of French windows with a phone on the floor. Further down the turns of the stone hall were two small bathrooms. In both bathrooms the shower curtains had been torn

off and the inside walls were revealed to be stained by a copper red fluid, like blood.

"I continued further. I realized that I had been holding my breath, so I took in a deep inhalation of dampness, neglect and an apprehensive memory which the castellated house manifested with certainty. I was at the bottom of the silo. I raised the beam of the light up into the watery shadows of a giant spiral staircase. The damp walls echoed my voice, "hello up there?" I offered the darkness, waiting above. A black, smooth sheen covered the stone walls, the narrow eyelet windows far up above, and the long, curving handrail which journeyed up and out of sight into the night of the house. It was a warm summer night, but a cold, damp chill permeated the chambers of the house. Stale air loomed all around me and it felt as if by walking that I was tearing invisible cobwebs of backwatered air."

Bruce disappeared into the kitchen and quickly returned with a bottle of Bowmore, and a bowl of ice, sitting down snugly close next to Helen, refreshing her drink, too.

"You lush," mocked Don comically from across the table.

"Look who's talking Donny boy," replied Bruce.

"Sssshhhhhhhhhhhhhhh!"   Came a voice from the gathering darkness.

"And so," Bill continued, "the rooms at the top of the spiral staircase stared down at me through the darkness beckoning me to climb up. At that point, every horror movie I had ever seen flashed before my mind and seemed pale in comparison to my present surroundings. There I was, Dr. Marquay in 'The Haunting,' but this was really happening! I was saturated with the flapping of bat wings, the damp earth must of the silo and the indelibly imprinted image of this castle whose severe turrets pined steep above against the starless, black sky. I could not shake the sensation that something or someone was following me. I climbed

up to the first plateau which was a small circular empty platform offering a view from the narrow slits of the windows. I looked down across the rooftops and yard below. I could see my car, and wished that I were in it. The beam broke across the steps as I continued to ascend toward the next platform, which again had the long, narrow windows almost a foot thick.

"One more level and I would be at the top. Once there, I realized that the silo had been constructed into the rest of the house to afford, up at the top, two bedrooms. Straight ahead the bedroom was vast. Stored furniture and objects were covered with sheets. I followed the interplay of object and light, standing with my back to an open room. As the beam of the flashlight moved exploring the large room and its contents, a sudden presence charged the air and the whole scene dissolved entirely from being surreal, to something that was actually happening, moving towards me now, watching me. A shadow blacker than the room itself gathered behind me. At that one instant, time froze. A split second seemed an eternity. The shadow lengthened, laughing, cackling eerily empty like a voice coming from the bottom of a well. Simultaneous images of moving my legs and running down the staircase, through the stone halls, passed the fireplace, out from beneath its solemn dark towers, brooding steep - panicking while running across the sidewalks, feeling the overwhelming weight of the presence of the house coming in all around me and scooping me up into its black wings while trying to run to the car afforded a glimpse of the impossible - while I stood in the darkness alone with this monster. The spectre leered: shining, deepening; folding capes and wings and claws of pitch black; black like the bottom of an ocean; black like being buried in the grave; black as mining caves dug into rock, ground and mountain; its breathing muffled and bated, labored and slow, like the thick, wet breathing of someone wearing a mask.

"For one long moment I both fled and screamed without even moving. I could not fathom ever escaping from this nightmarish house alive. I ran down the staircase. My legs were shaking so bad I almost fell. When I got outside the real world seemed

uncannily to mock me, indifferent, offering no instant comfort from the terror of the house. Nothing seemed normal. The presence of the entire house brooded in a menacing gesture of darkness, cold air and lonely isolation against my fleeing movements. I could not get out of the house and out from under its sinister gardens fast enough. As I turned my car around, I looked up at the long, narrow eyelet windows of the silo where I had been standing before, and they looked back at me. The castle-house was alive, breathing, watching me leave."

The quiet, crackling wood music popped and snapped from the fireplace across the room, and the incense from the burning timber filled their senses in a calm, natural pause in the story.

"I recognize this story," Helen said. "You took me there one night."

"Yes, and you ran out and locked yourself in the car, remember?"

"Ya," she said, laughing.

"What I found out about the house is that a family was murdered there, children and all. Their horses and dogs were shot, and the whole family had been tortured, before they were killed. I believe that there are other horrible events which stain the history of that house. There was a newspaper clipping once about a skeleton found buried in the yard, an entirely unrelated event to the family murder. It was the skeleton of a boy who either had been pushed or fell down that spiral staircase in an alleged dispute with his father. The father having discovered that the boy was not his - that the mother had had an affair. Every room in that house was saturated with a walking sadness. "

"Maybe there's an ancient burial ground under the house?" Asked Bruce.

Helen jingled her glass, adding this: "I believe that there exist places of historic malediction. That a place can just be bad because of events that are trapped there, a sort of camera flash imprint made from a sudden jerk or spasm of intolerable pain."

"You mean a sort of living memory?" Asked Don, presumably serious.

"Exactly. Something that can't be painted over or redecorated, or removed in any way. A real, living presence of evil and unrest evoked by unthinkable acts of violence. As if incredible moments of pain permanently leave a residue upon an environment, an imprint, a fingerprint: voices in a wall, shadows peopled with gross attractions to certain places reliving the same situations over and over again like a rewound reel replaying itself, until something breaks the patterns of torture, fear and guilt that were set into motion."

"Ghost Psychology 101," Don chuckled. "I think it's no more than an abandoned house that has some dust in it and broken windows."

"Well, you go there sometime."

"Tell us about the swamp creature that chased your car when you were in Louisiana last summer. Or about the time you brought a tape recorder into a graveyard at night and asked dead people questions. Bill, you *could* be a nut, ya know." Don said, raising an eyebrow at him.

"Yeah," Bill laughed, clicking his gums, "and when I replayed that same tape over again, I heard voices answering me dummy. Not just one voice, but voices. That was really scary. It was actually more scarey playing the tape back alone at home in my office, than when I was actually in the graveyard. I don't know why that is. Maybe I thought nothing would happen."

"Where's the tape, Bill. Where's the proof?" Don prodded him.

"Ya know Don, you could be eating a knuckle sandwich for dessert, if you don't back off buddy. Wanna hear it? I've got the tape! It's in my briefcase. You think I would leave it at home knowing I was coming to a Halloween party with you guys? It's over there." Bill pointed.

"What a relief, scientific proof is on the way." Don laughed.

"Please boys, don't fight! It's Halloween, let Bill have fun. I'm certainly entertained by these stories!" Maggie defended him.

"When are we going to get the power back? This is such a remote, uncivilized place," complained Don, lighting a new cigar.

"I think Don is scared." Helen teased him.

"Come 'ere, Helen, wanna see how scared I am?" Don winked at Helen. "I like beautiful women, sweetie. Why don't you come over here and sit on your uncle Don's lap for a while?"

"I don't care if you slump over your plate and have a stroke. I'm not going over there to comfort a caveman like you...go comfort yourself Don, I'm sure you're used to it!" She smiled.

...All of a sudden banging echoed throughout the house. A violent rapid pounding as if someone was striking the door with a crowbar...

CHAPTER FOUR: THE MYSTERIOUS GUEST

"Who could that be?" Helen asked, as everyone looked toward the door.

"In this weather, down this long and dangerous road tonight, probably someone in need of a brandy I assure you!" Nathan comforted them, as he went to the door.

"Or a punch in the face." Scowled Don. "They sure ain't got no manners, that's for sure."

"Oh look who's talking," laughed Helen.

Nathan opened the door. The wind blew in shrill whipping voices, and an explosion of wet leaves was thrown at him by mischievous hands of wind. "Hello! Who's there?" He asked, peeling leaves off his neck.

Wet darkness answered him. Thunder shook the ground and the trees wavered at him, the hands of gusting winds pulling at their branches like mad strings upon a harp.

He shut the door with a sudden chill and returned to the table. Expectant faces looked up at him.

"Well?"

"Who was it? Someone looking for directions?" Bruce wondered.

"There was no one there," Nathan replied.

"...but the banging *was real*, Nathan, we all heard it!" Helen said, looking worried and frightened as the arms of the evening embraced her, the room steeped in the wild storm and by the story of the haunted house.

"Maybe it was a branch that flew against the house," he offered, sitting down and pouring himself some whiskey. "This is the best Bruce, you've fine taste in spirits...you too William," he said, chuckling to himself, "such stories tonight! I'm afraid I won't sleep a wink!"

The candles burned brightly, flickering and rippling hard sending jumping shadows all around them. "Who will tell the next ghost story?" Aunt M pressed. "This is certainly the spookiest Halloween we've had in a long time, isn't it?" she said, looking at Nathan. "I want to hear about that swamp creature. You said something clawed the side of your car, Bill. And the UFO you said you saw with Jay VanSteen near Timberlake. What happened that night?"

"Ya," replied Bill, clicking his gums again and clearing his throat, "that was an interesting night. I was down in the bayou swamp land area in Louisiana. All kinds of strange creatures in those deep swamp woods. And long, dark roads with nothing about but forest for miles and miles..."

"Do you believe there is a real, actual devil?" Nathan asked Helen, with an air of academic inquiry which she liked.

"No, absolutely not. I think that the devil is the archetype of the Lesser Man, the man of hate and crime, a comfortable mythological symbol in which we identify good from evil; sanity from madness; and love, compassion and forgiveness, from hate and rage. The image of the devil with his ugly horned head is a token totem pole erected to remind us of the perils of being bad. A behavioral signpost."

"In the twilight zone," laughed Don.

"That's really funny Don, but what about documented cases of possession?" Nathan asked her.

"The psychiatric wards are filled with people diagnosed with schizophrenia and other psychotic problems, all who exhibit probably the same behavior as a 'possessed' person."

"But conventional science has failed to cure the symptoms, whereas exorcisms have."

"True, but it still could be a form of mental illness in which the patient believes in the delusion that he or she is possessed by an evil spirit. It is the power of belief that is cured, not the soul." Helen replied.

"Don't be so cock sure about things, Helen," Nathan warned her. "Paranormal activities have plagued our newspapers, our most prestigious news magazines, television programs, as well as books written exclusively about case histories in an effort to better understand paranormal phenomenon. Abnormal psychology has explored the behavior of "possessed" individuals searching for the remotest connections with schizophrenia and psychosis, with all recorded successful remedies to date having been performed by exorcisms. Telluric activity has been attributed as a cause of poltergeist phenomenon, yet its manifestations are so bizarre as to bend any contemporary scientific rules. UFO sightings have been documented by the United States government, and countless other credible individuals, that I believe we are immersed in a most amazing world of possibility."

Nathan walked over to the fireplace setting a couple logs over the crackling flames. He poked the fire with a large brass firepoker, dreamily, momentarily hypnotized by the glowing, flickering lights. The room settled as lightning scoped silver and blue outside the windows, scattering corners of darkness in dappling moon colors, pulsing here and there, shadowed by rolling thunder. The dark which had fallen over the room rested deeply, sleeping, as if it had been spinning invisible webs of quiet dreams cast by the hours which slipped and fell away.

"I wish something would happen tonight! I wish something would happen... I wish something would happen..." Begged Bruce. "Like all the things we've talked about: UFO's, ghosts, telepathy, life after death, heaven and hell, all of it, I want to know if it's real. *I wish I wish I wish* something would happen tonight..." The air was electric with the wonderful ideas that had invoked an energy field all around them, awakening the revenants of its dormant spaces.

Helen wrapped herself up in a thick wool sweater, taking a sip of her drink, thinking, when suddenly loud banging struck against the front door again echoing throughout the house.

"Whoever it is, why can't they just knock?" Helen complained.

"Someone's playing Halloween games with you Nathan!"

"Sounds like you got the Jolly Green Giant outside, Nathan." Said Don, looking not so glib anymore, the smirk wiped right off his face.

"I don't think anyone's playing any Halloween games with us tonight. We're 29 miles from town and there's no neighbors for about 8 miles. Highly unlikely," he said, amused, more than frightened by the thrilling crashes against the door. "This has turned out to be some kind of Halloween party to remember, guys! ...oh, and my ladies." He said, standing up with his glass.

Bill and Bruce got up from their chairs also, as Nathan emptied his glass winking at Helen, and they went to the door as a group, as if embarking upon some mysterious expedition, walking close together, bonding in their vigilant gesture of bravery for want of the unknown visitor.

"I'll protect the women folk," bragged Don, as he moved over and sat between them.

"You're a loveable caveman, you know that Don. We like to tease you. You're so handsome. You need some help in the language and brain department honey, but like I said, you never studied, son, you never went to college. You've *never* used your head." Smiled Aunt M affectionately.

"Was that a compliment?" Don asked Aunt M, smiling with a frown.

"Sure, honey, we all love you. You're a bit high-strung, but it's your lifestyle I'm sure. Really, *you should* spend some time with us, the fresh air, the peace and quiet. All that anger will just melt right away, dear, just like snow on a warm spring day. Get to meet some real people - down to earth people."

"He's so primitive," yawned Helen. "About as evolved as a bulk of seaweed swaying back and forth along the shore," she laughed, moving her hands in a swaying motion.

"You're drunk, little lady." He said with cunning device. "You forget, women like the primitive strengths in a man, even though they pretend they don't like it that way."

"I don't know what you're talking about." Helen snapped at him.

"Oh yes you do little girl. I believe that our rooms are right next to each other, should you get frightened tonight." Don comforted her.

"I wouldn't get *that* scared," Helen yawned, turning towards the front door. "Besides," she laughed, "what could you do? Hide in the closet?"

Bruce tried to turn on the hall light, but forgot the power was down. The storyteller turned the knob pulling the door open against heaving, gusting winds whose very tension attempted to keep it closed like angry hands fighting against them. The three men braced the door open, looking out into the whipping darkness and wet leaves.

And there before them stood a man.

He didn't seem too odd at first. In fact, it was a relief to know that the banging they had heard was real. But in another moment, they would know that there was something very wrong. He was long and skinny and somewhat bent over by a spine which had lumbered above the ground for indeed many years.

"Hello, can we help you?" Offered Nathan.

Bill smiled, clicking his gums, and Bruce stared.

"Like one of the characters out of your stories, huh Bill!" Bruce whispered, elbowing him.

"He looks like an evil Abraham Lincoln," said Bill.

Feeling kind of tipsy and light, Nathan asked, "are you lost?"

His expression changed like quicksilver, as hollowed features staring blankly lit up suddenly with an animated interest, as he replied: "I'm Ahriman, but my friends know me by many other names. I was traveling by and wanted to know how much further the next town would be?"

"I don't see your car anywhere, sir."

"I parked it back down the road, didn't want to get stuck in any muddy driveway, ya know. *It's a wild night out here, may I come inside?*" He spoke in a plaintively sinister, melodic manner - almost cunning, musically hexing, as if they really should have thought about the whole thing first - as if giving them a last chance. Indeed even the wind itself was trying to keep the door closed.

"Why yes, of course," and Nathan gestured for the man to come inside.

"Where are your manners boys?" asked aunt Maggie.

He walked inside passing them, as they winced.

Bill pinched his nose, "he stinks," following behind him as they went to the table.

"Like rotten meat," Bruce whispered to him.

"Like sulphur..."

"Aunt M, can you find us a chair for this man? He's traveling in this terrible night and wants some directions. Let's get a glass, too." And Nathan grabbed the bottle of whiskey pouring a neat two fingers. He pushed the glass toward the stranger and sat down.

"Looks like you just invited Dracula inside," Don whispered over to Aunt Maggie. "Wow. How'd he get like that?"

"Shhhhhhh, Donald, behave now," she scolded him.

Ahriman sat down, his long black coat completely dry, but no one noticed.

"By God you can drink man," and Nathan reached to pour him a little more. "I didn't even see your arms move to reach the glass. But our nerves are all wound up anyways from the tales of terror our good friend Bill has been weaving all night."

"Ghost stories on Halloween night. Why, that's as natural as holiday punch on Christmas Eve. I know a couple ghost stories myself," mused the stranger, suddenly revealing a more scrofulous expression to his face.

The entire table sat still, utterly captivated. They stared at this stranger whose changing face scared them and whose slight but definite odor winced even the candle flames with a weird new chemistry stirred into the air. A sullen miasma of impending doom loomed over them as shadows began moving in the room. It would happen just as they would look away from something, or the shadows would glide passed in peripheral blindspots of the darkening room like people or things drifting by suddenly without form as the room became cold. Intense black shadows gathered, like ravens and vultures flocking silently together in the nether worlds of the room, conjured up by the mysterious guest as if he were some mad conductor summoning notes and instruments to now play in this defiled room of the dead.

His fingers seemed supernaturally long, like spindles weaving together with the action of thought and word, his stories and pictures of faraway places. Mesmerized by his sophistication, and deft, agile words, the visitor cast them spellbound with swiftly flowing terror, from his quickly conjured tales which crept up from the subterranean depths of his mind to this table of faces.

END OF PART ONE

LaVergne, TN USA
29 September 2010
198957LV00006B/103/A